M000265686

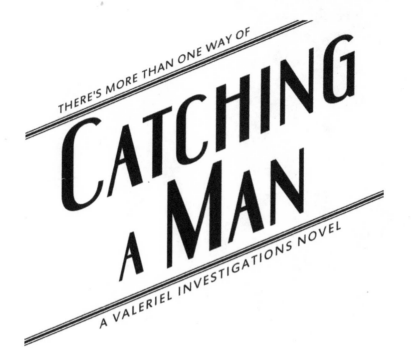

THERE'S MORE THAN ONE WAY OF

CATCHING A MAN

A VALERIEL INVESTIGATIONS NOVEL

ELIZABETH CORRIGAN

Catching A Man

First Print Edition: November 2014

ISBN: 978-0-9862573-1-5

Cover and Formatting: Streetlight Graphics

To Kevin,
Who may have wanted to see Kadin
in print more than I did

CHAPTER 1

CALLISTA DEVALERIEL GAZED OUT THE window at the two full moons that shone over the twinkling lights of Valeriel. Tradition claimed the twin orbs portended inauspicious events, but what mattered ill omens to the woman who ruled the city?

Most of the proletariat who scurried around the dirty streets thought her husband Ralvin reigned over them, but he only controlled the political arena. He and the uptight men of the Assembly, all those hereditary Imperials and elected Merchants, spent their days squabbling over what further scraps they could take from the working class. She cared nothing for that.

Callista lorded over the side of the city that mattered—the social side. Her image appeared in every glossy, and her name peppered every gossip column. Fashions and reputations depended on her. A year ago, Mabea Wage had dared wear a taffeta ball gown after Callista had declared the fabric passé. No self-respecting Imperial had invited Mabea to a gala for months, and then only because Callista had chosen to grant forgiveness.

Callista turned away from the window and sat in front of the looking glass. For once, she didn't take time to admire her flawless reflection. She knew she looked perfect. Earlier that evening she had pinned the curls of her blond bob in place with ruby-encrusted barrettes that set off the gold and white gown that seemed to all but flow from her alabaster skin. Her maid may have clipped the locks in place, but the queen could hardly credit the look to the person who had merely implemented it when Callista had created it and carried it off.

None of that mattered tonight, though, because she, the woman all men desired, would see the one man whose affections she returned.

She plucked the clips from her hair one by one and let the golden ringlets fall loose around her face. She hadn't felt his arms around her in so long. Almost a full year, in fact, but she had made up her mind to stop counting the days once she knew that she would no longer have to.

She picked up a hairbrush from her white and gold bureau—everything was white and gold for the royals of Valeriel, much to Callista's wearied dismay—and ran the rough bristles through her silky curls. She had had several lovers in the past year. Her husband hadn't been among them, of course, but any number of nobles had, men who wanted to brag about their experience with the most beautiful woman in the kingdom. She didn't care two pence for any of them, though several of them had convinced themselves of her affection.

She stood and unfastened her dress, the amber sillage of her perfume drifting into the air as she slid the gown down her hourglass figure. She almost felt bad for some of the men in her life, particularly her husband's cousin. Dear Baurus was so in love with her and had been since the moment they had met. She had strung him along like all the others, and sometimes in the past year she thought she might capitulate and commit herself to him, inasmuch as a married woman could devote herself to another man.

The bureau drawer creaked as she slid it open and pulled out a garment, a shimmer of ivory silk trimmed with golden lace that someone not troubled by its length might call a nightgown. As she pulled it over her head, she thanked the Deity that she had not pledged herself to Baurus. She would have had to break her promise now that her *true* lover had finally returned to her after a year with no word. Breaking faith didn't matter overmuch to her, but she would have had to manage the fallout from one of Baurus's rages. He wouldn't have harmed her, but his hysterics could damage lamps and one-of-a-kind antiques in his vicinity.

She smoothed the cool material over her flat stomach and sat back down in front of the mirror. She picked up the damp cloth her maid had left and swabbed it across her face. She didn't leave her boudoir without her face painted to perfection—foundation cream and powder to make her pale skin shine, dark eyeliner and mascara to widen her blue eyes, and lipstick as red as the rubies in her hair to shape her lips into a sultry smile.

As she finished wiping away the last of her makeup, she heard a whisper of fabric behind her.

She turned toward the door. She had wanted time to re-make-up her face, not in the ostentatious colors she had made popular in Imperial society, but in softer tones designed to highlight her natural beauty. But she didn't mind if *he* saw her without her tweezed eyebrows penciled in a perfect arch. He loved her with or without adornment. And when he stepped into view, thoughts of her appearance flew straight out of her head.

Her heart fluttered as she took in his familiar features. Callista had known many richer and handsomer men, but from the moment she met him, she had known that he could understand her like no one else. Others might call her shallow, callous, and selfish, but he understood her. And she saw the best and worst of her nature reflected in him.

She stood and took a single seductive step toward him. She met his eyes, and a cold smile formed on his lips.

"Callista. At last." He held out a hand to her.

She extended her arm to take it, but before their fingers touched, her chest began to burn. She pulled her hand back and placed it over her breast.

"Excuse me. I seem to have..." She gave a small cough as the fire intensified. "I need... water..." She tried to take a deep breath, but the air would not go into her lungs. She reached behind her to get a solid grip on the chair.

She looked up at her lover. "Help... me..."

The cool smile remained on his face, and she realized his eyes bore not even that chilly expression. "I'm sorry, my dear. It had to be this way."

She fell to her knees, still clutching her heart. "I don't... understand... How... could you?" She gasped again and realized she could no longer take in enough air to form words.

He knelt down in front of her and ran a delicate finger along her cheek. "If it's any consolation, I do love you. This wouldn't have been necessary otherwise."

She collapsed onto her side, and he continued to stroke her face. As her vision darkened, she fixed her gaze upon his remorseful expression. Because even though he had killed her, she wanted him to be the last thing she saw.

Eight hours earlier...

"Valeriel Investigations! How may I direct your call?" The perky brunette at the switchboard plunked the front cord in a jack near the top of the panel and flipped the "talk" key to ring the office at the other end of the line.

Someone's calling robbery, Kadin Stone thought, knowing that her fellow operator's switches matched those on every board in the row. She looked back at her own assortment of wires and lights and thanked the Deity for about the ten millionth time that in another hour her switchboard days would be behind her. She wouldn't miss the drafty basement office, with its grey brick walls and moldy scent, and the sooner she got away from the constant clacking of fingers on keys, punctuated by the occasional ding followed by the whirr of a carriage return, the sooner she could stop spending so much money on aspirin.

"You're so lucky, Kadin." Trinithy Gold studied her reflection in a pearly, gold-trimmed compact and poked a curl back into her blond beehive. "Working upstairs as an aide to a homicide detective, among all those men! I don't think I'm ever going to get out of this basement. This morning I actually considered accepting when Darson asked me out."

Anything but that! The postboy was good-looking enough, with his crew cut and scuffed white bucks, but he had been at the menial job when Kadin had started at the company three years ago and didn't seem inclined toward promotion any time in the near future. He could never support a wife on his salary.

Kadin mimicked Trinithy's movements and ran her fingers through her own dark red curls. "I kept telling you to take the training course with me."

Trinithy wrinkled her snub nose at her reflection, then snapped her compact shut. "An entire year of night classes? Given Ollie's tales of how much work he had to do, I am quite certain that I have better employed my time *meeting* people, not to mention getting my beauty sleep. This perfect complexion does not come naturally."

Kadin nodded and turned to her switchboard to ensure that none of the lights were blinking. The detective coursework had been quite intensive, and some nights she'd had to sacrifice more sleep than she'd wanted writing papers and completing assignments.

She glanced down the line of switchboards at the coifed women with their full skirts puffed out around their stools. If she looked behind her, she'd see rows of typists at cheap plywood desks, as done-up in the height of fashion as the operators. Kadin dressed to her best advantage, but with her strong features and sturdy frame she would never stand out among the sea of beauties desperate to impress any unsuspecting man who wandered into their lair by mistake.

Even Trinithy, the tiniest, most delicate flower in the cellar, couldn't find a man in this crowd. If the blonde had considered going out with Darson—an exaggeration, Kadin suspected—she might have done well to put up with the detective course.

Judging from past experience, though, within a few weeks Trinithy's mother or sister would introduce her to a new crew of eligible men, all of whom would be falling at the blonde's feet. Trinithy claimed she spent hours on her hair and make-up, but Kadin suspected her friend rose from bed looking lovely. Trinithy's blue eyes would always look more innocent than Kadin's brown ones, and Kadin could never get her rosy features to rival Trinithy's fair complexion. Trinithy's pink dress, solid except for the white and pink polka-dotted bow across her chest, would have clashed with Kadin's red hair.

Kadin sat up straighter. "Education is an investment in your future."

"So is taking the proper amount of rest so that I don't develop wrinkles before I've got a ring on my finger." Trinithy propped her bare elbows on the table in front of her and glanced at the clock on the wall. "Where is Ollie? He promised he'd skip out early to get drinks with us, and I'm dying to leave."

Kadin swallowed a laugh. No doubt Trinithy did want to leave—she avoided work more than she did the ugly men her grandmother kept setting her up with—but her eagerness had less to do with the end of the workday and more to do with Olivan's promised presentation.

Olivan worked in personnel and had a lax view of what information should remain confidential, as well as a keen mind for discerning behavioral trends. He knew more about the eligible men at the company than they knew about themselves. He had promised to give Kadin a breakdown of the bachelors she should look out for, with a special emphasis on those in the homicide department.

"Relax." Kadin's voice remained calm, but she, too, shook with anticipation. "You know Ollie. He probably ran into someone he knows and absolutely had to tell him some of the latest news from *Imperial Society*."

"Oh my Deity, Kadin." Trinithy splayed out her manicured fingers and set her palms on the desk in front of her switchboard. "Did you see the issue that came out yesterday?"

Oh, here we go. "You know I didn't, Trin. Octavira hates to see me spending money on something so frivolous as glossies."

Kadin sent a brief mental apology to her sister-in-law for once again using her as an excuse for not embracing her friends' celebrity gossip hobby. That Octavira did refer to their interest as an "overinvestment in the lives of people they would never meet" lessened Kadin's guilt.

Besides, Kadin didn't need to read the society columns. Olivan or Trinithy would regale her with the contents, whether she wanted them to or not.

Trinithy leaned forward and spoke in a softer tone. "Well, of course it covered Duke Chaise Imbolc's charity ball. You remember I told you about that, right? No one could believe that he, of all people, would have a charity event, but I heard that his daughter refused to consider another marriage proposal unless he donated something to the schools in Smoke Row. Which is absurd. I mean, it's one thing to want to help children get a better education or whatever, but Lady Elyesse is twenty-eight years old. She may be a duke's daughter, but she doesn't have forever."

Kadin vaguely remembered Trinithy telling her about this particular event, but the Imperials' galas ran together after the first hundred or so. And Lady Elyesse's unmarried status, though a constant scandal, was hardly newsworthy. People had commented on her perceived failure for the past three years. Though the reminder made Kadin all the more grateful that she was a good three years away from being twenty-five and shamefully unmarried.

"—the dress she wore was such an unflattering shade that it's no wonder she can't catch a husband. I mean, vermillion! As if her long hair weren't unfashionable enough! But Lady Elyesse is old news." Trinithy barely took a breath before continuing on her next item of gossip. "The big story is—"

"Let me guess." Kadin knew Trinithy could only get this excited about one woman's exploits. "The big story is who Queen Callista brought as her escort."

"Yes!" Trinity disregarded the note of sarcasm in her friend's tone. "You will never guess!"

Kadin waited for a few seconds before she realized that Trinithy actually expected her to guess. "Well, since it's not someone I would expect that rules out Duke Baurus."

The duke's affair with his cousin's wife was the worst-kept secret in the Imperial circle. The society pages only ever hinted at the romance, but since the commoners in the city followed every tawdry detail they could read between the lines, Kadin imagined the nobles did as well.

Kadin's gaze wandered to the door. "I guess I'll go for the long shot and guess that she showed up with her husband."

Trinithy pouted, and Kadin suspected her friend had practiced shaping her lips into that perfect bow more times than she would ever admit. "Don't be absurd. You know that King Ralvin doesn't attend social events. He never appears in public without full ceremonial garb, and you know that would be far too uncomfortable to wear to a ball."

Kadin had never been to an Imperial gala and knew no such thing, but Trinithy liked to pretend that she had close relationships with all the players in Imperial society.

Kadin studied her long, almond-shaped red nails. "It's as good a guess as any."

"I suppose." Trinithy fiddled with her popped collar. "Anyway, the truth was nearly as shocking as it would have been if she had come with King Ralvin." She held up her hands and clasped them to her chest to give the appearance of waiting with bated breath. "She came alone."

That's it? Well, I guess it is shocking.

"Why alone?" Kadin asked.

"That's the thing. Nobody knows." By "nobody" Kadin assumed Trinithy meant the many society columnists who had discussed the issue at length in the various gossip glossies on which Trinithy spent a significant portion of her income. "None of the people interviewed—" i.e. the minor nobility who were unimportant enough to value seeing their names in print but consequently had little inside information "—had any idea what statement she was trying to make. Because of course even Queen Callista wouldn't do something so scandalous without good reason." Trinithy sat back. "She danced with everyone just the same."

"Except Duke Baurus." A man came up between Trinithy and Kadin and leaned his quiff into their huddle. "Garson Gray thinks that she came unaccompanied in order to add greater insult to their most recent break-up. She was stating in no uncertain terms that even if she didn't have another escort, she wouldn't be seen with him."

Trinithy turned to face the speaker, as if grateful to have a more interested party than Kadin with whom to discuss the issue. "Please, Ollie. Garson Gray thinks that everything is to do with the DeValeriels. I give more credence to Nandra Colt's theory that the queen was showing Lord Dimka that she is still unattached. Everyone knows she's wanted to resume their affair ever since he got married last spring."

Kadin waved her hand in Olivan's face, knowing the conversation would continue for at least half an hour if she didn't intervene. "Are we still going for a drink?"

"We'd better be." Trinithy reached up and pulled a white cardigan off the hook to the left of her switchboard. "I've had the most trying day."

"I would apologize for my tardiness, but I assure you it is to good purpose." Olivan gestured toward the pile of folders that he carried in his hand. "In here, I have the confidential personnel files of everyone that Kadin will be working with come tomorrow, as well as that of at least one eligible bachelor in the ranks of this great company's detectives."

"Ooh." Trinithy's mouth formed a perfect O as she reached for the files.

Olivan held them up out of her reach. "These are for Kadin. I seem to recall you telling us not long ago that you did not need assistance in finding men because you had a constant stream of potential suitors from both your mother and your married older sister."

"No, I said that I wasn't going to bother taking an entire course on how to be a detective's aide when I had other avenues of finding potential husbands." Trinithy stood up but did not try to reach for the documents again. She shrugged on her sweater and straightened the pink flower on the shoulder. "At no point did I say that I had any intention of ignoring potential matches in the workplace."

"You get first choice of these, K." Olivan took Kadin's elbow and helped her to her feet, and Kadin reached to grab her fitted green jacket. "Trinithy is only allowed to come if she swears not to approach any of these men until you have already rejected a proposal of marriage and/

or dinner. Which you won't want to do, because I would never foist someone ugly upon you."

"If you idlers are planning to skive off work like the delinquents you are, can you hurry up and do it so that the rest of us can perform our job functions?" A strident voice spoke up from two switchboards over.

They all turned to look at the olive-skinned brunette in a high-necked green and brown plaid dress, who had contorted her face into an expression of such loathing that Kadin suspected it had to be uncomfortable.

"Aw, Les, do you need me to find you a husband too?" Olivan ran his finger along the burgundy velvet lapel of his otherwise brown drape jacket. "I am sure I could come up with someone desperate enough. Trin, what was the name of that guy in missing persons? You know, the one with the harelip?"

Leslina Wolfsbane sniffed with such vigor that Kadin could see her nose hairs. "I can assure you, if I spent as much time as any of you trying to improve my appearance, I could certainly have managed to catch a husband by now."

Trinithy twirled on her flannel-accented pump, causing her full, knee-length skirt to puff out even further. "Well, Leslina, if I put as much time and energy into my career as you did, I definitely would not have lost out on the job to Kadin."

Kadin dropped her eyes to the buttoned top she wore over a matching skirt that tapered at the knee. She and Leslina had both applied to work as Caison Fellows's aide, but he had offered Kadin the position. Only a few months before that, Kadin had scored higher on the detective's exam than Leslina. But the woman had hated Kadin since they started working at the call center within a week of each other three years ago, and Kadin had no idea why.

"Oh, I'm over that." Leslina addressed her words to Trinithy, but she directed her glare at Kadin. "Everyone knows that Caison Fellows hires the biggest sub-D who applies for the position."

Kadin didn't want to engage her, but she knew Olivan and Trinithy would give her grief if she let Leslina put her down like that.

"Then it's a wonder he didn't choose you, Leslina." Kadin's heart pounded inside her chest. "But I guess even the promise of extra favors wasn't enough to put up with you every day."

Leslina rammed a cord into the home jack of her switchboard. "You're so stupid, Kadin Stone. But you go off and enjoy being a glorified java girl for the menfolk. There's an aide position coming up in robbery that has my name written all over it. One that requires actual detective skills."

"Ignore her, K." Trinithy picked up her box purse with jeweled partridges on the side and slung it over her shoulder. "Caison Fellows's last aide got married six months after he hired her."

"I charted the wedding rate." Ollie swept past Leslina as they headed for the door. "Overall, the female aides in the homicide department have the highest rate of attrition due to nuptials, and within the last 20 years, only two of Fellows's aides left his employment without a wedding planned. I'll show you the graphs when we get to the restaurant. Where are we going anyway?"

Kadin pushed the button to call the lift and put on her coat. "How about that new place on the corner of Candlewick and Drawing? We haven't gone there yet."

"I don't know." Trinithy swung her purse. "Do they have a jukebox with a decent selection?"

The steel lift doors opened, and Kadin stepped inside. "I'm sure it's as good as any other."

"It'd better be, because I want to *dance*." Trinithy pushed the button for the ground floor. "You'll dance with me, won't you, Ollie?"

Olivan rose on the toes of his thick-soled creepers, showing off the suede tops in the exact color of the trim on his jacket. “Well, you’re about a foot too short and the wrong gender to be my type.”

Trinithy picked at her diamond-shaped “Queen Callista” neckline, as if her bulging cleavage would do anything to persuade Olivan. “Oh, you sideways boys! I don’t want you to marry me, just dance with me. And I promise if any eligible boys come along, I’ll let you go. Mostly because I plan to steal them for myself.”

Olivan stuck the hand that wasn’t carrying file folders into a velvet-lined pocket. “You think you can steal boys from me, Trinithy Gold? All right. It is *on*.”

Kadin sighed as the lift dinged and the doors began to open. “So we are going to the new place? Hatpin’s, I think it’s called.”

Olivan held the door so that the women could exit. “Might as well. I hope they stock the good whiskey.”

Cool autumn wind ruffled Kadin’s hair as she stepped out onto Candlewick Avenue, the main thoroughfare of the Business District. The most commercial of Valeriel City’s six districts held the headquarters of the most distinguished companies in the city, as well as those, like Valeriel Investigations, that were still working toward distinguished. Kadin stuck her hands in her pocket and pulled her arms in close to herself, wondering if the season grew late enough that she should consider wearing her shapeless woolen coat. She shuddered, thinking of the likelihood of attracting a man in *that* getup.

“Cold, K?” Olivan wrapped an arm around her shoulder, seeming, as ever, oblivious to the elements. She glanced down and beheld a goosebump-less ring of skin between the bottoms of his drainpipe pants and green socks.

Kadin ducked out from under Olivan’s arm. She couldn’t have any eligible men they might pass thinking she had an attachment.

Honking autocars lumbered past them down the street, leaving the scent of gasoline in their wakes. Trinithy ogled a sleek red and white model with a thick hood and a tapering trunk.

"I've been trying to get my daddy to buy an autocar like that, but he says I'll have to find a rich husband." She stuck out her lower lip and kicked a rock on the sidewalk. "Like I haven't been *trying*. I need—" She let out a squeal and grabbed Kadin's hand to drag her over to the closest wide-paned window set in the wall of red brick storefronts. "Look! They have *air conditioners*!"

Kadin recognized the display at Hasten's Electronics, whose offerings were always the best and most up-to-date—and the most expensive. Kadin couldn't even afford one of their transistor radios. Alongside the clunky, slat-covered grey window unit Trinithy admired stood a dishwasher, half open to show off both its shiny pink front and optimally-arranged wire drawers, and a black-and-white television in a mahogany case with five shiny gold knobs next to the screen.

"Who wants an air conditioner in this weather?" Olivan squinted to peer past the display.

"It's not about the temperature. It's about *having* one." Trinithy pressed her nose against the glass, steaming up the window with her breath. "When I get married, my husband is going to buy me an air conditioner and a dishwasher and a vacuum cleaner and..." She pulled away from the window and pursed her lips. "Come on, K. Aren't you even a little bit excited?"

Kadin watched the fuzzy footage on the television—Queen Callista on the arm of some noble Kadin didn't recognize. "I don't know, Trin. It's hard to get excited about cleaning. Though, I suppose Octavira couldn't make me wash nearly as many dishes if we had a dishwasher."

"Another advantage to getting married—no more Octavira! Or, at least, only on special occasions." Trinithy had disliked Kadin's sister-in-law since Octavira had made disparaging comments about Trinithy's flirtatious behavior at the Stone's barbecue last year. Trinithy had then accidentally-on-purpose spilled marinara sauce all over Octavira's white dress. Kadin had spent the next week listening to the two women complain about each other, and Octavira had blacklisted Trinithy from any future events at her home.

The blonde hooked her elbow in Kadin's and skipped down the street. "We're lucky, K. We're young and beautiful in this modern age. The world is our oyster." She wrinkled her snub nose. "Or maybe something less slimy."

"I don't know." Olivan sauntered along beside them. "In another twenty years, everyone will have a television and a dishwasher. Do you think we'll be too old to appreciate it?"

Kadin tried to imagine herself twenty years in the future and came up blank. Trinithy liked to imagine her life as a housewife, but Kadin hadn't thought much past getting married. She supposed she'd have children, and they'd be almost grown—sons looking to get jobs or go to college, and daughters looking for husbands of their own. But, then, if times changed enough that everyone could have the things that today seemed like luxuries, what else might be different?

Trinithy waved a dismissive hand. "I will never be too old to appreciate a dishwasher."

"Hey, we're here." Ollie stopped and pulled open the door to Hatpin's Bar. Trinithy ducked under his arm to enter, and Kadin followed.

Kadin's navy and white heels clacked to the beat of the Dawban Steel song ringing from the juke box as she moved across the room. Young professionals bellied up to the bar or sat at circular tables peppered throughout the dark space. Cigarette smoke and casual laughter filled the air. Kadin and her friends headed straight for the patch of bar in front of the bartender, who stood in front of a wall-length, gold-rimmed mirror with wooden shelves full of exotic liquor bottles on either side.

"What can I get you?" The man reached over his head and pulled down three glasses.

Trinithy giggled, her eyes on the tight white T-shirt that showed off his muscled chest. "Gin Rickey, emphasis on the 'gin.'"

Kadin ran her fingers along the bar. "Dirty martini."

"Whiskey sour. With the Oriole whiskey. None of that crap from Barring." Olivan pulled out his wallet. "First round's on me, ladies. In honor of Kadin's last day."

Trinithy threw her arms around him. "If only I could get rightways boys to buy me drinks so easily."

Kadin felt the heat rise to her cheeks at Trinithy's overreaction. Olivan frequently bought them drinks, but generosity had little to do with it. Society did not look keenly on men—even sideways ones—who made women pay for drinks. "Thanks, Ollie."

The bartender stuck a wedge of lime on Trinithy's glass and plopped a cherry into Olivan's, then slid all three across the bar.

Olivan threw a bill on the bar. "Keep the change." He lifted his glass, and the girls followed suit. The condensation from the glass dribbled down Kadin's thumb as they crossed the smoky bar to sit at a table in the corner.

Olivan took a sip of his drink and made an appreciative noise. He set his glass down and pushed it toward the center of the table, pulling his file folders in front of him. "Now, to the business of the day. The homicide department currently has eight members. Kadin will make it nine. Fortunately for K, the others are all male. Unfortunately, some of them are already married. I brought the married guys' files, too, but I don't know that you'll want to see them."

Trinithy's glass clinked as she took a gulp. "Eh, skip 'em."

Olivan raised his eyebrows at Kadin as she swallowed and set down her glass. “Maybe just the ones I’ll be working with?” she asked.

Olivan handed her two files. “Inspector Blaik Warring runs the department and has for the past two years. The only one who has been working for the department longer is your new boss, Detective Caison Fellows. The company offered Fellows the Inspector job, but he didn’t want to take it when he was so close to retirement. Rumor has it that you are the last aide that Fellows ever plans to hire.”

Kadin opened the first file and saw a click of a strong-featured man with greying black hair and a frown that implied he had better things to than sit for a personnel photograph. She didn’t bother glancing at Fellows’s picture. She had met the balding, older detective when she had interviewed with him.

“There are a few more, but...” Olivan threw the next few files onto the table in quick succession. “Boring, ancient, ugly, sideways.” He pulled the next file out of the stack more slowly and waved it in front of Kadin. “Feast your eyes, Miss Stone, upon this.”

He opened the file with a flourish.

“Ooh.” Trinithy sucked in a breath as she looked at the man in the click. He had dark brown hair parted on the side, piercing blue eyes, and strong, symmetrical features. “Who is that?”

Olivan grinned. “That, my dear Miss Gold, is the one and only Dahran White. Full homicide detective at only 28 years old and a rising star in the company. But he knows that he’s not going to get much higher without setting down some roots in the community, and for that he will need to find a nice girl to settle down with. And who is nicer than our Kadin?”

“I could be very nice to him.” Trinithy licked her lips.

Kadin felt an uncertain twinge in her stomach. White’s smile gave the impression that he took great pride in his ability to make women swoon. "He seems to be an interesting prospect." She peered at the short stack of folders Olivan hadn't presented yet. "Anything worth considering there?"

"The aides in the department. I wouldn't waste my time with them." Olivan wrinkled his nose at the files as he handed them over to her. "And a few far less attractive boys from robbery, but you can leave them to Leslina."

Kadin took a brief glance at the photos, then set them aside. *It's better than your options in the basement.* "All right, you've convinced me. So what do you recommend I do to win the heart—or at least the committed interest—of Dahran White?"

Trinithy elbowed Kadin. "First, make an *effort.* Seriously, Kadin, for all you've dated, you'd think you would be better at it by now. A man will want to hear your sarcasm about the same time the Society of Mages returns to Valeriel. Pretend you're besotted with him. Laugh at everything he says. Admire everything he's interested in. And by all the Deity blesses, don't correct him. You know that's what lost you what's-his-name."

"Sevuel." Kadin shuddered at the thought of the last man she had hoped might put a "Mrs." in front of her name. "But, Trinithy, he said the Assembly had 27 representatives. I couldn't let that go."

Trinithy held up a chastising finger. "There will be plenty of time to worry about how many members are in the Assembly after you've got a ring on your finger."

"But everyone knows there are three representatives for each of the eight territories! Three times eight is..." Kadin bowed her head at Trinithy's disapproving stare. "I guess it's not that important."

Olivan cleared his throat and swiped a piece of paper out of Dahran White's file. "Should you decide to progress to more advanced tactics than simply not insulting the object of your affections, I have picked up a few details regarding Mr. White's preferences."

Kadin took a sip of her drink and leaned forward. "I'm all ears."

Olivan flipped the paper around and pointed to a graph at the top. "First, according to the questionnaire that I may or may not have included as part of his employment paperwork, the first thing Dahran White notices about a woman is her legs. So keep wearing the tight skirts, and consider upping the height of those heels by at least two inches."

Kadin glanced down at the pumps that already had her towering over the girls in the basement. "But I'm so tall already."

Olivan smirked. "He's 6'2". You're safe."

Kadin thought back to the last pair of four-inch pumps Trinithy had convinced her to buy and realized she had gotten rid of them the last time Octavira had taken donations to the charity store. Which meant Kadin would have to borrow shoes from her sister-in-law, whose feet were a size smaller than Kadin's. She groaned but nodded. "I can make it work this week and go shopping on the weekend. What else?"

"On his list of interests, he includes autocar racing, and, fortunately for you, your best friend in the entire world managed to pick up the latest issue of *Racers* for you to peruse at opportune moments." Olivan pulled the glossy out of Dahran's file and handed it to Kadin. "I also have a list of his favorite television programs, but since your brother is too cheap to buy one, that's of little help."

Trinithy slugged down the last of her gin. "You need to think long-term, Ollie. Not having a television will be very useful in six months or so when she wants to finagle an invitation to his house."

Kadin felt heat rise to her cheeks, but she wasn't sure if

she was reacting to the idea of going to an unattached man's house or being so mercenary as to finagle an invitation.

"You raise a valid point, Miss Gold." Olivan slid the paper back into the file and closed it. "Well, that is all the information I can provide at this juncture." He picked up his glass. "So I propose a toast to Kadin and her new job. May we soon be toasting its end."

CHAPTER 2

KADIN ALIT FROM THE AUTOBUS in the Covenant District, where most of the middle class families in the city lived, and coughed as the retreating vehicle puffed exhaust fumes in her face. The twin full moons lit the way in front of her as she hurried down the two blocks to her house. She tried not to think they were a bad omen, when good things were finally coming her way.

She stepped through the wrought iron gate at #14 Springtown Lane, a not-too-shabby white townhouse with a green door and shutters, and went around to the back door. On the stoop, she exhaled into her hand and sniffed, checking to make sure her breath didn't smell like alcohol. Trinithy and Olivan had talked her into her a second drink, against her better judgment. Her palm seemed clean, and she felt some tension go out of her shoulders.

She unlocked the door and pushed it open. She stepped into the room her family used for dining, a cheerful space with yellow walls and a brown linoleum floor. Soft jazz drifted in from the radio in the other room, and the scents of buttered spinach and ham with brown sugar glaze filled the air.

"Where have you been?" An attractive woman in her late twenties with dark brown curls pulled back from the short fringe on her forehead stood in the entrance to the small kitchen to Kadin's right. The woman placed her hands on the cinched waist of her green and white striped dress, which had a frilly white apron covering the full skirt. "You know I need to get dinner ready for your brother by the time he gets home, and I can't do that and watch the children at the same time."

"Sorry, Octavira." Kadin wondered if her sister-in-law could have finished dinner faster if she hadn't waited at the door for Kadin. "What do you need me to do?"

Octavira pointed a wooden spoon toward the stairs. "Go check on the children. And then get back here and set the table."

The floorboards creaked as Kadin hurried through the living room and up the stairs to look in on her niece, Drena, and nephew, Aberon. At three and four years old, respectively, they didn't need to be in the presence of an adult at every moment, but Octavira worried over their safety even when she could see them.

The upstairs of Kadin's house featured a hexagonal-shaped space, where each wall contained a door that opened into a bedroom. Kadin opened first door to the right and beheld a small room with toys scattered all over the floor—robots and autocars for Aberon, doll dresses and dishes for Drena. She picked up the scent of watercolors, and noticed the papers hanging on the wall depicting colorful blobs that likely had great meaning for the children.

"Auntie K!" A small girl with her mother's brown curls ran toward Kadin from the pretend kitchen set up against the wall.

Kadin bent down to give her niece a hug. "What have you been doing today?"

"I've been taking care of Manzy." The girl held up a rag doll. "She's sick."

Kadin shaped her mouth into a wide "O." "Oh no! Did you take her to the doctor?"

Drena stamped her foot. "I *tried.* But Aberon said he didn't want to be a doctor. He wanted to be a 'vestigator."

Kadin looked over at the chubby boy who made noises for a tiny autocar as he rolled it across the carpet. "You don't want to be a doctor? But your father is a doctor."

"No!" Aberon shook his head but didn't look up from his toy. "'Vestitators are better! Mummy told Papa that if he was a 'vestitator, he would be able to buy anything he wanted."

Kadin crawled over and laid a gentle hand on her nephew's head. "Your father saves dying people. That's more important than buying anything you want."

Drena bounced up and down on her knees. "Aren't you a 'vestigator, Auntie Kadin? Does that mean you can buy anything that you want?"

Kadin reached out to tickle her niece, who giggled. "No, I'm just an assistant investigator, and I'm only doing that for a little while. Someday soon I'm going to get married and be a housewife like your mother."

"Mummy says that's going to be a zisaster." Aberon trundled his autocar over to Kadin and made it roll along her leg. "She says Auntie K can't step into the kitchen without burning something."

I'm going to have to talk to Octavira about what she's saying to the children. Kadin laughed to herself as she thought how well that would go over.

"Yes, well—"

"Kadin!" Octavira's strident tones came up from the ground floor.

Kadin gave Aberon and Drena each a quick kiss on the head. "I've got to go help your mother. I'll see you at dinner in a bit."

"Kiss Manzy too!" Drena thrust the doll under Kadin's

nose. Kadin obeyed her niece's wish and then hurried down the stairs.

"I don't ask that much of you, Kadin." Octavira turned away from the gas stove as soon as Kadin set foot in the kitchen. *Without burning anything,* she thought as she retrieved the brown floral dinner plates from the white cabinet and took them out to the table.

Octavira returned to stirring the corn. "But you know that your brother works diligently to save people's lives for very little compensation."

Imagine if he had a job like mine and could buy anything he wanted. Kadin placed the last plate on the table and returned to the kitchen for silverware.

Octavira lowered the heat on the corn and turned her attention to the spinach on the next burner. "The least we can do for him is make sure that dinner is ready when he gets home."

Kadin sighed as she folded a napkin and placed a fork on top. "I know, Octavira, and I really am sorry." Her brother, who was ten years older than she was, had done so much for her, looking after her when their parents had passed away and taking her in after their grandmother and guardian had died five years ago.

Octavira bent down and opened the stove, drizzling more brown sugar on the ham. "I hope that this new job of yours will allow you to spend the proper amount of time on your responsibilities at home."

"Oh, well, I think they said that I might have to work some extra hours with this position..." Kadin took in Octavira's narrowed eyes and tapping foot. "But I'm sure they'll understand that I can't do that." *Or at least hold off on the overtime until I can come up with a better excuse.*

Kadin had finished filling the last water glass when the door opened and her brother entered, a broad smile on his face. "How are my two favorite girls this evening?"

Like Kadin, Tobin was tall and sturdy, with brown eyes

and a strong nose and chin. His hair was several shades darker than Kadin's, more of a brown with a touch of red. He wore a white doctor's jacket over his plaid shirt and solid brown tie.

"Everything is almost ready. You're right on time, as always." Octavira wiped her hands on a dishcloth and gave her husband a kiss. "Kadin, would you be a dear and get the children washed up?"

"Oh, don't be silly. I'll do that." Tobin stepped around his wife and moved toward the living room.

"Darling, you should rest," Octavira said. "You've been at the hospital all day, up to your elbows in Deity knows what."

"Do you think I should rest, or do you think I still have blood and guts on my hands?" Tobin smiled and shook his head. "Believe me, I've scrubbed, and caring for my own children is hardly work. Besides, Kadin's been at the office all day too."

Drena and Aberon jumped up and ran over to their father as soon as they saw him and behaved in a far more cooperative manner with him than they would have with Kadin. The two adults got both of the children down the stairs and seated at the table as Octavira brought the final steaming dish out of the kitchen.

"How was your day?" Octavira asked Tobin as she spooned a portion of spinach onto each of her children's plates.

"Oh, the usual." Tobin speared a piece of ham and put it on his plate. "Lots of people needing surgery, but only so many resources available." As a doctor, Tobin was a Valeriel City employee, and he frequently complained about the budgetary restrictions. "I have one man who keeps calling me about his mother's kidney condition, and I don't have the heart to tell him I can't move her up on the list unless her condition worsens."

Kadin took a bite of her spinach. Like everything else

Octavira cooked, it was perfect. It had a buttery flavoring and just the right hint of garlic. "And yet you think criminal investigations should be run by the state as well? You want everyone to have to wait for years to find out who murdered a loved one?"

Tobin huffed and took a sip of water. "Better to have a slow time frame than what we have now, where many people can't get investigations at all."

"I don't want ham!" Drena crossed her arms and pouted, as her mother slid her daughter's plate in front of her. Aberon giggled as he picked up a piece of corn with his fingers and shoved it in his mouth along with half his hand.

Kadin sliced the skin off her ham and savored the smell of the salty meat laced with a hefty dose of brown sugar. "Most people have investigation insurance to cover the costs."

Tobin stuck his knife into the butter with more force than necessary. "But there are tens of thousands of people in the city without insurance, and they are forced to go into debt or else present in court with no sanctioned evidence for their case! And even for people who have it, premiums are going up every year! And where is all the money going? To rich merchants who want it to buy another beach house in Barring! Or to pay for giant corporate parties, while I have to deny care to non-emergency cases because the hospital is short on stents!"

Kadin smiled as she raised her water glass to her lips.

"You don't need that much butter." Octavira pulled Drena's knife away from her, as the girl tried to cut two tablespoons worth off the stick. Aberon made a chain of spinach and corn around the inner rim of his plate.

Tobin leaned forward and pointed a finger at Kadin. "It is unreasonable to expect a society to continue to function in this manner, and if the Assembly weren't entirely populated by wealthy Merchants protecting their own interests and selfish Imperials who have never had to work a day in their lives, people would see that. In fact—" Tobin broke off when he saw Kadin's expression and then resumed speaking in a calmer voice. "But you know all this and want to watch me rant for your own amusement."

"I know you like to get it out of your system every once in a while." Kadin didn't know which side of the debate to socialize investigations she stood on, but her pragmatic side knew that change wasn't going to come any time in the near future, so she had to deal with things as they were.

"I don't see why you complain so much." Octavira sat down in her chair and began cutting her own food while keeping a steady eye on her children. "The kingdom isn't perfect, but it's still better than anywhere else we could live. Imagine if we were in Ruathala, where the Church stones people for telling lies, or Crestor, where families are lucky to have a single room of their own. We're the most prosperous country in the world, and we should appreciate it."

Tobin reached over to help Drena butter her roll. "At least in Ruathala criminals are punished. The lower classes here live in anarchy, because no one has investigation insurance, and the courts won't admit any evidence that isn't certified by a detective."

Octavira made an exasperated noise. "But that has nothing to do with us. We're decent people who *do* have insurance, so we don't need to worry."

"But what if something happened to me? You would only have whatever insurance the territory was willing to pay for." Tobin shook his head. "I can't believe King Ralvin didn't veto that bill to cut spending to the widows and children investigation allotment."

Kadin sliced her ham into even pieces. "Well, King Ralvin only ever gets involved in the Assembly's affairs if he has to. He didn't veto the bill for the state to pay for all murder investigations either."

Tobin speared a piece of corn with his fork. "But he didn't need to because that one didn't pass. We would be so much better off if Duke Baurus ruled the kingdom. He at least passes legislation to help the people instead of sitting and doing nothing."

Kadin snickered. "Yes, but he forgets about governing the state entirely when Queen Callista isn't sleeping with him."

Octavira sniffed. "Kadin! Don't say such things in front of the children."

Kadin looked down at her plate. "Sorry. But the Assembly is full of people who have been wealthy for generations. None of them have any idea what it's like to be a regular person, and they don't care."

Drena bounced in her chair. "What's a 'ssembly?"

Tobin leaned his head down to be closer to his daughter's. "The Assembly is the group of people who make our laws. Each territory has three members. One seat is taken by the duke, who also rules the territory and inherits his position. The next representative is chosen from among the Merchants Guild, the group of businessmen made of anyone wealthy enough to pay for membership. And the last one, the assemblyman-at-large, is voted for by all the people, but in practice it's always an Imperial or a Merchant."

Kadin didn't think either of the children understood most of what Tobin was saying, but her brother never passed up the opportunity to teach his children.

"What territory do we live in?" Tobin asked the children.

"Hmmm." Drena put her finger to lips and made a show of thinking.

Aberon bounced up and down in his chair. "Baleriel!"

"That's right!" Tobin reached out to tickle his son's ribs. "Valeriel City is the newest territory. It used to be part of Sultan, but King Drakan decided that the city had enough people form its own duchy. So he made his second son Corwin the duke of the city, and now Duke Corwin's son Baurus leads the city."

Tobin opened his mouth, no doubt to impart further knowledge of government upon his children, but before he could Aberon knocked his cup of milk over, causing rivulets of white to seep into the green tablecloth. Octavira shrieked, and Kadin hurried to mop up the mess before the liquid damaged the pine table underneath.

When they finished supper, Kadin helped Octavira with the dishes and then assisted in getting the children ready for bed. When she finally had a moment to herself, she sat down on the chair in front of her bureau's floral-painted mirror and studied her face.

By nature, Kadin was not possessed of better-than-average attractiveness, but she had spent many years learning how to make herself appear to her best advantage. She couldn't make her dark red hair stop clashing with clothes that would otherwise look well on her, but she could select lipstick that complemented the unique shade. A subtler shade of blush accentuated her cheekbones, and mascara and eyeliner made her round brown eyes appear even larger. She must have been doing something right, because everyone knew Detective Fellows didn't hire homely aides.

She glanced at her closet and knew she had better finalize her choice of outfit for the next day, the day she would meet her—she hoped—soon-to-be fiancé Dahran White. She had settled on her most form-fitting black pinstriped dress with the tapered skirt and sweetheart neckline, but she couldn't decide between the green cardigan, which looked better on her, and the red one, which looked better with the dress. She had almost decided on the green when she remembered she needed to borrow Octavira's shoes.

Kadin crept across the landing to her brother and sister-in-law's room, careful not to wake the children, and had lifted her hand to knock on the door when she heard Tobin speak. "I am not having this conversation again, Vira."

"Yes, you are." Irritation rang in Octavira's tone, and Kadin suspected that, had the children not been sleeping, their mother would have spoken at a much higher volume. "We are going to keep having this conversation until you come to your senses."

"I think I am being sensible, as you well know." Tobin's voice was not as strident as Octavira's, but it held the same level of frustration.

"She's twenty-two years old. It is high time she was out of this house. It would be past time if she were living with her parents, and it's absurd for her to be staying with a brother this long."

They're talking about me. Kadin had long known that her continued presence in the house annoyed Octavira, but Kadin's eyes still stung at her sister-in-law's words.

"What do you want me to do, cast my only living relative out onto the street?" Tobin sounded almost amused at the idea.

Octavira made an exasperated noise. "She is not your only living relative. You have your children to think of as well. And she wouldn't be homeless. She has a job. She probably makes more money than you do at this point. She could get an apartment and live perfectly well on her own."

Kadin knew she should walk away. She didn't want to eavesdrop on her brother's conversation, but she couldn't make herself stop listening.

"No." Tobin's tone was serious again. "It doesn't matter how much money she makes. It's not safe for a woman living on her own in the city. You know that."

A bang sounded, as if Octavira had slammed a shoe on the hard floor. "Well, if you won't let her live alone, you could at least let her support herself. And stop looking at me as though you don't know what I'm talking about.

I know that she offered to contribute to the household income last week and that you turned her down *again.* There is no reason that you should feel obliged to pay for everything."

"Kadin can have a job or not as she chooses, and I will still feed and clothe her. It is my responsibility to do so," Tobin said. "And it's not as if she doesn't do anything to earn it. She spends most of her free time helping you with the house and the children. And don't think I don't notice the new additions to your wardrobe that are funded by her paycheck instead of mine."

Kadin could picture Octavira standing up straight and putting her hands on her hips. "And why shouldn't I let her buy me things, if she offers? Do you want your sister to be better clothed than your wife?"

Tobin sighed. "Of course not, Vira. In fact, I am glad that you and Kadin get along well enough that you can do these kinds of things for each other. My only point was that you benefit from her being in the household, so I don't see why you're so eager to see her gone."

Had Kadin been in the room, she might have commented that the purchases didn't reflect a friendship between herself and Octavira so much as the older woman's insistence that Kadin pay her dues in some manner. But she probably would have kept quiet, since Tobin liked to believe the two of them enjoyed each other's company, and both women expended quite a bit of energy to keep Tobin happy.

"And I don't see why you're so eager for her to stay here forever," Octavira said. "Any other brother would at least introduce her to some of the men he works with. But you don't seem to want her to get married."

Tobin was silent for a minute before he answered. "You don't understand. Kadin's special. When she was little, when our parents were still alive, everyone could tell that she could do anything that she wanted. My parents never wanted her to grow up like an ordinary girl, thinking of nothing but catching a husband. But after my parents died, my grandmother spent years convincing Kadin she was ordinary and average, and Kadin started to believe it too. I refuse to contribute to that perspective."

Kadin gasped at Tobin's speech, then clapped her hand over her mouth, hoping they hadn't heard. Tobin hadn't gone on about how special she was supposed to be for a long time, and Kadin thought he had given up the notion. Until about a year ago, whenever she dressed up or went out on dates, Tobin would try to stop her. *You're special, K,* he would say. *Mother and Father never wanted this for you. You could be so much more.*

Then one day, after yet another boyfriend had broken up with her over some offense that she couldn't remember now, Tobin had insisted it didn't matter because she didn't need a husband, and Kadin had snapped. She told him their parents had known a six-year-old child and of course wanted to believe in the superiority of their children. She missed them, too, but she and Tobin had to stop living according to what they thought the dead wanted.

Tobin had stopped his speeches, and she had hoped that he had given up his misplaced conviction that she was destined for greatness. Apparently not.

"Of course being a wife and mother isn't good enough." Octavira's voice was so tight, Kadin could imagine the flecks of spit spouting from her lips. "Oh, it's good enough for some of us, but not for precious Kadin."

Kadin heard the floorboards creak and realized that Octavira or Tobin approached the other side of the door. Kadin darted backwards, trying to look as if she had not eavesdropped on their argument.

Octavira flung the door open, and, from the way she pulled her head back, Kadin suspected her sister-in-law hadn't known Kadin stood in the hall. "What do you want?"

"I..." *I'm sorry,* Kadin wanted to say. *I don't want to be a burden on you and Tobin. I'm trying my best to get out of your way, honestly.* "I wanted to know if I could borrow your black pumps."

Octavira stomped back into her room and disappeared into the closet. Kadin avoided looking directly at Tobin. He would know that she had not just arrived.

Octavira emerged a few minutes later and practically threw the shoes at Kadin.

Kadin went back to her room and looked in the mirror. She hated this, being a burden on her brother's family that he refused to give up.

But I have a plan. I'm going to get married. I'm going to leave here, and Tobin will be able to focus on himself and his family.

Kadin looked her reflection straight in the eye. "I will not keep being a burden on my family. I'm going to marry Dahran White, whether I like him or not." She held her chin up and refused to acknowledge the slight quiver of her lower lip.

Kadin made it a point never to cry herself to sleep. The resulting puffy eyes could ruin her complexion for days.

CHAPTER 3

By the time Kadin got to Valeriel Investigations the next morning, she regretted her decision to borrow Octavira's shoes. She had wedged her feet into the pointed toes well enough, but after a ride on a standing-room only autobus and a block and a half walk to the office, she felt the pinch. She glanced down to remind herself how good her calves looked and renewed her vow to buy a pair of heels in her size that weekend.

She passed through the revolving door and veered left to head to Employee Medical Services. As a woman beginning a new job, the law mandated that she have her blood drawn before she could report for duty.

The woman at the reception desk was too busy applying a dark coral lipstick to look up when Kadin approached.

Plum would suit her better. But she probably doesn't want unsolicited beauty advice.

After the receptionist applied the third coat, Kadin cleared her throat. The receptionist added one more swipe, rubbed her lips together, and snapped her compact shut before turning to look at the new arrival.

"Hi, I'm Kadin Stone." Kadin put on her best friendly smile. "I start in Homicide this morning."

The woman made a check mark next to the first entry

on her schedule and said in a bored voice, “Dr. Combs will be with you shortly. Have a seat.” She flipped her compact open and pulled out a mascara wand.

Kadin had her choice of brown-polyester-padded chairs in the empty waiting room, so she sat down next to a low table covered in glossies. She might have been tempted to scan through *Imperial Society* to look at the dresses, if Trinithy hadn’t given her the full analysis the day before. Instead, she picked up *Professional Woman.* She flipped through the pictures of the latest business fashions, paying particular attention to the shoes. She read the advice column of how to gauge the sincerity of the interest of your male coworkers and skimmed an article about opportunities for women in primarily male professions. She smiled when she saw that detective’s aide was one of their top choices for marital possibilities.

A condescending female voice next to the reception desk interrupted Kadin’s satisfaction. “Marin, I need to speak to my husband immediately.”

The speaker had teased her dyed tangerine beehive to twice the height of Trinithy’s and wore a layer of foundation so thick Kadin could see the cracks in it. The woman had pulled her tight black skirt well above her knees, and a V-shaped neckline showed off her significant cleavage. Her purple heels had at least an inch on the ones Kadin had borrowed from Octavira, and the matching eye shadow rose almost to her eyebrows. The newcomer resembled nothing so much as a down-and-out Class D on a corner in the worst part of town.

Kadin realized she was staring, so she closed her mouth and turned her attention back to the glossy.

The phone clicked as Marin hung it up. “Your husband will be out in a minute, Mrs. Combs.” The receptionist sounded, if anything, even colder toward the new woman than she had toward Kadin.

The clacks of Mrs. Combs’s heels softened as she stepped

from the tile around the reception desk to the carpet of the main waiting room. She managed the movement with more ease than Kadin would have in such shoes, but her motions were still more gawky than graceful. She snapped open her clutch, and, after a moment of rustling paper, the sound of smacking lips accompanied the scent of fruit gum.

A few moments later, the door to the back room swung open, and the handsomest man Kadin had ever seen—head mirror on his brow notwithstanding—stalked out. His silky blond hair was a shade lighter than his tanned features, and his eyes were such a bright green that they looked like chips of emeralds. Kadin could barely make out his torso beneath his bulky white medical coat, but she could tell that his job at the agency left him plenty of time to work out.

The only thing marring the perfect visage was the scowl on his face.

His nostrils flared when he saw the woman in the purple heels. "What are you doing here, Joelle?"

If I were married to someone who looked like him, I would consider that my ultimate blessing from the Deity and never ask for anything again, Kadin thought.

Joelle apparently felt differently. "Don't you get huffy with me, Jace Combs. I told you I was getting my nails done today, and you didn't leave me the money for it. What did you expect me to do?"

Combs clamped his fist around the stethoscope dangling from his neck. "What happened to all the money I gave you earlier this week?"

"I told you I needed that to get clothes for the club opening last night." Joelle snapped her gum. "Which you missed, by the way. Everyone kept asking where you were, too. It's so embarrassing to have to make excuses for you all the time."

Kadin could practically see the fury radiating from

Combs. “I had to work, Joelle. You remember my job? The thing that gives us money so that you can do things like go to club openings and nail salons?”

Joelle stuck out her lower lip. “None of the other girls’ husbands work as much as you do. It’s not as if they pay you enough to make it worthwhile. Belina had one of the new Cotillion bags. You know, the one you keep saying that we can’t afford.”

Combs opened his mouth to respond but paused when he glanced to the side and saw Kadin gaping at their conversation. He pulled a wallet out of his pants pocket and counted out a few bills. “Joelle, I need to get back to work. Take this for your nail appointment, and we can discuss the other things later.”

Joelle grabbed the money with a huff, then turned and sauntered out without a word of thanks. Kadin snapped her head to the glossy in front of her and scrutinized the images of the season’s best outfits until a shadow fell into her light.

She looked up to find the blond man raising his eyebrows at her. She studied his face, looking for some flaw but finding none. *I wonder if Ollie knows about him and, if so, how he’s refrained from recounting his virtues at every occasion.*

“I’m Dr. Jace Combs, forensic examiner and occasional phlebotomist and upholder of social norms.” His tone was hostile, and Kadin hoped it was leftover anger at his wife and not any kind of judgment on her. “You, I assume, are Caison Fellows’s new aide.”

“Indeed.” Kadin smiled as she stood, so that he would know she wasn’t offended by his attitude. “I’m Kadin Stone.”

He looked her up and down, and she stood up taller, knowing she had dressed her best today. Except he must have found something wanting in her appearance because his scowl deepened before he spun away from her.

He took a few steps toward the back door and looked

back at her, which was all the indication he gave that she should follow. She tried match his pace but slowed when she felt her shoes digging into the back of her feet.

The cold white hallway seemed longer than it probably was, and of course Combs led her to almost the last door in the row. He turned the handle on the door and opened it, and when she caught up, she saw a small room with a paper-covered steel examining table and a balance beam height-and-weight scale. Papers and folders covered the small desk set into the wall, and yellow-brown cabinets hung over the serviceable metal sink. Kadin wrinkled her nose as the smell of antiseptic hit her.

Combs slammed the door as soon as they entered. "For the sake of the Deity, take off those ridiculous shoes! You can't even walk in them." His shoes squeaked against the tile floor as he went to fiddle with the syringe and empty test tube next to the sink.

Oh, yeah? You try to do any better! she thought, but bit her tongue. She didn't want to antagonize Combs any further, and besides, her feet practically cried out for a few minutes of freedom. So she sat down in the wooden straight-backed chair next to the desk and removed the offending pumps.

"All right, you've been through this rigmarole before." Combs handed her a clipboard and pen. "Read the front page, fill out the second, sign, and date. I'll draw your blood after that."

Kadin scanned the top page, and as far as she could tell the form hadn't changed since her last random blood screening. It probably hadn't changed in the thirty years since women had entered the workplace in sufficient numbers to necessitate the legislation.

Nearly a decade before Kadin's birth, the Assembly had decided that a woman's first priority would always be to care for any children she bore. Since she could not perform the duties of a career and be responsible for her children at the same time, legislators had deemed any woman who had children or had put herself at risk for pregnancy, i.e., had had sexual intercourse at any point in her life, legally unemployable.

Kadin checked the box indicating her status—Class E, never had sexual intercourse—and signed to indicate she could pass a drug test indicating she was not taking any contraceptive pills, which were illegal in any case. She skimmed through the other class descriptions. A's were married and supported by their husbands. Their positions were the most secure, which was why most women sought marriage. B's had been married but lost their husbands through legitimate means, usually death, and consequently qualified for a government stipend. C's had never been married but had children, for whose care the state would reimburse them. Neither B's nor C's made the kind of money most people desired, but they were better off than D's. Class D's were not virgins, were unmarried, and had no children. They had no means of acquiring legal income.

The system had its flaws, which Kadin had heard Tobin and Leslina, among others, detail many times. But in her experience, a woman who followed the rules and lived a satisfactory life didn't need to worry, so she tried not to get too upset about the bad cases.

Kadin handed the clipboard back to Dr. Combs. He ripped the paper out with more vigor than she thought necessary and stuffed it into a large manila envelope labeled "Stone, K." He grabbed her left wrist and pushed her left sleeve up above her elbow. Kadin would have offered to take her cardigan off to make the process easier, but he had already tied a rubber strip around her arm and was checking for accessible veins with rough fingers. He rubbed iodine on the inside of her elbow, then held up the syringe, giving her a suspicious look as if he expected her to flinch or look away. But Kadin didn't have a problem with needles, so she met his gaze straight on. She didn't so much as blink when the point pierced her skin and the rich crimson fluid filled the glass tube.

"Well, that's all I need from you, Miss Stone." Combs kept his eyes fixed on the envelope with her name on it as he slid the sample in. "If there is a problem with your blood tests, we should know within the week. Unless you have any questions, you are free to go."

Kadin thanked him with her brightest smile, but his sullen expression didn't change. She took a deep breath and stuck her feet back in her shoes, trying not to cringe as the nail from her pinky toe dug into the flesh of the toe next to it.

She had braced herself to rise to her feet when the door to the exam room swung open, and she found herself looking at a handsome man with eager blue eyes wearing a long beige trench coat. She couldn't place him at first, asa grey fedora covered his hair and shaded his features, but after a moment she harkened back to the photo Olivan had shown her the night before and recognized her would-be future husband, Dahran White. She stopped herself before her jaw had a chance to drop and craned her neck to check her hair as best she could from her distorted reflection in the doctor's head mirror.

Combs turned his scowl on the detective. "White, you know that you are not supposed to interrupt me during employee examinations. You can talk to me in the lab in fifteen minutes—"

"No time for the attitude today, Combs. We need to hurry." Dahran's eyes gleamed like Trinithy's would if someone told her she won a microwave. "Someone murdered the queen."

CHAPTER 4

THE ENVELOPE BEARING KADIN'S BLOOD dropped out of Combs's hands and fell to the floor with a swish. Kadin hoped the test tube hadn't broken. She didn't want to come down again.

Wait a minute. Did he say someone murdered the queen? That didn't make any sense. The palace retained so many guards Tobin often remarked that they lowered the city's unemployment rate by at least two percent. Who could get close enough to kill her?

"Someone murdered the queen? Were her bodyguards incompetent?" Combs's fingers twitched as he picked up the envelope and set it on the desk. "Wait. Better question. Someone murdered the queen, and *we* were called in to investigate?"

"That's right." Dahran made a circular motion with his arm. "So if you wouldn't mind stepping up the pace?"

Combs ripped the stethoscope from around his neck. "That doesn't make any sense."

That's what I thought.

The doctor flipped off the light and headed out the door. "If the queen was murdered, why would we be called in, of all the companies in Valeriel? I would think they would want CrimeSolve, or at least one of the other big companies."

Kadin, not wanting to be left alone in the dark, followed the men into the hall.

"Why shouldn't we be the ones called in?" Dahran's lope seemed less hurried than Combs's frantic tempo, but the detective kept up with the doctor. "We may be smaller, but we have an excellent quality record. It's not hard to believe that the king would take notice of that."

Combs barked out a laugh. "Yes, I'm sure the first thing that the king thought when he heard that his wife was murdered was that he should use this as an opportunity to promote small business."

"Don't be so negative, Combs." Dahran seemed awfully cheerful, considering he was talking about a murder investigation. But Kadin supposed the queen's murder had the potential to be a career-making case. "We should take the opportunity and be grateful for it. Don't you think so?" On the last question, he turned to look at Kadin, who traipsed behind them, cursing her shoes in her head.

"Oh..." She beamed at him as she struggled to think of the best thing to say. "I'm sure that if *you* are on the case, it will be solved in no time."

Kadin's stomach knotted as soon as the words were out of her mouth. He was bound to see right through *that* attempt at flattery. But he flashed his teeth at her without a hint of irony.

Combs glanced back at her as they crossed through the waiting room. "I can see that Fellows has continued his tradition of hiring from the brightest end of the secretarial pool."

Kadin flushed, but she couldn't fault him for thinking she sounded like an idiot when she had thought the same thing.

"Oh, are you Fellows's new aide?" Dahran eyed her

with more interest. “Excellent. He’ll probably want you to come to the palace with us.”

Kadin felt a rush of excitement. “I’ve always wanted to see the palace.”

“Deity’s sake!” Combs’s exclamation made both Kadin and Dahran jump. “We are going to investigate a murder, not take a tour of the Imperial estates. A woman is dead. Show some respect.” He muttered something about having to get his instruments, then hurried off ahead of them.

“Don’t mind Combs.” Dahran held back for a minute to walk alongside Kadin. “He gets like that sometimes. He’s one of those liberal types who think that we should perform investigations for free. I don’t know who he thinks would pay our salaries. Anyway, ignore him if he starts going on about how we should all be ashamed of making money off of other people’s misfortune. He’s a doctor, for Deity’s sake. If he wanted to, he could go work for the city, but you don’t see him doing that.”

“Mmm.” Kadin nodded, but she was paying more attention to her throbbing toe than to Dahran’s words. She gave a silent prayer of thanks that Dahran was matching her slow pace.

Kadin and Dahran strode into the lobby, and Detective Fellows, a stout older man with browline glasses and a bowler hat, nodded at Dahran, then looked Kadin up and down, nodding to himself in appreciation of her figure.

“So what do we know about the case so far, Fellows?” Dahran asked, with a distinct lack of deference.

Fellows frowned, presumably at his junior’s tone, until someone entering the building bumped against his back, nearly knocking the bowler hat off his head. “All we know so far is that the queen is dead and foul play is suspected. The king specifically requested that our team investigate.”

“And we don’t think that’s odd?” Combs joined the group, a black medical bag in his hand.

The detectives scoffed at Combs. “Of course not.”

Fellows clapped the doctor on the back. "We may be small, but we're the best the city has to offer."

As the group piled into company autocars and drove to the Imperial District, Kadin had to wonder whether Combs had a point. The king had a whole host of palace guards at his disposal, as well as the wealth to hire any investigation agency in the city. Why would he choose Valeriel Investigations, which had only solved a case that made it onto the front page of the *Valeriel Tribune* once since the company's founding?

As the painted gates of the Imperial Palace opened to let the autocars through, Kadin couldn't help but gawk at the estate. Trinithy and Olivan had once dragged her on an autobus tour that stopped at the gates of all the major Imperial estates, but she had never come this close to the royal palace. Even late in the autumn as it was, the lawns were impeccable, covered with a lusher green grass than most lawns in the city saw at the height of summer. Judging by the color and bareness of the trees, bright orange leaves should have littered the ground, but Kadin couldn't spot one. The palace garden staff was clearly more effective than the queen's guards were.

As they continued up the drive, they passed clusters of shaped ornamental hedges lining artificial ponds placed to provide pleasing views from the winding paths. Kadin gasped when the palace came into view. She had seen pictures, but none of them did justice to the sprawling white mansion lined with gold-crested columns and juniper trees. Even the government buildings in downtown Valeriel, which took up whole city blocks, were not so large. Kadin marveled that such a huge façade housed only two people—or one, since Queen Callista was dead.

Captain Azram Carver, the leader of the private defense force paid to protect the royal family and the palace, greeted the team at the white and gold double doors that stretched up three or four times Kadin's height. He and two of his guards escorted the detectives inside.

Have to love the fuzzy hats. Kadin stifled a smile as she looked at the formal white and gold uniforms that matched the foyer. *White and gold* are *the royal colors. And "foyer" is not the right word for this room.*

The ceiling of the palace entryway arched far above their heads, and carvings of the royal crest of Valeriel—a lion passant surrounded by a ring of stars—covered the walls. Captain Carver led the team down a hallway lined with gold-plated doors interspersed with lion statues on white pedestals. Between staying upright in her increasingly impractical shoes and trying not to stare at every golden painting and fresco that she passed, Kadin had a hard time keeping up with the party.

At the end of the hallway stood a sweeping staircase.

Captain Carver turned back to the detectives. "This way. The queen's chambers are on the second floor."

Kadin gave a mental apology to the sculptor of the staircase's decorative railing. But if he hadn't wanted passing climbers to clutch his work, he should have consulted with the designer who picked the carpet and the women who planned to walk on it. Two-inch-thick plush did not go with stiletto heels.

"These are the queen's chambers." Captain Carver opened a door on the second floor that led into a sitting room featuring a wide gondola sofa with white cushions and a gold base, two matching chairs, and a round painted end table in between. The carpeting matched that on the stairs, and Kadin trod as carefully as possible, not wanting to fall over now that she had no bannister.

As they passed into a luxurious bedchamber with more modern furniture in the royal colors, the mixed aromas of several expensive perfumes struck Kadin's nose. She might have found the effect of each individual scent pleasant, but the combination nearly made her choke.

The entire party came to a halt when they turned the corner to the queen's boudoir and encountered the reason for their presence. Kadin had never seen a dead body before, but she couldn't imagine mistaking the form lying there for anything else.

The blond figure lay crumpled in front of the bureau wearing an ivory and gold lace nightdress, spread out on top of a silky white fabric that looked to be a ball gown. She had Queen Callista's unequaled face and form, but her head lolled in a position that would wake any sleeper, and her blue eyes were open and staring.

If Fellows had asked her in her interview how she would react to such a gruesome site, she would have told him she expected a mix of fear, sadness, and disgust, but not enough to incapacitate her. As she faced the first of what she presumed would be many such corpses, she experienced a cold burning in her chest she could only describe as a desire to see whoever had done this brought to justice.

Captain Carver stepped between the investigation team and the door to the dressing room, as if trying to protect her from their stares. "The queen was found in this room at approximately midnight last night by her assigned personal guard."

"The guard's name?" Fellows pulled a notepad out of his pocket and licked his finger before opening to a blank page."

Carver cleared his throat. "Corporal Herrick Strand."

"Where had Corporal Strand been before that?" Fellows asked. Kadin watched Dahran and Fellows scrawl down the captain's words and, realizing she should do the same, retrieved her pad from her purse.

"He had left her alone for what he claims was no more than five minutes." The captain pulled at his collar, revealing the beads of sweat dripping down his neck. "When he returned, she was as you now see her. He immediately sought me out and didn't move anything in the room. He claims that he saw no one on the premises between the time he left her and the time he returned."

That doesn't sound likely, Kadin thought.

Fellows coughed into the hand holding the pencil. "You don't find this suspicious?"

Captain Carver stood up straighter. "I do not, for several reasons. First of all, under normal circumstances, Corporal Strand is not an internal palace guard and certainly not Queen Callista's regular guard. Though he formerly worked inside the palace, he received a promotion several months ago that transferred him to external guard duty. He was only with the queen tonight because her regular guard did not report as scheduled, and the duty sergeant determined that Corporal Strand could most easily fill in. Unfortunately, I was not there to approve the assignment, or I would have insisted on someone with more experience."

Why did the sergeant choose Strand? Kadin wrote on her pad and underlined it twice.

The captain's fingers curled and uncurled. "Due to his lack of experience, Corporal Strand was unaware that his only duty was to accompany his charge everywhere. Her Majesty wanted him to run an errand for her and was quite adamant that he do so. He claims that he didn't think anything would happen, and under most circumstances he would have been correct.. You may question him further about this if you wish."

"We intend to." Fellows flipped his notepad closed with a snap. "However, first I would like to speak with His Majesty, King Ralvin."

Carver sniffed. "You can't demand an audience with the king. He decides whom he will speak to, not the other way around."

"I think he'll see us. Because otherwise we will be forced to rely on journalists and less discreet nobles for our information, and I'm sure he'd rather we hear his business without the embellishments of third-hand accounts." Fellows didn't wait for Carver to reply. "Combs, while we're doing that, get a full analysis of the body. White, you question any staff who worked in this area last night. See if they saw anything peculiar."

One guard remained in the queen's bedchamber with Dr. Combs, while another directed Dahran toward a side room from which he could interview the members of the staff who, according to Captain Carver, had been on duty that night.

Check list of duty staff for completeness, Kadin wrote.

Fellows and Kadin followed Captain Carver back down the plush staircase, which somehow seemed even less supportive on the way down than on the way up. They crossed the main hall again, and Carver opened two massive doors that led into a hallway wider than Octavira's kitchen.

Portraits of Valerian nobles lined the walls. The images appeared modern, as if the hall's purpose was to give the Imperials something else to brag over. *Oh, yes, my picture is on the wall of the palace, you know.*

Captain Carver asked Kadin and Fellows to wait outside while he checked that the king was prepared to meet with them.

Fellows glanced at Kadin and jerked his head back a bit. He looked her up and down, as if he had forgotten her in the hour since he had done so back at the office. "What was your name again?"

Kadin did her best to look earnest. "Kadin Stone, sir. And may I say it is an hon—"

Fellows waved a hand. "Yes, yes. Mind you keep to your own business in there. Don't want you saying anything foolish in front of the king."

Kadin gave a brief nod, though Fellows was no longer looking at her to see it. *No sense getting offended by that.*

After all, I don't know anything about questioning someone. Even if he could *have been nicer about it.*

Kadin turned her attention to the pictures closest to the door. The largest one, set in the middle of the hallway, caught her eye first. The painting featured King Ralvin and Queen Callista as they appeared on the day of their coronation. Both wore full gold and white regalia with matching greasepaint caked on their faces. They looked cold and austere, more like statues than living, breathing people. The king was of average height and slight built. His hair was covered by a thin golden helm, and his aristocratic attire covered every inch of him from the cravat at his neck to the white leather boots that encased his feet and lower calves. Queen Callista wore similar garb, except that her golden curls framed her face, and not even the white face paint could hide her beauty.

Kadin let her eyes wander from the portrait of the cold monarchs to a small photograph positioned next to it. The click showed two dark-haired teenage boys who looked alike enough to be brothers. The larger one laughed with abandon, unintimidated by the presence of the camera. The smaller one also seemed amused, by the other boy's behavior if nothing else, but he bore a subdued expression, as if he knew these walls would memorialize his image and he might appear foolish.

The casual nearness of the boys' hands and the way they each seemed to watch the other out of the corners of their eyes suggested to Kadin that they were the best of friends. She glanced down at the caption, which identified the image date at twelve years ago and the smaller boy as Prince Ralvin and the laughing one as Lord Baurus.

After staring at the teenaged Imperials for long enough to capture every nuance, Kadin turned around to observe the images on the other wall. Opposite the portrait of the king and queen, in a similar, nearly-as-large frame, hung a painting of Duke Baurus. The two pictures of King

Ralvin looked so unalike each other that, without the labels, Kadin might never have known they depicted the same man. The oil work she now beheld clearly depicted an older version of the boy in the click, though in this image he glared out of the canvas as if the artist had enraged him beyond reason.

Trinithy had often giggled about how handsome she thought Duke Baurus was, but Kadin had always thought the real attraction was to his title and net worth. He wasn't unattractive, with slicked-back brown hair parted at the side and intense hazel eyes, but he had nothing on someone like Jace Combs. In person, Duke Baurus would have been at least several inches taller than she, even in her heels, and twice as wide, with the kind of musculature one would expect from someone who had performed heavy labor his whole life.

Kadin marveled at the skill of the artist, capturing the duke's raw emotion, but she also suspected the subject's excitement had been far greater than what appeared on the canvas. She stood transfixed, reaching her hand out to touch the painting, wanting to get closer to the pure passion, but before her fingers brushed his black-clad arm, she remembered where she was and stopped herself.

As Kadin broke free of the painting's mesmerizing hold, the door at the end of the hallway opened, and Captain Carver, appearing disgruntled that the king had consented to see them, indicated they should enter. "The king will see you now. Please understand that he is distraught over the loss of his wife and grant him the infinite respect due his station."

Kadin followed Fellows into what she would have known was the throne room, even if she had not seen her statuesque monarch sitting on a golden chair at the other side of the room. Or if she hadn't seen a hundred clicks of the chamber before.

Oh, my Deity, she thought. *I'm standing in the Imperial throne room.*

Wooden benches sat alongside the walls of an open space so large it required ivory columns, placed at intervals, to hold up the ceiling. Light reflected off the solid gold walls and ceiling a hundred times, making the room glow. Kadin tried to get a glimpse of the images engraved in the gold—every school child in Valeriel knew the throne room walls illustrated key events in the kingdom's history. She craned her neck, searching for her favorite—the founding of the Assembly—but when she couldn't find it within a few seconds, she gave up, not wanting to gawk at the grandeur in front of the king. She listened to her heels clack against the hard marble and breathed a sigh of relief that it provided a balanced surface to walk on. She didn't think she could live down falling flat on her face in front of the king.

When she reached the throne, Kadin managed something resembling a curtsey in echo of Fellows's and the captain's. Tight skirts did not make the action easy. Her grandmother had ingrained in her long ago that polite girls did not look on Imperials' faces, so she studied the king as circumspectly as she could. She may as well have continued to look at the portrait outside, though, because the king appeared the same as he had in the official painting—dressed head to toe in formal white and gold, with white greasepaint covering his face, pristine calfskin gloves, and a shiny, sunburst-patterned cape draped over the seat's right arm.

The facelessness of the king's appearance reflected his politics. He had begun his reign nearly ten years ago, when he was in his early twenties, and since then had rarely exercised his executive power to make a major policy decision. As king, he had the power to veto any action of the Assembly not endorsed by 75% of members, but Kadin couldn't think of a single time he had used this power. He only voiced an opinion when the Assembly was deadlocked, and even then gave them ample time and incentive to reconsider their votes. His few forced votes always supported the status quo.

"Thank you for coming." King Ralvin's cold tone indicated annoyance more than gratitude. If his wife's murder influenced his state of mind, as Captain Carver had claimed, Kadin couldn't tell from his voice. But, then, Carver had also indicated the king couldn't be bothered to meet with commoners, even in light of the dire situation, and that Kadin could well believe.

"The people of Valeriel face a great tragedy this day." The king sounded as he did when he made a public speech advocating an unpopular policy—"using empty words to placate the masses," Tobin always said. "While nothing can bring back our beloved queen, we must do everything within our power to discover who has committed this terrible act and bring him to justice. I want no expense spared in this pursuit, and any assistance that We or anyone in our employ can offer is entirely at your disposal."

"I thank you for that, Your Majesty." Fellows gave another obsequious bow. Kadin wondered whether she should do the same, but by the time she thought to mimic her boss, he had straightened. "My name is Caison Fellows, and I will be leading the investigation, though another detective is also assigned to the case full-time. He is interviewing your staff at present, but if you wish to meet him, he can join us now."

King Ralvin's expression shifted into something Kadin couldn't quite call a sneer. "That will not be necessary."

The king turned his curled lip on Kadin. His gaze roved over her, and she straightened, forgetting for a moment not to look directly at his face. She expected to see disdain in his eyes, but the expression in his eyes didn't harbor any of the hostility the rest of his face did.

"Who is this?" The scorn in the king's voice shocked

Kadin out of any nascent thoughts that his mien might not match his true feelings.

Fellows looked confused for a moment, until he realized that the king referred to Kadin. “Oh, that’s my aide...” Kadin could practically hear the wheels turning in his head.

“Kadin Stone, Your Majesty.” *The king of Valeriel may be an Imperial snob, but, I mean, he’s the king. And he’s addressing me. Me!*

Fellows cleared his throat. “If you don’t mind, Your Majesty, I need to ask you a few questions.”

King Ralvin stilled, and Kadin expected the detective to turn to ice under the monarch’s glare. “You are welcome to ask.”

Fellows swallowed, and his next words spilled out of his mouth. “I assure you, we at Valeriel Investigations understand the vital importance of maintaining strict confidentiality regarding any information we receive, and, barring an immediate threat to the public welfare, our company policies forbid the disclosure of information gathered during the course of an investigation to any parties not directly involved in a court of law regarding that case.”

The king arched an eyebrow. “Then by all means, ask what questions you will.”

Fellows stared at his notepad, and Kadin felt a flash of gratitude that she wasn’t the one who had to ask her monarch the kinds of awkward questions that come up when one’s wife has been murdered. “Can you please describe for me your relationship with Queen Callista?”

“She was my wife.” The king snapped the words, and Kadin didn’t wonder at his defensiveness. He must have known about the queen’s amorous exploits. “We may not have had the most amicable of relationships, but both of us understood that our marriage benefited the kingdom.

We're different from the lower classes. We don't marry for *love.*" The last word sounded like poison on his lips.

Political marriage, wrote Kadin, thinking that King Ralvin was fooling himself if he thought the average Valeriel woman married for love.

The king glared at Fellows, as if daring the detective to comment. "I suppose our lives might have been easier if we had gotten along better, if Callista had been less selfish and shallow. But she was beautiful and didn't interfere in affairs of state, and that, it seems, is all the masses require from a queen."

Fellows continued writing for a moment after the king had finished talking, and Kadin wondered what had so interested him about the king's words. *I wonder if King Ralvin killed the queen. He seems to have disliked her enough. But somehow I think Queen Callista was too* useful *to kill off.*

Fellows flipped to a fresh page and looked back up. "Did your wife have any enemies that you know of, or had she received any threats?"

"Do you have any idea how many death threats personages like myself and Callista receive on a daily basis? How many violent protestors my guards discover sneaking onto the premises each year?" The king waved a dismissive white-gloved hand. "If you want to waste your time pursuing that avenue, Captain Carver can provide you with information about the most recent threats."

Fellows opened his mouth to ask another question, but the king continued. "Sooner or later, some indiscreet member of my staff will tell you about Baurus. Callista broke off relations with him yesterday, and he was in quite the rage, storming all over the palace and ranting at anyone who would listen, myself included. Yes, I knew about their affair. I am at least as informed about the doings of my own household as the average reader of glossies." At the last words, he looked down at Kadin.

Right, she thought. *I'm a woman, so I must be obsessed with society gossip.*

Fellows tapped his pencil on his notepad. "Do you believe it's possible that Duke Baurus killed your wife either before or after his conversation with you, when he was, as you put it—" Fellows glanced down at his notes "—'in quite the rage.'"

"I don't see how." The king gave his head a short shake. "Baurus left the palace late in the afternoon, and I saw Callista an hour later for dinner. After we finished eating, I didn't see her again before Captain Carver brought me the news. Baurus didn't return in that time. If he had, everyone would have heard it. Baurus doesn't do subtle. And besides, I have guard posted at every entrance."

Doesn't everyone do subtle when they're plotting murder? Kadin made a note that they should question Duke Baurus and also investigate the entrances. The king might have thought his doors secured, but no doubt he had also considered the queen protected.

Fellows made a few jots in his notebook, then gave a slight bow. "I believe that those are all the questions that we have for you at this time, Your Majesty. We would prefer if you would make yourself available for any questions that we will certainly have over the course of this investigation. Please contact us if you recall anything further that may be of use to our investigation."

King Ralvin's expression indicated that he would as soon scrub his own toilet as talk to them again, but before he could contradict his expression with the necessary platitudes, the door to the throne room swung open. Captain Carver, his face flushed red, hustled across the room. "Forgive the interruption, Your Majesty. Dr. Combs has finished his analysis and would like a word with Detective Fellows. He claimed it was urgent."

The king made a circle with his hand. "By all means, admit him."

Carver hurried out, and a moment later Jace Combs strode into the throne room, flanked by Captain Carver and one of the guards from before. Combs was frowning, but Kadin couldn't tell whether the case had upset him, or if he simply wore his accustomed countenance.

By the time Combs reached the king, his perfect features had smoothed into a neutral expression. He bowed in the king's direction. "Forgive me for interrupting, Your Majesty. Due to the seriousness of the situation, Detective Fellows asked that I find him as soon as I completed my analysis."

Everyone else turned to the king to see his response, but Kadin kept her eyes on the doctor's handsome features for an extra moment, as any self-respecting woman would have. Only when she realized that the expected reaction from the king was delayed in coming did she glance back at the inscrutable monarch.

Except that when she did, his face was not quite as neutral as she had expected. In fact, she had to describe his expression as a subdued version of the slack-jawed dumbfoundedness she had surely worn when she had first encountered Combs that morning, minus the tripping over her own shoes and gaping at his wife. Kadin glanced around to see whether anyone else noticed, but her colleagues seemed unwilling to look upon the king's face and consequently remained oblivious to the king's attraction to the doctor.

Kadin started to make a note but then thought better of it. Even speculation that the king was sideways would put Imperial gossipmongers in a tizzy. The average man could have romantic attachments to as many men as he wanted. Imperials, though, needed to produce heirs, and people would always suspect the heirs of a sideways man of illegitimacy.

Though, wouldn't people suspect the paternity of any of Callista's children? Kadin wondered. But, then, she suspected the Imperial obsession with its men proving their virility by fathering children ran deeper than logic.

"Not at all." The king's words sounded the slightest bit less clipped as he addressed the doctor. "We are all interested in getting this case behind us as soon as may be."

"At this point, I have only conducted a cursory analysis." Combs cleared his throat and kept his eyes on his notes. "I can say with some certainty that she was asphyxiated, but I will have to investigate further to determine the exact cause. I will have to ask Your Majesty to permit the transfer of the body to the lab at Valeriel Investigations so that I may conduct further examinations."

King Ralvin gave his head a slight shake. "Unacceptable. My wife's body must be laid to rest as soon as may be, both for her own dignity and the comfort of her people. I cannot sanction subjecting her to disfiguring procedures not befitting her person."

The doctor sniffed, and Kadin suspected if he had put the slightest amount more vigor in his breath, he would have snorted. "I understand, Your Majesty, but it's standard procedure in cases like this. I will not do anything to the body that would impede a full state funeral, once I have completed my tests. I assure you that without collecting more data, I have no hope of ascertaining cause of death and, consequently, of catching the killer."

"Then it seems I have no choice." King Ralvin's tone indicated he was unaccustomed to not getting his way.

But, then, if he's sideways, and he has to pretend otherwise, how much power can he have over his life? And if his sexuality is a lie, how much of this snobbery is real, and how much is a front?

Kadin glanced at her boss's puffed-up face and suspected that, were the king not present, Fellows would have gone after Combs with strong words and possibly fisticuffs. Combs returned Fellows's look with equal severity.

"Thank you for your assistance, Your Majesty." Fellows gave a bow so deep, Kadin thought his nose might touch his knees. "If it is not a problem, we will now take our leave and continue the investigation. We will keep you apprised of absolutely any further developments."

The trio trailed out through the shining gold room. When Kadin reached the door, she turned back to see whether the king would give some indication of his true feelings, but his face remained a stony mask.

Maybe there's another reason he wants a no-name investigation company on the case, she thought. *Maybe he knows a more competent team would uncover the truth.*

CHAPTER 5

Fellows stormed into Queen Callista's personal library, which Carver said the team could use for consultations. His red hot rage seemed at odds with the mauve and mahogany room. *The queen must have gotten sick of the white and gold, too,* Kadin thought.

The wallpaper bore thick pink stripes interspersed with matching rosettes. Across the room from Kadin stood two sturdy bookcases, their shelves filled with hardcover copies of recent romance novels and women's fiction. The air smelled of flowers, and the irises on the side table next to the boxy loveseat looked as if a maid had refreshed them only a few hours previously. Kadin guessed no one had told the woman responsible that Queen Callista wouldn't need the room aired that morning.

Scattered papers and envelopes, most of which bore the shiny engraving of formal invitations, covered the desk in the corner. Lying amidst them was a scrapbook open to pictures of the queen in elaborate ball gowns. On the floor next to the desk lay a pile of glossies, the latest issue of *Imperial Society* on top.

Fellows turned on Combs as soon as the door clicked shut behind them. "What were you thinking, ordering the king around like that?"

"I was thinking I need to further examine the body in order to determine the exact cause of death, which I was thinking might help the investigation." Combs ripped the head mirror from his forehead. Kadin realized he had worn it since she'd first seen him and wondered if he needed it for the examination or if it was more of an affectation. "You have seen me say the same thing to any number of family members."

"You said taking possession of the body was standard procedure." Fellows voice grew loud enough that Kadin worried anyone outside the room would hear him. "You know we only need to bring the body to our facility in a small percent of cases."

Kadin looked from one man to the other, from the handsome doctor, even more attractive without a metal circle covering his features, to her puffed-up boss.

"Well, obviously this case is in that small percent, or I wouldn't have said it!" Combs's tone almost matched Fellows's in volume.

Fellows's nostrils flared, and, given the cherry shade of his skin, Kadin half expected fire to flare from his nose. "Well, maybe you should have looked a little closer, because the press is going to have a field day over us taking the queen's body into private custody."

Combs crossed his arms and tapped a finger against his elbow. "Oh, well, I am so sorry that the murderer's desire to cover his method will garner bad press for our mercenary superiors."

I guess this is what they meant in class when they said external factors could interfere with an investigation, Kadin thought. *I wonder if I should write any of this down.*

Fellows opened and closed his mouth several times, and the doctor held up a finger and took a few deep breaths. When Combs spoke again, he had replaced the ire in his tone with quiet intensity. "This case is like nothing I've ever seen. I can tell she was suffocated, but the symptoms don't resemble any obvious poisons, and there aren't any marks that I would ordinarily associate with strangulation or smothering. I need to take her back to the lab to test for other poisons." He ran his fingers through his blond hair, disarraying its slick-backed perfection. "Believe me, I know the case is important, and the last thing that I want to do is make it more difficult. But I need to take that body to the lab if you want an accurate cause of death."

"Well, His Majesty has already given permission, so I suppose we may as well take advantage of it." Fellows sighed with the air of someone making a great sacrifice. "All right, Dahran is still questioning staff upstairs, and I want to talk to the delinquent substitute guard and the sergeant who assigned him before we leave today. I'll take the guard—" He glanced at his notes. "—Corporal Strand. You!" He waved to the guard in the hallway. Fellows scribbled something on a piece of paper and handed it to the man. "Give this to White. Tell him to talk to the sergeant when he finishes with the staff. Combs, go back to the lab, and do not leave until you get the answers you need for us to release that body."

Captain Carver escorted Fellows and Kadin—she assumed her boss wanted her to go with him—out of the palace to another building that served as barracks. They trekked for what seemed like hours. As they passed lush green grass and beheld the royal forest in all its autumnal glory, Kadin could only pay attention to the pebble from the rocky path that had found its way into her shoe. As if enough blisters hadn't formed on her toes and heels, now one was developing on her instep as well.

The dark interior of the guard house smelled stale, and Kadin suspected the room didn't get much use. Either the guards didn't have a lot of extra space for this kind of thing, or the sergeant in charge of allocating space wanted Strand to suffer. She thanked the Deity for even musty respite, and when they entered the interrogation room, she collapsed into one of the utilitarian plastic chairs with what she hoped more closely resembled dignity than desperation.

After she had slipped off her shoes, Kadin stared at the man seated across the faux mica table. He wore his light brown hair unfashionably mussed, though Kadin supposed he hadn't had time to style it that morning. His skin bore a sallow hue, but the situation may have affected that, too. His eyes and nose—the former a little too close together, the latter a little too large—didn't have circumstance to excuse them. So likely even on the best of days, he would have been as unimpressive and unassuming a man as Kadin had ever seen. She almost pitied him the glaring spotlight about to shine down on his life. The frenzied media would soon be upon him with a vengeance. His negligence had caused the queen's death.

Fellows set his notebook down on the table. "Corporal Strand?"

The man nodded and lifted his shaking hands from his lap to the table.

Fellows kept his cold eyes trained on Strand. "My name is Detective Caison Fellows. I need to ask you a few questions about the death of Queen Callista."

"Y-yes, of course." Strand straightened and looked Fellows in the eye for a moment, but his gaze flickered back to the bare table. "Please, I want to help in any way that I can. You can't imagine how it feels, to know that I caused her death..."

"You were assigned to guard Queen Callista last night." Fellows's voice held none of the delicacy it had with King Ralvin.

I guess he reserves the respect for royalty... or people whose incompetence didn't get someone else killed, Kadin thought.

"Yes." The soon-to-be-former guard hesitated, as if attempting to gauge what information Fellows sought. "It was a new assignment for me, or, rather, a temporary one. And last minute. I mean, I was about to go on duty at the west gate, and Sergeant Dervish ordered me to protect the queen. I guess he thought I would be okay to do it, since I used to be a door guard inside the palace." He sighed. "But he was wrong."

Fellows made a brief note. "According to Captain Carver, you were instructed to remain with the queen at all times. Why did you disobey your orders?"

Strand opened and closed his hands a few times. "I don't know. I wasn't supposed to leave her alone. But she seemed safe in her room, and she was so insistent, and it was only for a few minutes..." Tears formed in his eyes. "She asked me if I would retrieve a book she had left in her library. I told her, I said, I couldn't leave her alone. I tried to get one of the hall guards, but none were around. I offered to escort her down. She insisted she wasn't leaving, that she needed to prepare for bed, but that she needed to finish the book that night because she promised Lady Beatrin..."

Strand took a deep breath, and by the time he spoke again, his voice had steadied. "She... she ordered me to go, and she was getting rather... loud...about it. I had my orders, but it's the DeValeriels who sign my paycheck. I figured it would only take me a few minutes to go down and get it, and where was the harm?"

Sounds to me as though she was trying to get rid of him, thought Kadin, making a note.

Fellows leaned back in his chair, narrowing his eyes. "Did you suspect she was trying to get you to leave the room? Perhaps to meet someone or to engage in a behavior that she did not want you see?"

Strand's head jerked backwards, as if the idea had not occurred to him. "No... No, I don't think so. I mean, I suppose it's possible, but I was only gone for a few minutes. I wouldn't have thought there was even enough time for someone to come in and..." He closed his eyes and took a second to pull himself together again. "I used to work in the palace, though not directly with the queen, and she was well-known for being... insistent. Bordering on demanding. I had been called on to obey a whim of hers a few times. I honestly think that she just wanted that book and didn't see any reason why she couldn't have it."

Must have been some book, Kadin thought. She moved her foot and accidentally kicked over one of her shoes.

Fellows gave Strand a level glare. "You said that you didn't think someone had enough time to come in and, I assume, kill her. How long were you gone, exactly?"

"I wouldn't have said more than ten minutes, though I wasn't keeping track." Strand's gaze grew unfocused. "It must have been longer, I guess. I mean, you can't kill someone like that in ten minutes, can you? So that there's no sign? I mean, you could get a ject shot off, or stab somebody, or..." Strand's hands shook harder.

The killer didn't just leave no sign. He ensured that no one would notice the crime was occurring. A projectile weapon shot would have made noise, and the victim of a stabbing would scream. Kadin used her toe to maneuver her shoe upright again as Fellows waited a full minute to see if Strand was going to pull himself together enough to continue. The guard, who suddenly struck Kadin as quite young, appeared to be finished, if not prepared to answer another question.

Fellows cleared his throat. "Did she behave in an unusual manner earlier that evening?"

Strand started. "I don't know. I mean, I don't know what normal behavior for her would have been. She seemed the same as what little I saw of her before, but I don't know what normal behavior is for her, or any Imperial."

Can there be normal behavior for a noble? Kadin jotted down something about confirming Queen Callista's behavior with her regular guard, if the team ever found him.

Fellows tapped his pencil against his notebook. “Well, did she appear to have any signs of illness?”

Strand’s mouth opened in realization. “Oh, you mean, did she seem to be poisoned or something?” His brow furrowed. “No, I don’t think so. She wasn’t wincing or limping or anything.” His head jerked up. “She did seem irritable, in how insistent she was that I get the book and all. Irritable can mean pain, right?”

Fellows flipped back a page in his book. “But you said that being ‘insistent’ was an accustomed behavior of hers. Now you claim it was unusual?”

Fellows is good at this. Kadin tried to peek over at his notes, wondering what other tidbits he had picked up that she had missed.

“No, no, I don’t mean that!” Strand’s breath came faster, as if he had just realized he might be a suspect in this case and might be facing more trouble than the consequences of being negligent on duty. “I mean, from what I knew of her, tantrums weren’t unusual. I didn’t think anything of her behavior at the time, except, you know, that I’d better not upset her more. But you asked if I noticed any signs that she was sick.” He lifted his shoulders with effort, then let them fall. “I don’t know what else to tell you. I left because she was yelling at me to go, and I came back, and she was dead. I didn’t see anything. I don’t *know* anything. I wish I did. Maybe if I could help find whoever did this, I could stop seeing her face...”

Either Fellows took pity on the man or he had all the information he needed, because he snapped his notebook shut. “Thank you for your time, Corporal. I trust that you will remain available for questioning at a later date, and if you think of anything, I want you to contact me immediately.” He handed Strand a card.

Strand looked up at Fellows with haunted eyes. “I will, Detective. And please, please, tell me as soon as you find out who did this.”

Kadin tried not to wince as she slid her feet back into her shoes, stood up, and tottered toward the door. Before she left, she turned back to look at Herrick Strand. He stared at Fellows's card in his hand, but Kadin doubted the guard could read the words in his current state. She allowed herself one last pang of empathy before she closed the door on the man, leaving him alone with his guilt.

When Fellows and Kadin arrived back at the palace, Dahran waited for them outside the queen's bedchamber. Kadin had hoped the detectives would compare notes back at the office, or at least in a comfortable sitting room at the palace, but Fellows deemed the palace hallway a good place to deliberate, stiletto-unfriendly plush carpeting and all. She lifted her right foot out of its shoe and cringed as the blister on her heel rubbed against the too-tight back of the pump.

I wonder if anyone would notice if I shrank by a few inches.

Fellows either didn't notice or didn't care about his aide's pain, because he turned to Dahran. "What have you got?"

Dahran flipped through his notebook. "According to Sergeant Dervish, Queen Callista's regular night bodyguard didn't report for duty last night, so he had to rearrange his roster at the last minute. He assigned Corporal Strand to watch the queen."

Fellows raised an eyebrow. "Did he give a reason for the assignment? Why put a gate guard in charge of the queen? There must have been someone better suited to the position."

Dahran snapped his fingers and pointed at Fellows. "Exactly what I wondered. The corporal was assigned to the west gate, where Dervish felt he could most easily spare people. Corporal Strand was also being considered for a promotion, so Dervish thought this would be a good way to test out how he handled additional responsibility."

I guess his move out the palace last year wasn't a demotion.

"Apparently not too well," Fellows said. "Anything in the queen's room?"

Dahran flipped to the next page. "No sign of a struggle or forced entry that we could see. The queen was either poisoned before she went into the room, or she knew her attacker and let him get close enough to strangle her before she realized he planned to kill her."

Fellows clapped Dahran on the back. "That makes sense, given the corporal's story. He claims he wasn't gone for more than ten minutes—fifteen at the outside. If she had made any kind of fuss, he probably would have been close enough to hear it during the necessary window. What did you get from the servants and guards?"

Dahran glanced in Kadin's direction, which reminded her she had worn these accursed shoes to impress Dahran, and she hadn't done a thing to impress him since her awkward attempts at flattery back at the office. She met his gaze and smiled for all she was worth.

Dahran winked at her and turned his attention back to Fellows. "None of the staff were in the immediate area at the time, so they didn't hear anything. But when I asked if they believed anyone might have wanted to hurt the queen, a large number of them immediately named someone who had expressed displeasure with her that day." Dahran smirked. "I'll give you three guesses who."

"I don't think I'll need them." Fellows gave a small smile of his own. "Duke Baurus?"

"One and the same." Dahran grinned, and he turned to include Kadin in the expression. She did her best to look as though she admired his cleverness.

"The duke came up in my investigation as well." Fellows flipped back a couple of pages in his notebook. "According to the king, his wife and the duke had been having an affair for some time, an affair that she ended yesterday."

According to the king and every gossip rag in the city, Kadin thought. *Don't detectives keep up with that kind of thing?*

"Indeed, several servants commented upon an angry duke raging through the palace this afternoon, though he left several hours before the murder took place." The corner of Dahran's mouth quirked upward again. "Of course, I got the impression that this was not an entirely uncommon occurrence. The relationship between Queen Callista and Duke Baurus was not what one would call a secret, and it had its dramatic moments. The servants all expected him to do something violent long before this."

Well, at least he *is up on celebrity news. Although I'm pretty sure something like the relationship between Duke Baurus and Queen Callista would better be called "olds."*

"Well, I think that we will want to speak with Duke Baurus as soon as may be." Fellows frowned at his notebook. "However, I don't think we can rule out other suspects quite yet. After the breakup, the duke went to discuss the affair with the king, and I'm certain that we can both see how his wife's infidelity might provide a motive."

When the men gave each other knowing nods, Kadin had to clap her hand over her mouth to prevent a snort. "I don't think he minded so much."

Blinking, the men twisted their heads around to look at her.

Fellows cleared his throat. "I'm fairly certain that King Ralvin is man enough not to want his wife spreading her favors around."

Dahran reached out and patted Kadin's arm. "Miss Stone, you're a woman, so you may not understand. He couldn't help but be upset by it."

Kadin resisted the urge to bristle at the condescending tone. "No, seriously, I think that—"

"Okay, that's enough." Fellows held up his hand as Dahran smirked. "We've all had a busy day and are obviously tired. Starting tomorrow, White, I want you to check out the financials of every guard and servant working here. If anyone got paid to look the other way, I want to know about it. I'll set up an interview with Duke Baurus, and possibly his sister, as soon as may be. Dismissed." Without another word, Fellows strode off in the direction of the entrance.

Dahran turned to study a fresco on the wall. Kadin thought about taking the opportunity to strike up a flirtation, but the allure of going home and getting out of Octavira's shoes proved more tempting. She turned and followed Fellows.

I guess I shouldn't have expected them to listen to me. With no one to look at her, she let herself cringe with every step down the stairs. *It* is *my first day, and they've got a lot more experience than me.*

By the time Kadin got to the first floor, she realized she had no idea how she was supposed to get home. She couldn't see Fellows ahead of her, but if he had planned to wait for the team, he wouldn't have rushed out.

Guess I'll have to wait for Dahran to come down, so we can split an autotaxi. She trudged down the main hallway, the unsteady click of her heels providing evidence of the poor state of her feet to anyone listening. *I can't walk to the nearest autobus stop. Do they even* have *autobuses in the Imperial District?*

Kadin made it to the palace's front door, but among the ornate columns and lions head frescos, she could not find anywhere to sit. The queen's library was only a little ways down the corridor, though, and she figured she would still hear the other detectives come down if she waited in there. With the determination of one who knows that, if she suffers for a few minutes more, her swollen feet will get a respite, she headed toward the room and opened the door.

"Get out!" a deep, commanding baritone shouted.

Kadin froze. *Oh Deity, I hope I didn't offend someone important.*

"I'm so sorry, sir." Without looking up, she backed away and started to pull the door shut behind her.

A white and green object flew through the air, and she heard a papery *fwap* as whatever it was struck the wall next to her head, then *thumped* on the floor. Kadin stopped her retreat and looked down at the object lying next to her.

"Did you... Did you throw a book at my head?"

She lifted her gaze and gasped. She recognized the thrower from the pictures outside the throne room, as well as any number of clicks in any of number of publications Trinithy and Olivan had shoved under her nose. Same dark hair. Same hazel eyes. Same forbidding build. She even thought he might be wearing the same red-vested black suit as he had in the painting.

She had snapped at Duke Baurus DeValeriel.

The fury of his presence came toward her in a flood so powerful she almost felt the need to step back. His face, his posture, everything about him from his side-parted hair to his shiny black wingtips, radiated rage, as though he were so overcome by his emotions that he could not contain them inside his skin.

He clenched and unclenched his fists. "What are you doing here? I said get out!"

Get out of here, Kadin, the rational part of her brain told her. *He might have* murdered *someone last night.*

But the waves of his temper had seeped into her skin, daring her to stay.

She put her hands on her hips. "I *was* leaving, and then you threw a book at my head."

His lip curled. "That wasn't incentive enough to listen to me?"

Her heart pounded in her throat. "No, generally a man's attempting to hurt me doesn't sway my opinion in his favor."

True, fair, excellent logic, she thought. *You have made your point. Maybe you should go.*

The duke's hazel eyes flashed. "Do you always wander around other people's homes uninvited?"

Her jaw tightened. "It's not your home either."

She wanted to clap her hand over her mouth as soon as she spoke. *Please, please tell me you did not contradict a duke.*

Judging by the way his eyes bugged, Duke Baurus had the same response to her words as she did. "I have a standing invitation to my cousin's home."

Kadin held up her head. "I was invited, too. I'm part of the team from Valeriel Investigations looking into the death of Queen Callista." He didn't need to know that she was no longer on the clock. Or that the other detectives didn't value her contributions.

His countenance changed; the anger remained but was accompanied by surprise, guilt, embarrassment, curiosity, worry... A parade of emotions scattered across his open face, though none of them remained in place long enough for her to capture the thoughts behind them.

His face cleared, and he focused a simple glare on Kadin. "Fine. You won't leave, then I will."

She bristled, but before she could speak, he whipped the door out of her grasp and stormed out of the room.

She sank down into the mauve loveseat, her hands trembling more than Herrick Strand's had. *I cannot believe I said all those things to Duke Baurus. To a murderer.* She took a deep breath. *Except...*

Her detective's brain raced past her shock. *If he were a murderer, why would he come back here, to the scene of the crime? I mean, criminals don't do that, really. He has to know he's a suspect.*

There must have been something he needed to do here. Some object to retrieve. Her eyes darted around the room, looking for anything suspicious or out of place. But though the queen's sunburst clock indicated dubious taste, Kadin couldn't see anything that would draw a former lover—or a killer. She resolved to tell Fellows about the encounter in the morning. Maybe he would have a better idea of what to look for.

Kadin hobbled outside the palace just in time to breathe in the last fumes of the autotaxi carrying Dahran away. She sighed, realizing, as she had feared, she would have to pay for a ride across the city herself or else walk to the nearest autobus stop in her heels.

Of course, I'm not likely to see anyone I know in the Imperial District. With a sharp thrill in her chest, she stepped out of her shoes and breathed a sigh of relief as she felt the cold pavement through her stockings. She picked up her shoes and headed for the gate.

CHAPTER 6

KADIN SKIDDED INTO THE OFFICE about two minutes before her scheduled start time of 9:00 a.m. Her plans to entice Dahran with her shapely legs had hit a snag when Octavira flat-out refused to allow Kadin to borrow the pumps again. She couldn't tell whether Octavira was most upset about the mud and scuff marks on the outside, the blood stains on the inside, or the fact that her shoes had visited a more prestigious part of the city than she had. Kadin knew she should be disappointed, but her most comfortable soft-soled cognac kitten heels wore into her blisters as it was. She couldn't imagine what another day in Octavira's shoes would feel like.

These shoes are better for solving murders in, anyway, she thought as she stepped off the lift onto the fourth floor. *And that* is *what I'm getting paid to do.*

The wooden beads on Kadin's handbag clinked as she set it on the grey metal desk of her new office. It served as an antechamber to Fellows's office, so she could act as the detective's secretary. The door to his office was closed, so she assumed he wasn't in, though she didn't peek through the little window to verify. The filing cabinet and short bookcase matched the desk, and altogether the room gave off an empty, depressing feel. Listening to the steady tick of the clock, Kadin wondered if she shouldn't bring something in to spruce up the place.

She pulled a crumpled pile of papers—primarily documentation personnel had given her regarding her new job— out of her bag.

"Ah, Miss Stone."

Kadin jumped and dropped her papers. She spun around and discovered that none other than Dahran White had stuck his head into her office.

Great, if I had to look like a spaz in front of one person.

"I'm so sorry." She tried to find a dignified way to pick the papers up off the floor. *Mental note: tight skirts bad for curtseying* and *bending over in front of attractive men.* "You startled me."

"No, I'm sorry." Dahran smiled at her, and Kadin resolved to think his expression friendly, rather than smarmy. "I thought you must have heard me approaching." He knelt and gathered some papers, giving them a cursory glance. "Are you interested in autocar racing?"

What? Why would he think I...?

Dahran held up a glossy with a man in bright red on the cover, and she recognized the issue of *Racers* that Olivan had given her. Her breath caught. Maybe this mishap wasn't as inopportune as it seemed. She couldn't have come up with a less obtrusive way to let him know about her "interest."

"Oh, yes." She scooped up the rest of the papers and straightened, smoothing her skirt with the backs of her hands.

He flipped through the glossy. "Who do you support in the drag on Saturday?"

"Oh, the Yellow Comet." she said, naming the first autocar driver that came into her head. Her breath caught in her throat when she realized she had named the fashion laughingstock of the racing community. Olivan and Trinithy only mentioned him to mock his outrageous yellow hair, which seemed to grow out of his head at the exact same shade as his garish autocar.

Dahran laughed, which could have meant anything, since Kadin had no idea if her new favorite's racing skills were on par with his style. "Well, it just so happens that I have an extra ticket for the drag." He handed her the papers. "I was supposed to be going with a friend of mine, but he had to cancel. Would you like to go with me?"

Kadin's heart beat faster. She couldn't believe he had asked her out already, with so little effort on her part. "That would be great! I was so upset that I was going to have to miss it! I usually watch at my friend Olivan's house, but he's busy this weekend." Kadin worried she might be laying it on a little thick, but Dahran seemed to buy it. Besides, Olivan would back her up.

"That works out for both of us, then," said Dahran. "Write down your address for me, and I'll pick you up at 10." She tore a sheet out of her notebook and did as he asked. As she handed him the paper, he winked at her in a manner she decided to find endearing. "I look forward to seeing you in your drag colors."

Deity curse me! When she had named the Yellow Comet as her favorite racer, she had forgotten that she would have to wear his colors to the race. She looked terrible in yellow. *I'll have to make it work. I think Octavira has a yellow dress.*

"Did you want something when you came in?"

"Oh, right." He snapped his fingers. "I wondered if you were in yet because no one had made the java. The early starters need it by eight. But the last girl forgot all the time too."

"Right." *Did anyone tell me I was responsible for the java? More importantly, how will I convince Octavira to let me out of the house that early?* "I'll get on that now."

Kadin made her way over to the office's makeshift kitchen and inspected the java maker. It didn't look *too* different from Octavira's, though that might have been a more reassuring thought if Octavira let her prepare java. But how hard could it be?

After a few minutes, she had a brown liquid that smelled awful and tasted even worse.

This would be so much easier if I liked *java.* She stared down at the steaming liquid. She didn't think it was supposed to have little bits of grind floating in it, but she had no idea what to do about them. She decided to retreat to her office and be grateful no one could get food poisoning from poorly prepared java. She didn't think.

Fellows hadn't arrived by the time Kadin returned to her desk, so she decided to type up the notes that she had made yesterday. She coughed at the thick layer of dust that flew into her face when she lifted the black pleather cover off the typewriter on her desk. *Fellows's last aide must not have been a big typer.*

She had keyed most of her notes when Fellows breezed into the office, whistling a jaunty tune. He didn't say anything to Kadin, just hung his trench coat on the hook outside his door and headed into the back. As if he had awaited the detective's arrival, Inspector Blaike Warring, head of the homicide department, stormed past Kadin's desk and into Fellows's office.

Kadin had time to hear Warring shout, "*Why* is the queen's body downstairs in our lab?" before one of the men slammed the door. She heard raised voices through the wall but couldn't make out what they said.

The door remained shut for another ten minutes, and Kadin resisted the urge to move closer to listen in. A loud thump sounded, like someone throwing something on a desk, or perhaps a body falling, and Kadin was wondering whether she should check on the investigators when Inspector Warring stuck his head out and pointed at her. "You! Go get Jace Combs."

Kadin got about halfway down the hallway before she

realized she didn't know where to find Combs. *Fellows told Combs not to leave the lab until he knew what had killed the queen, so I guess I should head down to the basement.*

For three years, Kadin had operated a switchboard down the hall from the suite that housed Valeriel Investigations' forensic examination center, but she had never visited the lab. Her shoes clicked against the cheap tile of the basement floor, and she turned into a room that looked much as she expected—lots of hard steel cabinets covered with sharp-looking equipment that she could not identify, much less use. The air stank of formaldehyde, and a device that looked like something straight out of a horror film, all knobs and red wires, hummed in the corner.

Queen Callista's body lay on a wheeled table in the center of the room, though Kadin barely recognized her with her face shorn of makeup and her naked body covered in a sheet instead of some trend-setting fashion. Kadin felt like she should be disturbed, but she found, once again, that the sight of the body made her want to seek out whoever had taken away the queen's vitality.

Even if my place in the pursuit of justice is as a not-so-glorified errand girl.

Combs leaned over a microscope, so intent that he didn't notice Kadin come in. She cleared her throat, and the doctor blinked bleary, red-rimmed eyes before turning to look at her.

Fellows did *tell Combs not to leave the lab until he had determined cause of death. But surely Fellows didn't mean literally.*

"Inspector Warring would like to see you up in Detective Fellows's office." Kadin found her voice shook a bit as she spoke, and a pit formed in her stomach. She wasn't sure if she feared the doctor's temper, or if she was just nervous performing her first official task as a detective's aide.

Combs rubbed his eyes, even as he lifted them

heavenwards. "Fabulous. Do you know what about, as if I couldn't guess?"

The pit grew, as if her stomach acids solidified around it. "Well, they didn't say anything to me, but I suspect that it regards your choice to bring the queen's body here rather than release it to the Imperial Morgue."

"Right." He slammed a clipboard on the counter. "After all, it is much less important to find out what killed Queen Callista than it is to make sure we don't offend any future Imperial clients. Because solving the crime doesn't impact our reputation as much as how courteous we act."

Kadin's mouth went dry. "Um... You didn't stay here last night like Fellows ordered, did you? Because I'm fairly certain that he was exaggerating, and you look as if you haven't slept in weeks."

"I wouldn't be so sure of that." Combs swiped a folder off the table then called out, "Corkscrew!"

Kadin wondered for a moment whether the doctor had invented his own swear word, but then a small man with white tufts of hair over his ears came out of a room adjoining the lab.

"Yes?" the man—Corkscrew, Kadin presumed—said.

"Where are you on the tox screen?" Combs opened a drawer and rummaged around in it.

"I'm going as fast as I can, sir." Corkscrew's voice quavered, and the paper in his hand shook loudly enough that Kadin could hear the rustle across the room. "I'm not sure about these toxins you're looking for. If they had killed her, there would be other signs. I'm sure of it."

"Yes, well, let me know when you have any better ideas of what could have suffocated a person and left no marks." Combs pulled a large syringe out of the drawer and thrust it in Corkscrew's direction.

The small man jumped. "I should go back and finish the tests."

Combs rubbed his forehead with his free hand. "I need

you to take the rest of the samples now. I suspect we're going to lose the body in the next half hour."

"Oh, dear." Corkscrew tsked. "I don't think that's the best idea. The samples won't be fresh by the time we finish the tests I've already got going..."

"I know that, but we don't have a choice. The powers that be are going to order me to send the body to the morgue, and old samples are better than no samples." Combs shook the syringe at Corkscrew again.

This time Corkscrew took it. "Maybe we should..." He turned his head in Kadin's direction, and when he saw her, he jumped, nearly sticking himself with the needle. "What is *she* doing here?"

"That's Fellows's new aide, Kadin Stone." Combs waved a dismissive hand in her direction.

Surprised the doctor had remembered her name, Kadin forced a smile at Corkscrew.

The strange man took a few steps backward, his eyes bulging out of his head. "No, she can't be here. They said she wouldn't be here."

Combs closed his eyes and looked to be counting to ten. "Please tell me you haven't stopped taking your medication again. You remember what happened the last time. You're lucky they let you keep your job after that."

Corkscrew frowned. "Well, let's see, I took..." He counted on his fingers. "That one, and then the other one..."

Combs whacked the folder in his hands against his thigh. "Just don't forget again. And take those samples. I have to go let Warring bite my head off."

Combs strode across the room. From the hallway, he turned to Kadin. "You coming?" he asked.

Kadin spun on her kitten heel—then cringed at the pressure on her blisters from the day before—and followed the doctor to the lift.

Combs pushed the button for the fourth floor, and the doors hissed shut.

Kadin decided remaining silent would feed the pit in her stomach more than awkward conversation would. "So, you're going to turn the body over to the Imperial Morgue?"

"It appears that way."

"Well, at least you have all the records and tests that you wouldn't have gotten if you hadn't had her for this long." Kadin watched the elevator dial tick to floor 1.

Combs gave her a sideways glance. "You don't think I was wrong to bring the body here?"

"No, of course not. You said that you needed it to find the cause of death, right? Well, we need that to determine who killed her. Seriously, we seemed to offend the king by existing anyway—" *Though he probably would have let* you *do pretty much anything.* "—and Detective Fellows said we needed to solve this case quickly. I don't know what they're making such a fuss about."

"They're making a fuss because even if studying the body does help us solve this case, it will lead to bad publicity for the company. We're delaying the queen's interment and possibly defiling her body by cutting it open. Plus, the press, no doubt aided by the moguls who profit off of quick investigations, has created the myth that *competent* investigators can determine cause of death from a cursory examination and that only the hacks and con artists need to hem and haw with *tests*." He sighed and for a moment seemed unsteady on his feet. "If news of the queen's temporary sojourn here gets out, there will always be rumors that we doctored the evidence to cover for someone. I talked to Fellows last night and asked that he consider bringing another investigation company in on the case, so we have witnesses, but he doesn't want to risk sharing the credit with someone else."

The pit in Kadin's stomach jumped to her throat. "Isn't it more important that we figure out what's going on? Someone killed the *queen*. Granted, he's probably not some serial killer who's about to strike again at any moment, but this murder affects everyone in Valeriel!"

Combs's eyebrows flew upward as he held the lift door open for her. She huffed, not knowing what was so surprising about her statement, until she caught a glimpse of the girl with the tight dress and the traffic-stopping make-up reflected in the silver lift door. A ninny one step up from a sub-D, who cares more about men looking at her than listening to her.

And that's good, she thought. *I'm not here to solve murders. I'm here to get a husband.* Though, as long as the company kept paying her, she had planned to do both.

She picked up her pace to keep up with Combs's long strides. "Do you want some java before going in?"

Combs gave her a wry smile. "The homicide department doesn't like us lab rats messing with their java. Not after what Corkscrew did last time."

Kadin made a dismissive noise. "I made the java. I can offer it to anyone I want."

"Well, I'm certainly not going to say no."

She led him into the kitchenette, and he poured himself a cup. He took a sip, and his eyes opened wide for the first time that day as he spit it back into the cup.

"Oh, I'm sorry!" Kadin moved toward the refrigerator. "Did you want cream or sugar? I should have offered some..."

"Um... no." Combs stared down at his mug. "It's, um, fine. Just, you know, kind of hot."

"It's horrible, isn't it?" *Oops. Octavira was right about my java-making skills.*

"No, no! It's fine, see?" He took another sip and almost managed not to wince as he swallowed it. "Now I should probably go meet with Fellows and Inspector Warring."

Kadin's heart sank as she stared at the java machine. If her java was undrinkable, she didn't think the detectives would be as nice about it. *I'll have to pretend I forgot for today. And as for tomorrow...* She poured the java down the drain. *I guess I know what I'll be doing tonight.*

Fellows emerged from his office with Warring and Combs an hour later. Kadin hadn't heard their conversation, but judging by Combs's frown and Warring's puffed-up chest, she suspected the queen's body would soon be on its way to the Imperial Morgue.

Fellows retreated into his office, and after a moment of indecision, Kadin went to the doorway between their offices. She watched him shuffle through some papers for a few minutes before she tapped on the jamb.

Fellows looked up and narrowed his eyes. "Do you need something?"

The pit in her stomach that had almost subsided in the previous hour returned with full force. "Um... I was wondering what the plan was. For the investigation."

"I'm going to speak with the duke's sister, Lady Beatrin Oriole, this afternoon." Fellows dropped the papers into his outbox tray. "I suppose you can come, if you'd like."

"Okay."

Fellows scribbled a note on a piece of paper.

Kadin swallowed. "Do you... do you want to review my notes from yesterday? I typed them up."

"I don't think that will be necessary." Fellows, dismissal evident in his tone, kept his attention on whatever he was writing.

"Oh, okay." Kadin shifted her weight. *I should tell him about seeing Duke Baurus.* "I..."

"Yes, Miss Stone?"

She shrank back at the hostility in Fellows's tone. "I... Do you want me to contact the Oriole estate and let them know that we plan to go over and talk with Duchess Beatrin?" *It's not as though the duke said anything important. I can always tell Fellows about it if it becomes relevant.*

Fellows looked at her as though she were a dog who had happened to pick that day's issue of the *Tribune* out of a pile. "All right, that may be advantageous. Tell them that we will be there after lunch, about 1:00."

"What do you want me to do after that?"

Fellows made an exasperated noise and snapped his pen down on the desk. "Miss Stone, I am extremely busy right now. I'm sure that you can find things to do to amuse yourself."

Does that mean I have to be self-directed in my work or that he doesn't want me to do anything?

She returned to her desk and called the Oriole estate to schedule an appointment for that afternoon. When she hung up the phone, she read through her notes from the day before, making sure she hadn't left anything out of the typed version. She slid the clean copy into a file folder from the cabinet, wrote "Callista DeValeriel" on the tab, and set it to the side of her desk.

She glanced at the clock. *Three hours. Well, two until we have to leave. Does Fellows expect me to do nothing for two hours? Why would he hire and pay an aide to sit here and look pretty?*

Well, isn't that why you wanted the job? she could imagine Leslina asking.

It is, I guess. But I still expected to do *the job.* She eyed the clock again. Three minutes had passed. *I might as well look into the case on my own. But where can I get more information about the people involved?* She laughed to herself as the obvious answer occurred to her.

She took the lift down to the basement for the second time that day, but this time she turned left at the bottom and went to visit the switchboards.

Trinithy squealed when she saw Kadin. "Did you really get to go to the palace yesterday? Was it fabulous? Did you meet any Imperials? Did someone really murder Queen Callista? Please tell me you swiped a souvenir for me."

Kadin laughed. "Yes, I went to the palace, and it was fairly magnificent. But where would I have gotten you a souvenir? It's not as if the Imperial Palace has a gift shop, and, besides, I was investigating a murder."

Trinithy stuck out her lower lip. "You could have swiped me one of Queen Callista's perfume bottles or something. It's not as if she needs them anymore."

A rush of warmth filled Kadin. She wished she'd had a running commentary from Trinithy at the palace yesterday. "Yes, because the best thing for me right now would be getting caught stealing something from a dead woman."

Trinithy held up a staying hand. "All seriousness, though, Kadin. Did someone murder the queen?"

"Indeed, someone did." Kadin sat down in her old chair. "And I need your help with that. I don't know too much about Queen Callista—or Lady Beatrin, who I have to go see this afternoon—so I thought you might have some articles or something that could help."

Trinithy put a hand over her heart. "Lady Beatrin..." She sat up straighter. "If I'm going to give you enough information about Lady Beatrin for you to meet her, I need reinforcements."

She moved a wire to the jack for the personnel department and flipped the talk switch. After a moment, her face brightened. "Ollie! Get down here, and bring everything you've got on Beatrin Oriole. It's an emergency."

She didn't give him time to answer before she hung up and turned back to Kadin. "So did you meet anyone at the palace? I need details!"

Kadin leaned forward and lowered her voice. "Well, I was there while Fellows interviewed the king."

Trinithy made a series of high-pitched noises so shrill that Kadin feared temporary deafness, and more than one switchboard operator turned to look at them. "What was he like? Did he say anything to you? In all the pictures he's always all done up in full royal apparel. Does he dress differently when he's not in public? Did he have the face paint?"

Maybe I don't wish Trinithy had been there after all. If she had made these noises in front of the king, we never would have gotten anywhere with the investigation. "Yes on the face paint, no on the dressing differently. Maybe he wears normal clothes when he's alone, but we were enough of a public appearance that he had on the full regalia, cape included. He did ask who I was, but he didn't talk to me other than that. Fellows asked the questions, and Dr. Combs, the forensics specialist, spoke to him a bit, too. No one expected me to interrogate anyone on my first day." *And they still won't expect it today or tomorrow or the next day or any day, even if I'm here for years.*

"Oh, my Deity, Kadin, you are so lucky!" Trinithy's tiny body shook so much her stool squeaked. "Did you meet anyone else?"

"Well..." *Duke Baurus threw a book at my head and shouted at me some.*

Olivan appeared behind Trinithy, sparing Kadin the decision of whether to reveal that particular factoid.

"Ollie, Kadin met the king!" Trinithy reached out to grab some of the glossies that spilled from Olivan's hands.

Olivan set the rest of the pile down in front of Trinithy's switchboard and faced Kadin. "Oh, who cares about the king? I heard her say she met Jace Combs. Would you introduce me?"

Twin lines formed above Trinithy's nose as she paged through Olivan's glossies. "Who's that? Is he famous? I haven't heard of him."

Olivan's jaw dropped. "You haven't told her about Jace? He is only the hottest guy in the entire company. Or possibly the entire city of Valeriel. Maybe even the kingdom." He and Trinithy stuck their lips out at Kadin.

A twinge of guilt fluttered in Kadin's stomach. "Well, Trinithy was asking about the king. Besides, Combs is married, which is pretty fair evidence that he's not sideways."

Olivan waved a hand. "Oh, as if his sub-D of a wife counts."

Kadin rolled her eyes. "If she's got the ring and the certificate, she counts, Ollie. Let's not have this conversation again. Although I did mean to ask you, what's the story with them? I'm fairly certain she's not his dream girl, and she didn't seem overly devoted to him either."

Olivan's eyes lit up. "They've been married for a few years now. The story goes that she was totally Class D, or well on her way, and she set her sights on him. One hundred percent evil seduction until he had his wicked way with her. Then she threatened to cry rape if he wouldn't marry her. So he could have a wedding to save his reputation or get dragged through the courts and have the nuptials court-ordered. He picked the former. So now the sub-D cheats on him all the time, but he won't divorce her because that would be like throwing her out on the street, and he's too nice."

Trinithy winkled nose suggested she wanted to vomit, but her eyes held rabid fascination. "So he's hot and decent, but he's married to a sub-D?"

"And not even sideways. It's one of life's great injustices," Olivan said. They exchanged pitying glances.

Kadin thought back to Combs's behavior that morning, and the day before. "I'm pretty sure his bad attitude would turn both of you off within minutes."

Trinithy put her chin on her hand and sighed. "But he wouldn't need to be unpleasant if he were married to me. I'd be the perfect wife."

Kadin coughed to cover a laugh. "Regardless, I didn't come down to discuss Jace Combs, pretty though he may be. I need to know what you know about the queen."

"Oh, the queen! That woman was a sub-D and a half!" Olivan's excitement dimmed a bit. Kadin supposed that was the difference between Olivan talking about someone he had a chance of meeting, instead of someone he never would.

Trinithy twisted her lips. “I’ve never understood what you mean by that. I mean, wouldn’t being a half more than a D make her close to an E?”

“Not the point, Trinithy.” Olivan’s clipped words belied the animation in his face. “I meant that she made someone like Joelle Combs look as if she could be employed in the Merchant District.”

Trinithy twirled a curl around her finger. “I’m saying it doesn’t make sense, is all.”

Snipe, snipe, snipe. “So the queen wasn’t faithful to the king. Everyone and his sideways cousin knew about her affair with Duke Baurus.”

“He was just the tip of the iceberg.” Olivan pulled out a glossy and pointed out clicks of Queen Callista at various social events. In each one, she was attired in the latest fashions; her shining blond hair was perfectly coifed; and she had a different man on her arm. “This is her with Count Mikache Fox. And this one is Lord Dimka Fiesta. Oh, and do you remember this one, Trinithy? Groven Sophist? He’s a Merchant, K, so you know that was a total scandal. And let’s not forget—”

“Ollie.” Kadin held up her hand, knowing that if she let him go on, she would get the full list of every man with whom Queen Callista appeared in public since her coronation. “I get the idea. But going to parties with different guys isn’t the same as... engaging in inappropriate behavior with them.”

“True enough,” Olivan said. “Especially since King Ralvin was well-known for not going to Imperial events, and he couldn’t expect her to spend the whole time alone. And usually she did go with Duke Baurus.” He picked up a new glossy and flipped through it. “Oh, here’s one with the two of them.”

In every other click, the beautiful and charming queen drew Kadin's eye. But she faded into the background when Duke Baurus's sheer vibrancy attended her. His rapture shone forth from the page, almost as strongly as it had in person, and the emotion overwhelmed Kadin. *How can everyone have said he hung on her every word? Compared to him, she was nothing...*

Fingers snapped in front of her face. "Earth to Kadin! Did you hear what I said?"

Kadin blinked several times, clearing her head. "Sorry, Ollie, guess I zoned out for a second. What were you saying?"

Olivan pressed his lips into a line. "I *said* that everyone knew Queen Callista was sleeping with Duke Baurus, but the gossip writers could only speculate on the others. Some of the glossies speculate that she only went out with other men to make the duke jealous." Olivan flipped through several magazines until he found a click of Duke Baurus glaring at the camera. Kadin recognized the expression, since he had given her that look the day before. The facing page showed three pictures of Queen Callista dancing and laughing with other men. "Then out of the blue they would be back together."

"Hm." *If Queen Callista broke up with Duke Baurus all the time, what was different about this time? What could have made him enraged enough to kill her?* "Tell me about Lady Beatrin."

Olivan pulled out a glossy he already had folded open and handed it to Kadin. "Duke Baurus's older sister, married to Duke Frasis Oriole. No children, but Duke Frasis has two sons from an earlier marriage. The family's wealth comes from the vast mineral mines of Oriole Territory, which means Lady Beatrin always has the best diamonds. And that the Territory gets a cut of every electronic device we buy to fulfill the cravings of our modern hearts."

Kadin skimmed the article in front of her. Rather than

recounting yet another Imperial gala, the piece described some nobles' endeavor to raise funds for the city's charity food bank. Such gestures were pointless, Tobin often said. If the Imperials really wanted to help the poor, they'd redistribute some of their wealth and create a balanced economy. But Kadin knew most women, even noble women, didn't have control of their wealth, so she liked to see them doing what they could.

The click next to the article showed a woman in her late thirties with a severe dark brown pixie cut, an austere set to her lips, and a high-necked white dress. Some of her features had the same shape as Duke Baurus's, but Lady Beatrin's sheer lack of expressiveness made Kadin wonder how the nobles could be related at all.

"Duchess Beatrin is an Imperial of the old order. She believes in keeping up appearances at all times and snubbing the upstart Merchant class. Your basic boring Imperial. Although..." Olivan tapped his finger against his chin.

Trinithy leaned forward, her chest heaving under her light blue sweetheart collar. "Ollie, please do not tell me you know gossip about Lady Beatrin. You've been holding out on me!"

Olivan grinned, and his eyes shone with a wicked light. "Rumor has it that in her naïve DeValeriel days, Lady B had an affair with Garson Grey."

Kadin thought back to where she had heard that name. "Isn't he a gossip columnist?"

"The gossip columnist. For the *Valeriel Tribune.* And freelance for *Imperial Society."* Olivan reached over and turned back a couple of pages in the glossy in Kadin's lap. He pointed to a black-and-white click of a dark-haired man with a mischievous smile. "The story goes that Lady Beatrin's mother, Lady Augustille, found out about the relationship and hit the roof. She made Lady B marry Duke Frasis in a hurry, even though he was twice her age,

because he was the only one who would have her. I would have thought more people would have jumped at getting that much closer to the DeValeriel name."

Trinithy's jaw slackened. "Oh. My. Deity. How is it possible I did not know this? Lady Beatrin. I mean, she... she... she *goes* to parties, but she never *does* anything. How can she have been a rebel in her youth?"

Ollie shrugged, and he couldn't hide the grin spreading on his face. "It's just a rumor, and not one that will help Kadin in her search. These days, Lady Beatrin is as upstanding a member of the community as you're going to find. She doesn't approve of her brother's goings-on, and she's even less likely to approve of his being a murderer."

Kadin stared down at the stern woman on the page in front of her, with her tight lips and eyes that brooked no opposition. If *she* could have a fiery scandal in her past, what secrets could someone like Queen Callista have had?

CHAPTER 7

When Kadin and Fellows reached the Oriole estate that afternoon, a servant escorted them to Lady Beatrin's library. The main hallway seemed less grand than the entrance to the palace, but Kadin suspected that had more to do with the muted blue and green décor—Oriole colors—than any difference in quality. If anything, the woven tapestries and understated cedar furnishings that lined the walls probably cost more than the garish gold of the palace.

Lady Beatrin's library was similar to Queen Callista's in that both had bookcases lining the walls, but the similarities ended there. The light blue sofa and chairs did not conform to modern styles, and the antique desk in the corner was bare except for a simple gold lamp. The leather-bound volumes on the shelves reflected the tastes of a woman who preferred last century's classics to contemporary pulp.

Either Lady Beatrin likes antiques, or Duke Frasis is less inclined to indulge his wife's tastes than the king is, thought Kadin.

Kadin and Fellows sat in the room long enough for the gold clock on the mantle to chime both the hour and the quarter hour. As the echo of the delicate hymn faded for the second time, Lady Beatrin strode into the room wearing a smart blue suit. Fellows stood up to shake her hand, and Kadin noticed that, in her heels, the duchess had an inch or two on the detective.

"I apologize for keeping you waiting." Lady Beatrin, sounding about as sorry as the average Imperial who inconvenienced a commoner, gave Fellows's hand a brisk shake, then did the same to Kadin's. "I regret that I have another appointment in half an hour, so this will need to be brief. I assume you wish to discuss Callista's death."

"Of course, of course. I shall make this as quick as possible." Fellows situated himself on the sofa again. "Could you please tell me about your relationship with Queen Callista?"

Lady Beatrin sat down in a faded blue chair and crossed her long legs. "We had known each other for years, since her engagement to my cousin Ralvin, and we ran in the same social circles."

"Would you say you were friends?" Fellows asked.

"After a fashion." Lady Beatrin laid her hands on the arms of her chair. "We often attended events together, and we each had our Imperial duties, though we did not always agree on the method of carrying them out."

Party line all the way, then, Kadin thought, though she couldn't help but think that the duchess had expressed as negative an opinion of the queen as decency would allow.

Fellows wrote something in his notebook. "How did you feel about the relationship between the queen and your brother?"

A tingle ran down Kadin's spine at the mention of the duke. She decided to attribute it to guilt over not mentioning her encounter with him to Fellows. She certainly didn't find him *interesting.*

"I try never to have an opinion about Baurus's affairs." Lady Beatrin's hazel eyes looked as if they could see right through Fellows. “He is a grown man and may manage his life as he sees fit.”

“Then you were aware of your brother’s relationship with the queen?” Fellows voice sounded detached, disinterested. As if he were discussing his grocery list, rather than the torrid affair that may have led to the crime of the century.

Lady Beatrin raised a pointed eyebrow. “If you’re asking me to confirm society page rumors, I am going to have to decline.”

Kadin glanced down at the blank paper in front of her. She wondered how Fellows was finding so much to write about.

Fellows met the duchess’s gaze. “Are you going to tell me that Duke Baurus did not spend the evening here the night before the queen’s murder?”

Kadin’s head darted up to look at Fellows. Then she mentally chastised herself for being surprised. Fellows had worked all morning, so it only made sense he would have tracked down what the duke had done after he left the palace.

Lady Beatrin pressed her lips together, the only sign that Fellows’s question had discomfited her. “Yes, he came here the night Queen Callista died, but he left long before the guard found her. So if you’re looking for his alibi, you won’t find it here.”

Fellows made a noise that sounded like a muffled “Aha.” “So you are saying that we should be investigating your brother as a person of interest in the queen’s death.”

Lady Beatrin blinked twice. This time Fellows had caught her off guard. “You have made it clear you see reason to link Baurus’s and Callista’s names.” The duchess’s voice could have frozen the engine of an autocar. “Given that, I don’t see how you would not see him as a suspect.”

Wow. Even the king was willing to be explicit about the affair, yet Lady Beatrin feels the need to keep it secret. That doesn't make her look dignified or circumspect. It makes her look foolish. Is it because women aren't supposed to talk about these things?

Fellows tapped his pencil against the notepad. "Perhaps you can tell me what you and the duke discussed when he visited that afternoon."

Lady Beatrin's features smoothed, though whether she preferred the conversation's new turn or wanted to school her expression, Kadin couldn't tell. "Baurus was angry with me. He had had an unpleasant conversation with Callista that afternoon, and he blamed me, as he had visited her in order to retrieve a book I had lent her."

Kadin glanced at the bookshelves in the room. She wouldn't have thought the two Imperial women would have shared literary tastes. Further fodder for her theory that Lady Beatrin had little say in the room's décor.

Fellows narrowed his eyes. "You sent your brother, *the duke*, on an errand to retrieve a book?"

Lady Beatrin's jaw clenched ever so slightly. "The task required some delicacy, as Callista was unlikely to respond to the request of a mere servant, and I had promised to loan the volume to Elyesse Imbolc. Elyesse is such a sweetheart. One hates to disappoint her. Baurus had said he planned to see Callista in a few days. I did not ask him to make a special trip to see her, though he chose to do so."

That was almost legitimate information from her, Kadin thought. *Maybe she's starting to crack.*

But Fellows eased back a bit in his seat rather than press forward. "Did anything else happen between you and your brother that afternoon?"

The duchess's features returned to a collected mask. "No. He expressed his anger and then left. He told me he was going home. I had no reason to doubt his words, though I can neither confirm nor deny their veracity."

Fellows met Lady Beatrin's eyes, his mouth set in a

grim line. "Do you believe that Duke Baurus murdered Queen Callista?"

Lady Beatrin shifted her eyes and fixed her gaze on a point over Fellows's shoulder. "You could hardly expect me to implicate my closest relative in murder, Detective."

Lady Beatrin thinks her brother is guilty. Kadin put her pencil to her notepad but couldn't bring herself to write the words.

Lady Beatrin stood up. "I think this conversation is finished. Now, if you'll excuse me, I have another appointment."

"Of course." Fellows stood and stuck his notebook in the pocket of his trench coat. "Please, call us if you think of anything else that could be of use in the investigation." He handed her a card.

She stuck the card in her beaded clutch. "I'll be sure to do that."

More like she'll forget about us the moment we're gone, Kadin thought as she stood up.

"If you'll follow me, I'll have someone show you out." Lady Beatrin strode over to the door and summoned a servant from the end of the hall.

She wants to be cool, calm, and collected, but there's obviously more going on below the surface. Kadin thought back to Olivan's story about Lady Beatrin and Garson Grey and looked at the austere sitting room with the blank desk and outdated furniture. *I wonder if anyone in the Imperial sphere is who they seem to be.*

An image of Duke Baurus flashed through her mind. She'd heard tales of rages, and seen a firsthand example of one, but she felt a momentary relief that he, at least, was exactly as he appeared.

Kadin tugged the paper out of the typewriter and, squinting, brought it close to her eyes. The letters on the last lines of her notes had come out uneven and barely legible.

Great. I have to replace the ribbon. If only I knew how *to replace a typewriter ribbon. Between this and the java, I'm starting to suspect I don't have any skills at all.*

She pulled open her drawers and rifled through the contents until she found a ribbon in a plain white box. She opened the top of the typewriter and tugged at the spools holding the ribbon. When they didn't budge, she fingered around until she found the latch that unsecured them. After that the old ribbon came out easily. She needed a few tries to wrangle the new ribbon between the wires, but in short order she had snapped the spools into place.

She felt a rush of satisfaction, which lasted until she picked up a piece of paper to test her handiwork. Her ink-covered hands left black smudges on the white surface. She sighed and went to the bathroom to wash her hands.

On the way back from the ladies' room, the words "... Fellows's new aide..." floated from the kitchenette.

I shouldn't eavesdrop, but... She tiptoed closer to the door.

"Oh, yeah, I saw her." A man whose voice Kadin didn't recognize let out a whistle. "Boy, is she a stunner. She may well be the best-looking one he's had, at least as long as I've been here."

Kadin stood up straighter, until she heard a gruff tone. "She may be attractive, but I'm fairly certain she doesn't have the smarts to fill a breadbox. She forgot to make the java this morning. I miss Auriel. She made those crumbly muffins, and she didn't interfere with serious investigations."

Kadin's mouth fell open. *I didn't* forget *to make java,* she wanted to say. *I just... don't know how!* Somehow, that didn't vindicate her, even in her own mind.

"That's easy for you to say, Euston." The first voice laughed. "You have a gorgeous wife already. Some of us don't have something that nice to look at back home and like to see it at the office. I vote we let her do whatever feather-brained things she wants, as long as she keeps wearing those tight skirts."

Kadin ran her hands down her skirt. *They aren't* that *tight, are they?* But of course they were. She wore them to emphasize her shape.

"And some of us don't have anyone at home at all." One of the men opened the refrigerator as a new voice spoke. "I don't suppose you homicide boys would be willing to share her with us? We could use a good laugh down in assault."

"Eh, Dahran might have something to say about that," said the first man. "Got a date with her on Saturday. Maybe the next one, Corners."

Corners groaned. "I should be so lucky."

You should *be so lucky,* Kadin thought. *No woman would give you the time of day if she knew what you said about her!*

But, then, you knew that Fellows hires his aides for their looks, thought another part of her. *What did you think that meant?*

The man who wasn't Corners spoke again. "Anyone hear how the big investigation is going? Did they meet any Imperials?"

Euston coughed. "White didn't get any good interviews, but he said Fellows got to meet the king. White got sent to the DeValeriel estate today, but he knew Duke Baurus would have disappeared by now. No one's seen him since yesterday morning.

Kadin gasped. *No one except me.*

"Fellows has moved finding Baurus DeValeriel up to our number one priority," said Euston.

Kadin's hand flew up to cover her mouth. If Duke Baurus had disappeared, she was the only person involved in the case to have seen him.

I have to tell them what I know. Except...

She didn't actually know anything. And even if she did, how could she get the team to listen?

CHAPTER 8

"Now, Drena is asleep and should be okay if you leave her alone. Aberon has been fussy lately, so if he wakes up, give him a glass of water, but don't let him have any juice or he'll be up all night." Octavira crossed the kitchen and picked up her purse from the counter. "The Sanders live down the road, and we're only going to be there for a few hours. You shouldn't have any problems, but I left their ringer number on the counter. Oh, and if anything..."

Kadin tuned out the rest of Octavira's speech, wishing her sister-in-law would have some faith in her. The two women didn't always get along, but Kadin wouldn't have wanted anything to happen to the children.

"Calm down, Vira." Tobin came up behind his wife and began to rub her shoulders. "Kadin knows all this. It'll be fine, right, K?"

"Absolutely." Kadin gave Octavira what she hoped was a reassuring smile.

"The emergency and poison control numbers are on the counter as well," Octavira told Kadin as Tobin dragged her toward the door. "And don't eat anything out of the refrigerator, because we're having leftovers for dinner tomorrow."

"Bye, Kadin." Tobin gave Octavira a little push out into the night air.

"Bye!" Kadin waved and shut the door behind them.

Kadin collapsed against the door and breathed a sigh of relief. She didn't mind spending most evenings with her brother and sister-in-law—well, with her brother, at any rate—but her career and marital prospects were contingent on having the kitchen to herself this evening.

She headed into the kitchen and regarded her nemesis: the java machine. An average passerby would have thought it an innocent, slightly tarnished appliance, but such a bystander had not spent two years avoiding it.

"You don't look so tough."

Kadin peeled off a filter from the stack and placed it in the top compartment of the machine. She scooped some java grounds into the white paper, poured water on top, and pressed the red button. She closed her eyes and braced for an explosion of wires and wet brown powder.

Nothing happened. The machine didn't even make the hissing noises it did when Octavira started it. Or the horrible whirring noises the old one had made the last time she had tried to make java. Which had led to Octavira forbidding Kadin access to kitchen electronics. Kadin opened one eye and realized that the button hadn't lit up.

Oh, brilliant, Kadin. It helps if you plug the thing in.

She groped around for the plug and stuck it into the outlet in the pastel blue wall. She pressed the switch again, and this time the machine buzzed to life. She kept her attention fixed on it as it hissed, steamed, and trickled its way through the java-creation process. After a few minutes, the aroma of java filled the air, the machine fell silent, and the light went off.

Kadin jumped to pour the brown liquid into Octavira's least favorite cracked mug, then raised the cup to her lips. As soon as the java hit her tongue, she yelled and yanked the beverage away from her face, splashing steaming hot water onto her hand and the floor.

Idiot! She ran to the sink to run herself a glass of cold water, which she applied to her scalded tongue. *What did you think was going to happen if you drank boiling java?*

She wiped the water off the floor, and then started pacing across the kitchen, waiting for the pot to cool. She began next to the aqua-green refrigerator, passed the matching stove, and turned at the end of the row of dark brown plywood cabinets. Back and forth, in perfect time with the ticking wall clock above the steel sink. She tried to picture the admiring look on Dahran's face when he tasted her perfect java, but an image of him dismissing her when he learned her non-existent culinary skills didn't even extend to java making kept surfacing in her mind's eye.

After five minutes, the steam rising from the pot had dissipated. Kadin poured herself a new mug and took a sip.

She gagged and spit the java back into the cup, realizing the flaw in her plan. The java could be better than the finest roasts in an Astrevian tea house or worse than the swill she had made that morning, and she would never know the difference, because all java tasted terrible to her.

She scrutinized the liquid in her cup. The color seemed a little lighter than what Octavira served Tobin every morning, and she didn't think sediment was supposed to settle at the bottom of the mug.

I guess I could... Fudge. I have no idea.

A knock sounded at the back door.

Who could that be? She headed toward the sound, her mind still half on the java problem. *Octavira retrieving her keys? Some neighbor making sure Octavira's unmarried sister-in-law didn't smother the children in their sleep?*

She opened the door, and her heart stopped.

Standing on the other side was Duke Baurus DeValeriel.

He looked the same as he had when she saw him yesterday, still tall and broad enough to seem larger than life, with his thick hair looking desperate to break free from its smooth side part. He even wore the same suit, or one just like it. The Imperials did love their family colors. He probably didn't leave his estate wearing anything other than DeValeriel red and black. The only thing that had changed was his face. She could only describe his current expression as one of total devastation. The energy rolling in waves off him made tears spring to her eyes, and she had to force herself to focus.

He raised his hand in a half-wave. "Hello. I came by to apologize."

"Apologize?" *For what? What is he doing here? Why is there a duke at my house?*

"For yelling at you yesterday. And for throwing a book at you." He looked around the yard and peered into the house. "Look, can I come in?"

He might be a murderer, her brain yelled at her. *You can't let him into the house!* She knew she should close the door in his face, but she remained in the entryway, unmoving. "I don't think that's a good idea."

He huffed. "Do I need to remind you that you're alone in the house with two small children, and I'm wanted for murder?"

He's threatening me. She knew she should listen to him, but somehow she didn't feel intimidated. His words said she was in danger, but his face, his posture, said that if she insisted he go, he would go. "So you're going to kill me? The way you killed Queen Callista?"

At that, he looked angry. "Let me in, and you won't have to find out."

Shut the door in his face, Kadin thought. *He won't really do anything, will he?*

He won't hurt me. I'd bet my life on it. She stared into his flashing hazel eyes. *But I can't bet Aberon's and Drena's.*

Cursing herself, she held the door open and stood aside so that he could enter.

The duke's gaze flicked around the room, and for a moment, Kadin considered what her house must look like to him. The simple faux mica table and plastic chairs, the kitschy poodle lamp, the department store family click, all of them must have screamed "commoner" to someone of his standing.

She moved to pick up some papers Tobin had left scattered on the table. "How did you find me? I don't remember leaving a posting address with you. Or a name, for that matter."

"It wasn't that hard to find your name—you were the only woman on the investigation team. Your address was in the ringer guide." The corners of his mouth quirked upward. "Besides, you kind of stand out."

Her heart beat faster. *What does* that *mean?*

But his smile faded, and whatever he had thought about her had gone. He looked toward the framed family portrait on the wall, and a wave of despair washed over his face.

Well, of course, Kadin thought. *Didn't he just lose the love of his life?*

Didn't he just kill *the love of his life, more like.*

"I realize how this all looks. Me, Callista, her... death. I came by because I wanted to tell someone my side of the story, and I figured you would be more inclined to listen than the rest of those... gentlemen."

Kadin wasn't sure what word the duke had intended to insert in place of "gentlemen," but she suspected Octavira would not approve of its presence in her kitchen.

Duke Baurus sniffed at the air. "Isn't it a little late for java?"

An idea struck her. She pointed to the table. "Sit down."

The duke raised an eyebrow but pulled out a chair and complied with her request. Kadin went into the kitchen, pulled another mug—one of the best. Octavira would flip, but she would be even more upset if a duke thought she used chipped dishes—down from the cabinet, and poured a fresh cup of java.

Kadin put the cup in front of Duke Baurus. "Drink that."

With an amused gleam in his eye, he picked up the cup and put it to his mouth. Kadin barely had time to feel an inexplicable burst of pleasure that she had improved his mood, however temporarily, before he sputtered and sprayed java across the room.

Kadin waited until he was done making faces. "What's wrong with it?"

"It's disgusting!" He gagged and stuck out his tongue.

Kadin tapped her foot. "I know it's disgusting. What specifically is wrong with it?"

"You can't tell?"

"No, I think all java is disgusting." Kadin made an exasperated noise. "Look, they expect me to make java at work, and I don't know how. My sister-in-law doesn't usually let me use the java machine, after it exploded that one time—"

He smirked. "Exploded?"

Kadin felt heat rise to her cheeks. "Yes, but I still maintain that it wasn't my fault. She hadn't told me that she had already put water in it, and I'm fairly certain that the machine was faulty anyway. Anyway, it was two years ago, so it shouldn't matter anymore." She sighed. "But my java is undrinkable, and I need to learn to make it before I get fired. So tell me what's wrong with it."

The duke sat back in his chair. "You do realize I've never made a cup of java in my life."

Snobbery is not helpful. "Well, neither have I. You at least drink the stuff, so you have one up on me." Kadin pointed at the mug. "Now tell me what's wrong with it."

He furrowed his brow and stared down at the cup. "I

think there's something wrong with your filter. There's java sediment in the cup."

"Hm." Kadin spun on her heel and headed back toward the kitchen. When she got there, she opened the top of the java machine. She pinched her nose to block some of the odor of java and peered into the container. Sure enough, the filter had torn, allowing some of the grounds to seep through. She scooped the mess out as best she could, and then started peeling off another filter to try again.

She didn't need to turn around to feel the duke's presence behind her. "What are you doing?"

She looked over her shoulder. His tall, broad frame leaned in the doorway. She swallowed, then held up the filters. "I'm getting a new filter."

"I gathered that. I meant, why were you ripping it apart." Kadin must have looked confused because he took a step forward. "This thing here?" He reached out to grab the pile from her. "This is one filter."

He leaned in past her, so close she felt the hairs on her arms stand up to get closer to him, and dropped the filter into the top of the machine. As he backed up, his arm brushed hers, and her breath caught.

Because I'm afraid of him, she reminded herself. *Because he's a* murderer.

She added the water and turned the machine on again. As she leaned against the counter, she thought she heard a noise outside. She jumped, terrified that it was Octavira returning. She didn't want to imagine what her sister-in-law would say if she came home and found Baurus DeValeriel at her kitchen table.

Kadin, did you let a duke *into my house? But I haven't dusted in nearly a week, and I don't think I remembered to wipe the counters after dinner. And what if he notices the rip on the back of the sofa? It's against the wall, I know, but imagine if he dropped something back there. And, didn't I hear that he killed the queen? How could you let a murderer into the house with my children? Especially with the playroom such an absolute mess! I simply cannot get Drena to—*

Duke Baurus cocked his head to the side and regarded her. "You have the oddest look on your face. What are you thinking?"

Make something up. Anything. "You don't want to know."

For a moment, his face looked as it had when she saw him in the library the day before. "I wouldn't have asked if I didn't want to know."

He stood so close to her in the tiny kitchen, and she could feel his anger radiating off him. She felt defiant. "I was wondering whether my sister-in-law would be more upset that I had let you into her house because you were a duke—and she hadn't had time to clean or, you know, buy completely new furniture—or because you were a murderer."

He scowled and leaned even closer to her. "I did not kill Callista."

"Yes, well," Kadin's irritation fled, and she concentrated on taking even breaths. "Octavira doesn't know that. And, quite frankly, neither do I."

He glared at her, but the intensity had left his expression. "Why would I kill Callista? How *could* I kill Callista? She was the only thing I ever wanted." His gaze lost its focus as it roamed to the blue checked curtain framing the top of the kitchen's only window. "Well, almost the only thing."

"Almost?" *What else could a duke possibly want? What doesn't he have?*

He stayed silent for so long that Kadin thought he wasn't going to answer, but then she heard him whisper, "Magic."

Kadin blinked. "Magic, as in the Society of Mages?"

He nodded once, still staring out the window at the red swing on the back porch.

She couldn't quite keep the incredulousness from her tone. "You do realize that there haven't been any confirmed members of the Society in Valeriel in twenty years, don't you? And even before that it was just hearsay. Most people don't think that they even exist anymore."

Baurus's jaw tightened, and she could tell she'd hit a sore spot. "They're not gone. At least, not forever. Historically, they've been in and out of Valeriel society. They've disappeared for as long as a century before, but they always come back." He got a faraway look in his eye. "If I traveled to other countries, I bet they would have records of the Society for times we have lapses. And maybe I could find them there and ask to join."

"Ah. I see." The java machine beeped, and the light went off. Kadin reached for another mug and surreptitiously inspected it for cracks. When she felt sure it was intact, she poured a fresh cup.

Duke Baurus followed her with his eyes. "What do you mean, 'I see'? What do you see?"

Kadin shrugged. "You want what you can't have." He opened his mouth to protest, but Kadin held up a finger. "The one thing that you wanted more than anything else was Queen Callista, who, in addition being engaged to marry your cousin since before you knew her, was, by all accounts, incapable of emotional attachment. And now you tell me that you, who have wealth and influence most people only dream about, want the kind of power unavailable to you."

He leaned forward and grabbed the java out of her hand. When he straightened he seemed too close again, so she backed up an inch.

He gave her a level stare. "Maybe you're right," he said, surprising her. "But what's the point in wanting something you can have? What do you and other people waste your time wanting that's so attainable?"

Kadin pondered this for a second. Her goal of finding someone to marry her so she could move out of her brother's house was attainable. *But is that really what*

I want? She wasn't sure, and she still didn't want to lie to him.

She settled for the short-term instead. "I want to know whether that java is drinkable."

He raised his eyebrows with a smirk that said he knew she was avoiding the question, but he took a sip of the java.

Again he cringed but swallowed, so Kadin decided to interpret that as improvement. "Drinkable? Possibly, but it's the weakest java I've ever tasted. I don't think you put enough grounds in the machine."

"But I put in how much it said on the side of the canister." Kadin picked the canister up again. Right there on the side it said to put in four scoops for every four cups of java.

Kadin eyed the java pot. It did look larger than four cups. Estimation of volume wasn't her strongest suit. She squinted to read the raised print above the light, and, sure enough, it said that the machine made eight cups. Which meant she needed *eight* scoops of java grounds.

Kadin swiped the used filter and grounds out of the machine, noting with some satisfaction that this time the filter hadn't ripped. She then set up the entire process again, this time using two scoops of java.

Duke Baurus watched the process with an amused glint in his eyes. "So what are you going to do if this pot is perfect? Your life's work will be achieved, and things will get awfully dull from here on out."

She crossed her arms. *Smartass.* "Okay, you know what else I want? I want to know who killed Queen Callista."

He sobered, and the haunted, desolate look came back into his eyes. "You and me both."

Kadin's breathing slowed. "And by that standard, I should be bringing you to the office for questioning right now. After all, you are a highly involved party who has to this point remained unquestioned."

"Ah, but you won't." His tone was light, but his face

remained serious. "Because you aren't sure capturing me is urgent enough to justify the expense of emergency responders. Besides, you're watching your brother's children, and you can't afford to leave them alone should I choose to run, or to protect them should I choose to respond with violence. Why do you think I came here tonight instead of dropping by your office?"

Kadin froze. *He's not going to hurt me. I know he's not going to hurt me. But what was I thinking, joking with him, giving him java. He killed someone. And even if he didn't, he's unstable. Did you forget about the book throwing incident? You shouldn't do... whatever you were doing with him.*

Duke Baurus leaned back. "Calm down. I'm not going to hurt you. I told you, I came to tell you my side of the story. But I have no intention of allowing myself to be taken anywhere, as I suspect it would be a long time before I saw the light of day again."

Kadin's heart didn't slow. "Well, at this point, you are only wanted for questioning, though that is likely to change the longer you avoid the investigation team."

He gaped at her. "I knew Callista better than anyone, and I have a pretty good guess what all your interviewees said about both her and me during your investigation. They don't just want me for questioning. I can't let them take me in." He studied her face, as if expecting her to give something away. "I do want to help with the investigation, so I came here so you could ask your questions."

Kadin almost laughed in his face. *I can't tell Fellows that Duke Baurus was in my house but I didn't take him into custody, even if he would listen to me. That's if this whole visit isn't a plot on the duke's part to throw me off his trail.* Her brain considered everything for a moment, then came to a decision. *I might as well collect what evidence I can. Maybe someone will want it at some point.*

"Why me? I'm hardly the senior member of the team."

She went into Tobin's study and opened the top drawer of the desk.

Duke Baurus followed her. "You seemed the least threatening."

Well, I did ask. Kadin pulled out a notebook and pencil, returned to the kitchen, and sat down. "Tell me about your relationship with Queen Callista."

Baurus sat down in the chair he had vacated, pushing it back from the table to give himself room to stretch out his legs. "I loved Callista." His voice held a grim fierceness, as if he thought Kadin would deny what he was saying. "Everyone said I was crazy for it, that I wasn't seeing her for who she was, but I did. I always knew exactly who she was, from the first time I saw her. I was visiting her father Count Reuben on some matter of business when she entered the room, and it was as though I had never seen the sun before."

He ran his hand over his face. "It sounds like ridiculous and superbly trite hyperbole, I know, but it's the only way I can think to describe the effect she had on me. She was always harsh, incredibly searing, and she always had a dozen other satellites orbiting her. But it didn't matter because without her, my world was cold and dark, and I would rather be one of her hangers-on than be without her. I'm not saying that I didn't wish she could love me as I loved her, because I did, more than anything, but what she was willing to give was better than nothing."

He loved her, Kadin wrote, though that seemed insufficient to describe the emotion he laid before her. *What would it be like to love someone that much? I doubt I even could. I don't have that kind of... emotional capacity.*

Duke Baurus stared straight ahead, as if he were lost in a memory. "If I had been wise or politic or anything that my parents or Beatrin ever wanted me to be, I would have kept my feelings to myself rather than acting upon them. The gossip that our relationship created would have scared off many other men, and more than a few of her other lovers left for fear of damage to their reputations. But I've never seen the point of hiding my feelings and doing things because someone else wants me to."

He snorted, but still he did not come out of his reverie to look at Kadin. "Of course, the affair was not all sweetness and roses. Callista only ever accepted my affection in the absence of anything else to occupy her time and mind. I think she liked having someone who adored her so absolutely. Had I not been ready and willing to take her back every time without question or complaint, I'm certain that she would have been finished with me long ago. And thus did she develop a kind of fondness for me and our relationship."

Kadin rolled her pencil in her fingers, feeling the bevels against her skin, unsure how to capture his emotions as dispassionate evidence.

He cleared his throat. "Objectively, I knew that's all it was, but emotionally... Somehow I always managed to fool myself into thinking that it meant more, that this time she had realized I was more to her than some convenient groupie. Then every time she would decide to end things and shatter the delusion. I would get so angry, mostly at myself for being such an idiot, and I would lash out at everyone around me. Eventually I would stop being angry and just miss her. Then, after a few weeks or months, she would come back to me, and the sun was back in my sky. And the cycle would continue. Until two days ago."

"When she died," Kadin whispered.

"No." He shook his head but still didn't look at her. "Before that, in the afternoon, when I went to see her. Beatrin asked me to get something from Callista—I don't even remember what—and I used that as an excuse to go see her. Stopping by unannounced to see Callista was always a bit of a risk. Sometimes she was fine with it, but sometimes she was irritated by my presumption. This time she said she was glad that I had stopped by. She even looked happy. I had seen her in any number of moods over the years, but I had never seen her look so joyful."

He closed his eyes. "She told me that during one of our off-again periods about a year ago, she had been with someone she had fallen in love with. I don't know who he was, just that he ended things with no explanation. She said that he was back now, and for the first time she understood how I could keep going back to her every time, because she wanted nothing more than to go back to him. She told me that it was over between us, permanently this time."

His eyes opened, and he stared back into space. "The whole thing made no sense. The Callista I knew was too hard to love anyone, and if she did love someone, why wasn't it me, who loved her more than anyone else possibly could? But I could tell that she meant it, that she loved this other man, whoever he was, and I knew that we were finished for good."

"Okay..." Kadin knew she should be writing it down, but she kept getting caught up in the story, in his emotions. She found she felt... jealous. Because she knew no one would ever love her as much as he had loved Queen Callista, and surely she, who didn't make a habit of stringing men along for the express purpose of breaking their hearts, deserved it more. "What did you do then?" The king and Lady Beatrin had already told her, but she wanted to hear his side.

"I got angry." He frowned, remembering. He turned his attention to Kadin for the first time since he started telling his story. "That's what I do when things go wrong, I get angry. You got to witness some of that the other day." His lips held a trace of a smile.

His eyes lost their focus, and he was gone again, back into the past. "I was angry with Callista for being so cold, for not loving me the way I wished she would. When I shouted at her to try and have a heart for once, she asked me to leave, as she always did. I was angry with Ralvin for not bothering to control his wife, for letting this happen in the first place. I probably accused him of insane things like trying to keep us apart, which he never did. I was angry with Beatrin for sending me over in the first place, allowing Callista to end the relationship and my delusions a full day before she otherwise would have. Mostly, though, I was angry with myself for being idiot enough to believe, yet again, that she would eventually love me if I kept trying. And underneath all that was heartbreak and despair that this time, we really were finished."

He met Kadin's gaze again. "So I railed at Callista. I railed at Ralvin. I railed at Beatrin. And then I went home, stared in the mirror, and railed at myself. I consumed enough alcohol that I should have forgotten the name Callista DeValeriel. But when I finally passed out, I dreamed of her. I slept straight through to the morning, when someone finally woke me to tell me that Callista was dead."

Claims he was passed out drunk at time of murder, Kadin wrote, glad to have something as stable as an alibi, even if she couldn't confirm it. She supposed she could go to the duke's servants and ask them if he had stayed home all night, but she couldn't trust them not to lie for their master. Nothing she could do could outweigh the money and intimidation he could use to make them keep their stories straight.

Duke Baurus fiddled with a button on his jacket. "I didn't believe it at first. I had been angry with her and devastated by her, but never for a moment did I want her dead. A part of me, which probably would have been a larger part as time went on, was glad to see her happy for once. Even if she didn't love me, even if I couldn't be with her, her existence was still a light in an otherwise dark world.

"But I went to the palace, and I saw people from your little company carrying out the body, and the reality of her death hit me. I was so angry, angrier than I'd ever been in my life, angrier than I thought I was capable of being. I wanted to find whoever had done this and choke the life out of them with my bare hands." His jaw tensed, and Kadin feared he might look for things to throw. But then he took a deep breath and unclenched his fists. His gaze met hers. "That was pretty much the state I was in when you saw me."

Kadin stared into his eyes, and what she saw in their depths nearly overwhelmed her. All the emotions he described—love, rage, despair, regret—he felt them, all at once, with a passion she, in her relentless pragmatism, could never match. The intensity became too much for her, and she turned her head back to her notes. "What were you doing in Callista's library when I saw you?" Queen *Callista. Just because you're having java with someone on first name basis with the royals—who is practically one of the royals himself—doesn't mean you get to drop the formalities.*

Duke Baurus leaned back in his chair, and the light made the shadows under his eyes stand out. Kadin wondered whether he had slept since he heard about the queen's death. "When I came by the afternoon of her death, she had written me a letter. That's how she had planned to break things off with me, before I showed up in person. It may seem silly, but I wanted that letter. Still do want that letter. I know it will contain words that will break my heart all over again, but it's the last thing she wrote to me. Besides, I thought that it might have further information on her new-old mystery lover, who I'm sure is in some way connected to her death."

If she really had a mystery lover, Kadin thought. *But, then, the king also commented on his wife's good mood.*

"Do you have any idea who he was?" she asked.

The duke hesitated. "Yes and no. I don't have a name. She wouldn't give me one, no matter how many times I asked. Which makes sense, since I was a raging psychopath at the time, and who knows what I would have done to him? But when we weren't together, I kept obsessively close tabs on her relationships. Creepy and stalkerish, I know, but probably helpful for a murder investigation, because I can tell you the people she was involved with about a year ago, when she was with this guy she loved."

He reached into his jacket pocket and pulled out a piece of paper. He handed it to Kadin, and she read a list of four names. She had heard a few of the names, but she suspected Olivan and Trinithy could tell her more.

"Those are the men. I don't know which one she thought was her true love. I wouldn't have thought that she was particularly attached to any of them, but obviously I was mistaken." Duke Baurus sat back, glaring at the paper as if it had killed his best friend. Which, Kadin supposed, it may well have.

Kadin opened her mouth to ask him a question about what he had been doing since she saw him yesterday, when she heard the sound of a key turning in the back door.

She jumped up. "Octavira and Tobin are home! You need to leave."

He threw back his head and laughed, his sudden change in emotion lighting up the whole room. "But of course. We wouldn't want your sister-in-law to know that I had seen her imperfect furniture."

Kadin grabbed his arm to drag him toward the front door, her heart racing, this time more from fear of getting caught than of the duke's proximity.

"You have no idea how funny that is not." She opened the door for him and shoved him out as she heard the back door open and Tobin and Octavira step inside.

He turned around on the front porch to smile at her. "See you around, Kadin Stone."

Before she could respond—or figure out what he meant by *that*—footsteps started toward her. She slammed the door in his face and locked it, then whirled around in time to see her brother enter the room. She smiled at him and inched away from the door, hoping he didn't think to ask why she was there.

"Hey, Kadin." He bent over and picked up a brown throw pillow from the wooden floor. "How did everything go? The kids all right?"

"Yes, they're fine. No problems at all." Kadin wondered if it counted as a lie, since the children *were* fine, and she hadn't had any trouble with them.

His brow furrowed, and he opened his mouth to ask a question, but Octavira stormed in before he could.

"Kadin, what did you do while we were gone?" Octavira waved a hand back toward the kitchen. "There are java grounds all over my counter and mugs everywhere. The machine is full of cold java, and I could swear someone sprayed something toxic all over my kitchen table."

Kadin hurried past Octavira into the kitchen. "I forgot about that! Would you mind trying it to see if it's drinkable?"

Octavira trailed after Kadin. "Of course it's not drinkable. It's cold! And that doesn't answer my question. You know that you are not supposed to touch the java maker. Not after what happened last time."

Kadin spun around to face her sister-in-law. "Wings of the Deity, Octavira, that was two years ago, and the repairman said the wiring was faulty! Stop treating me like a child!"

Tobin had followed his wife into the kitchen, and both their heads shot backward at Kadin's words.

Kadin resisted the urge to clap her hand over her mouth. *Curses on Baurus DeValeriel. He's gotten me all out of temper.* "I mean, I'm sorry, Octavira. I needed to learn how to use the java maker at work, and I didn't think you would mind if I practiced on yours. I'll clean everything up now."

Octavira looked slightly mollified, but Tobin took a step forward. "Are you all right, Kadin? You seem a little... off."

Kadin took a deep breath and smiled. "I'm fine, Tobin. Nothing wrong at all." She wondered why those same words she said every day felt more like a lie than usual. "I'm going to go clean up the kitchen now."

As she lay in bed that night, Kadin wondered how much she could trust the duke's story. She planned to investigate the names he gave her, if she could find a way to introduce them to Fellows in a way that didn't get her fired. The team would also want to look for the letter from Callista he had mentioned.

But even after she had resolved everything that concerned the case in her mind, she couldn't help but smile at the notion that she had entertained a duke in Octavira's kitchen that evening. And to think, he had all the things in the world, but the only things he wanted were Queen Callista and magic.

The juxtaposition of those two things made her sit up straight in bed.

Combs couldn't find any physical evidence to explain the queen's suffocation. Corkscrew had said any of the possible poisons would have left traces. The colloquial expression would have claimed her death was "almost like magic." But if Duke Baurus was right about the Society of Mages returning to Valeriel, maybe she could get rid of the "almost."

CHAPTER 9

As Kadin locked her purse in her desk drawer, Darson stopped by with Fellows's post and a heavy, oddly-shaped parcel for her. She ripped off the brown paper and found a wine-red foil bag covered in a language she didn't recognized. She whipped the package around and found a small section in Valerien that indicated the package contained Astrevian grounds, known among anyone rich enough to afford it as the best java in the world.

She dropped the bag and snatched up the note that had fallen out of the package. "This probably doesn't come with a scooper, so you may have to use the one that came with whatever swill they've been drinking. - B.D."

Kadin stared at the lumpy package on her desk and felt her breath come faster. *I have a gift from a duke and a murder suspect on my desk.* She would have bet on the "murder suspect" part getting her in more trouble, but the "duke" part might lead to more questions. Either way, the wisest course of action was probably to throw the java in the nearest garbage bin.

She picked up the brown paper and shiny red bag and held them over her trash. *What are you doing? Your job depends on how well you make the java, and you're going to throw out the best stuff in the world? Besides, it's already bought and paid for. You shouldn't waste it.*

Kadin dropped the paper in the bin and made her way toward the kitchenette with the java. Fifteen minutes later she had a pot that smelled as unappetizing as ever but looked more like Octavira's morning offerings than any of her previous efforts. Kadin couldn't see to the bottom to tell whether any sediment rested there, but when she dumped out the filter, it hadn't torn.

Satisfied, she retrieved a mug from the cabinet and filled it with steaming java. She carried it down to the lab, where she found Combs shuffling through an array of papers.

"Good morning!" She gave him a broad smile, content that her salmon lipstick matched her full-skirted dress. "I come bearing java."

He, no doubt remembering yesterday's drink, gave the mug a wary look

Kadin laughed and held out the cup to him. "It's better today. I promise. I practiced all night." *When I wasn't interrogating Imperial murder suspects and trying to remember everything I knew about magic. But I'd probably better tell Fellows about that before I say anything to anyone else. And I'm going to tell Fellows. Any day now.*

Combs took the beverage and raised it to his lips. His eyes widened. "This *is* better. No wonder homicide doesn't like to share their java if this is what they're holding onto. It's nectar from the Deity."

"Uh-huh." She glanced around the lab, and then looked back at the doctor. "So, I was thinking about the queen, about how she might have died."

He raised his eyebrows at her as he took another sip of java, and Kadin couldn't help but notice the circles under his eyes.

He'd probably be insulted if I asked if he wanted to borrow my concealer to cover those up. She had put a healthy coat of the make-up under her eyes that morning to make it look as if she had slept better than she had.

"You and me both." He turned his attention back to the papers. "If you've come for a report, I've identified some rarer poisons that could have caused suffocation. But the symptoms don't match exactly, and I'm out of specimens. So if Fellows wants any more concrete answers, he's going to have to get me that body back."

Fellows hadn't sent her, but since Combs was treating her as though she was part of the investigation, she didn't bother to correct him. "Well, you said it looks as if she was strangled but with no visible marks, right?"

He nodded, not looking up from his papers. Kadin heard movement and looked up to see the small man who had been in the lab the day before—Corkscrew, Combs had called him—emerge from the side room with a metal tray in his hands.

Kadin tried to keep her voice casual. "Do you think it might, you know, theoretically, have been magic?"

A clang echoed through the lab as Corkscrew's tray clattered to the floor.

"What? No, no, no! No magic!" Corkscrew turned toward Combs. He had spilled a blue-green liquid over his lab coat and the abstract red tie and uneven blue-striped shirt underneath. "Jace, please, tell me, not the magic again."

Combs closed his eyes and took a deep breath. "No, Corkscrew, of course there's no magic." He opened his eyes and gestured to Kadin. "You remember Miss Stone, Caison Fellows's new aide. You met her yesterday."

Kadin smiled and offered her hand for Corkscrew to shake, realizing too late that if he took it, she would get that nasty blue stuff on her.

To her relief and dismay, Corkscrew looked at her as if she carried some horrible disease. "I don't think you're supposed to be down here."

"She came down to offer us some java." Combs held up his mug.

"Oh, well, that's nice." Corkscrew wiped his hands on his coat, getting more liquid on his fingers than he wiped off. "But I'm not supposed to have java. The doctors say it upsets my system." He looked down at his sticky blue hands. "Maybe I should go get cleaned up."

"Maybe you should." Combs gave Corkscrew a patient smile and watched the small man amble out of the lab. Then Combs whipped his head around and glared at Kadin. "Don't ever say the M-word down here!"

Well, how was I supposed to know he would react like that? "I'm sorry. I thought..."

"I know what you thought." Combs rubbed the bridge of his nose. "The same thing crossed my mind, more than once. This case looks like the kind of unsolved case that tends to pop up when the Society of Mages is reported to be in Valeriel. But it doesn't matter."

How can it not matter? Kadin wanted to ask. *Don't we need to do whatever we can to find the queen's killer? Isn't that what you've been fighting for?* "I don't understand—"

"No, you *don't* understand." Combs's shoulders sagged. "Let me put it this way. About twenty to twenty-five years ago, Dexter Corkscrew worked for CrimeSolve, Inc. as a forensic examiner." Kadin recognized the name of the largest and most successful investigations company in the whole kingdom. "He was brilliant, top of the field, and maybe he got to thinking that he could do no wrong."

Combs took a long sip of his java. "Then he ran into this one case that he couldn't solve, and he became convinced only magic could have caused the symptoms he saw. The detectives all told him to let the case go unsolved, but he refused to give up. He even looked into cold cases and insisted that magic was responsible for them as well."

Kadin swallowed past the lump in her throat. "What happened?"

"That depends who you ask." Combs set his mug down and stared into the brown liquid. "The official story goes that he had a nervous breakdown. He spent the next seven years in an institution, and it took years for him to be stable enough to work here. He knows more about forensic investigations than anyone, but he's nothing like he used to be. And he's terrified of even the mention of magic."

"That's the official story." Kadin took a deep breath. "But what do you think?"

Combs met her gaze. "I don't know. Sometimes I think that he was getting too close to something and that the Society of Mages did something to destroy his mind. After Dexter went to the institution, the Society disappeared from Valeriel, almost as if they wanted to lay low for a while. Of course, the fact that no one has seen a mage in twenty years discredits the notion that they're responsible for a murder now, especially a high profile one like this."

Kadin's heart pounded. "Would it make a difference if I told you that Duke Baurus's greatest wish is to join the Society of Mages?"

Combs gave a mocking laugh. "I would say that you shouldn't use fodder from the tabloids as evidence in a murder case."

Since she could hardly tell him that she had heard the news from a more direct source, she nodded, conceding his point. "But Duke Baurus isn't one to keep his desires to himself. Is it possible that someone is trying to make Queen Callista's murder look like magic, in an attempt to frame him?"

Combs cocked his head to the side, as if he were trying to figure out what was going on inside her head. "Whether someone killed the queen with magic or not, I am going to continue to look for a more concrete cause of death. And even if I can't find one, I'm not going to be crying 'Magic' anytime soon. No good can come of going down that road."

Well, if the only person who thinks I'm part of the team won't consider magic, I might as well forget it.

Exiting the lab, she bumped into Corkscrew. His hands were clean, but stains covered his front. She couldn't believe that he'd once had the finest forensic mind in the kingdom. But if he had, and if the mages had brought him down, didn't the investigative community owe him justice?

CHAPTER 10

I'M GOING TO TELL FELLOWS *about Duke Baurus.* Kadin marched from the elevator into her office. *Even if I get fired, he needs to know for the sake of the investigation. But I hope I don't get fired.*

She came to a halt at Fellows's door and rapped on the door jamb.

Fellows snapped his head up. "Miss Stone, what is wrong with this picture?"

"I have to tell you I— What?"

The noise Fellows made when he exhaled suggested she had all the intelligence of a squirrel, though he supposed he hadn't expected any better. "My aide is standing at my door first thing in the morning without a cup of java for me."

"Oh." Kadin's shoulders slumped. "But I..."

Fellows raised an eyebrow. "Yes, Miss Stone?"

"I... Do you take cream and sugar?" She tried not to cringe at the squeak in her voice.

Fellows sneered. "Does any self-respecting detective take cream and sugar?"

Kadin took that as a "No" and slunk off to the kitchen. *This doesn't change anything. I have to tell him. I just... have to get his java first.*

She pulled a mug from the cupboard and poured the last of the java from the pot into the mug. Apparently the drink was popular when made properly, or maybe the detectives had figured out that she'd made the good stuff. She set another pot to boil and returned to Fellows's office.

She set the mug on his desk and braced herself with a deep breath, but before she could get a word out, Fellows said, "Miss Stone, go find White." Fellows waved toward the door.

Should I tell him? Or wait until after he talks to Dahran? I should tell him first. She opened her mouth.

"*Now*, Miss Stone."

Out in the hall, Kadin realized she had no idea where Dahran's office was. After a moment's hesitation, she decided to check the offices next to the kitchenette first.

I'm sure they would have given me a proper tour if they hadn't had such a big case. I can hardly get upset at Fellows for not finding time to show me the ropes when I can't seem to find the time to tell him about Duke Baurus.

She peered into the first office on the left and breathed a sigh of relief to see Dahran sitting at the desk. "Fellows wants to see you in his office."

Dahran gave Kadin a broad grin and stood up. "All ready for the drag this weekend?" He scooped his fedora off the coat rack and put it on in one smooth motion.

Kadin hoped her expression didn't look too much like a grimace. "Absolutely." *I need to remember to get something yellow to wear.* Octavira owned a yellow dress, but Kadin wasn't sure her sister-in-law had forgiven the damage to her pumps yet.

Dahran swept past her, handing her a mug on the way. "Get me some more java, would you?"

"Sure," Kadin said, but he didn't have time to hear her response before he breezed down the hall. *I wonder if* he's *a self-respecting detective so far as cream and sugar are concerned.*

She refilled Dahran's mug from the fresh pot of java and sidled down the hall to Fellows's office.

"—open and shut case," Fellows was saying. "We need to make finding Baurus DeValeriel our number one priority. Any questions?"

Kadin cleared her throat. "Well..."

Fellows narrowed his eyes at her. "I'm in a meeting, Miss Stone."

"Right. I needed—"

Dahran laughed. "She was bringing me my java." He reached out and took the cup from Kadin. "Didn't mean to interrupt, Caison."

"Indeed." Fellows shuffled past Dahran toward the door and shut it in Kadin's face.

Kadin blinked. *I should knock on the door and insist on talking to them. But... would they even listen to me? Maybe I should... get some more concrete evidence and then present it to him.*

She pulled the notes from the night before out of her bag and scanned them. The best leads she had to go on were the names of Queen Callista's lovers from the year before. Duke Baurus believed that the queen had a special attachment to one of them, so the trick would be to find out which one. Fortunately, she had access to one of the best indexed archives of Imperial tabloids in the city.

Kadin took the lift to the ground floor and strode through the glass-paneled doors of the personnel office. She smiled at the secretary as she sashayed into Olivan's office and closed the door. Looking around the office, she felt a burst of pride, rather than her accustomed envy. She, too, had an office, instead of a switchboard cubby, with the same institutional white walls, grey metal furniture, and drab brown carpet. Maybe Olivan had a few more filing cabinets than she did, and she would probably never get that classy citrus scent to permeate her space, but she was moving up in the world.

"I need your help." Kadin swept past her sandy-haired friend's desk and opened one of his filing cabinets.

Olivan stood up so fast his chair skidded across the floor. "K, you can't go in there! Those are confidential personnel files."

Yeah, right. She pulled out a file. "Oh, so Valeriel Investigations has hired Duke Cobalt Fan's wife's dressmaker?" she asked, reading the paper on top. "Interesting. I'll have to get him to design my outfit the next time I have to go question someone at the palace."

Olivan snatched the file folder out of her hand. "It could have been confidential personnel data!"

"No, it couldn't." Kadin yanked another file out of the drawer. "In my experience, 'confidential' doesn't mean much to you, so if I had opened personnel files, you wouldn't have batted an eyelash. But if I were to get a few files in your Imperial index out of order. Well, then, you might not look like the gossip expert your reputation suggests."

Olivan grabbed the file out of her hand before she had a chance to open it. "Okay, fine. You don't have to invade my files. I'll tell you whatever you want to know."

Kadin sat on the edge of his desk and crossed her legs. "I know. I just like watching your reaction. You have to be the most neurotic gossipmonger in the city."

Olivan slid the folders she had removed back into the cabinet, checking twice to make sure that each was in the proper place. "What are you looking for? More information on the murder case?" He turned to her, his eyes glowing.

Maybe this wasn't the best idea. "You can't tell anyone."

He pantomimed zipping his mouth shut and throwing away the key.

"I mean it, Ollie." She did her best to look stern. "The detectives don't know I'm doing this."

Olivan slid the filing cabinet closed and opened the one beneath it. "You're doing work you don't have to? Have I taught you nothing?"

Kadin glanced at the closed door. "It's not that I don't have to! It's..." She looked back at his raised eyebrows. "Okay, so they want me to sit there and look pretty and stay out of the case, but I've stumbled onto a few things they don't know about. So I figure I'll investigate, and if I come up with anything, I'll let them know."

Olivan gave a low whistle. "I don't know, K. I mean, everyone knows that Baurus DeValeriel killed Queen Callista, so I don't know what more information I can give you."

Kadin considered telling Olivan that Duke Baurus had visited her house, but decided against it, if only because she would never get Ollie back on topic if he knew she had met one of his Imperial crushes. "You're right. My investigation probably won't make a difference. But it's something to do other than rearrange my paper clips for the fiftieth time."

"Okay." Olivan eyed his own paper clip collection. Kadin knew for a fact its disarray had nothing to do with his work ethic. "What do you want to know?"

Kadin pulled out the scrap of paper Duke Baurus had given her and passed it to Ollie. "I need to know which of these men Queen Callista was in love with."

Olivan made a disbelieving noise in his throat. "Queen Callista wasn't in love with anyone. It probably would have ruined her nails."

"Well, I have evidence that suggests otherwise."

Olivan had been scanning the list, but his head shot up. "I don't know whether I should laugh in your face or interrogate you about your sources."

Kadin closed her eyes and took a deep breath. "You should look at that list and tell me whether the queen was in love with any of those men."

"Okay, okay." Olivan turned his attention back to the paper. "First one is ancient, second is happily married, and the last is a total jerk who's cast two wives out onto the street so he could marry younger women. The second wife really should have seen it coming."

"Hm." Kadin suspected the queen too shallow to go for a man Olivan described as "ancient," even if she did know her friend's perception of age was a bit distorted. A happily married man probably wouldn't have returned to Queen Callista in the last week, but the third... Queen Callista wasn't very nice herself, so she might find a similar man appealing. "What's the name on that last one? In case I wanted to talk to him?"

"You can't. He had a horseback riding accident and has been laid up with a broken leg in Scanty for three weeks."

That rules him out. "I gave you one more name. Tell me he's a better prospect."

"Lord Landis Imbolc." Olivan thumbed through the folders in the drawer. "You should know this one. Heir to Duke Chaise Imbolc, Assembly member and ruler of Imbolc Territory. Lord Landis is a notorious playboy whose name has been coupled with every unmarried Imperial woman's and more than a few of the married ones." Olivan pulled out a thick file. "I've got more information on him than practically anybody else. Do you want me to go through this whole thing?"

Kadin eyed the stack of papers. "Maybe I could borrow it?" Olivan drew his head back as if she had asked to borrow his first born, and Kadin laughed. "I promise not to tell anyone where I got it. Or lose any of the clippings. Or get any of the pages out of order."

"No java stains on it either." Olivan handed over the folder.

Kadin weighed the heavy file in her hands. *I guess I've got work for the next few days. Even if Fellows doesn't need his java refilled.*

CHAPTER 11

FELLOWS WON'T CARE THAT *I left work early... right?* Kadin shivered as she hurried down the deserted street. *I need to get home on time* and *replace Octavira's pumps if I want her to lend me her yellow dress for the drag on Saturday. Just my luck she bought the shoes at a store on the edge of Smoke Row.*

Kadin wondered if the time wouldn't be better spent buying her own yellow dress, but between the poor chances of finding one this time of year and her inherent horror at spending money to add such a thing to her wardrobe, she decided the shoes were a more practical choice. *Especially since this way I can get a pair in my size, too.*

Kadin wrapped her arms around herself as much to protect herself from any would-be attackers in the worst part of the city as to ward off the autumn chill. She wrinkled her nose at the oily stench that permeated the street, appreciative that the neon graffiti on the grey stone walls was the only sign of life in the area.

The welcoming glow from the window of the shoe store caused Kadin to pick up her pace, and as soon as the bell above the door stopped dinging, Kadin rubbed her hands together, grateful for the warmth. She only needed a few minutes to select the two pairs of shoes, and within no time, she was back out on the street.

She glanced at her watch and swore under her breath. *I'm going to be late.* She glanced down an alley next to the shoe shop. She had never taken that street before, but theoretically it should get her to the autobus stop faster. *Ah, well,* she thought as she turned down the alley. *If I get mugged and murdered, at least I won't have to worry about what to wear to the drag.*

She reached the end of the T-intersection. *Right or left? Left, I think.*

Even as she made up her mind to head toward the stop, her attention shifted to the right, as if compelled by some kind of sixth sense. Out of the corner of her eye, she saw one of the buildings emit a blue haze. *It's just exhaust. This* is *Smoke Row, after all.* But somehow she couldn't stop herself from taking a few steps toward the building to examine it more closely.

It looked like any other abandoned store front on the street, with cracked glass windows that had faded gold writing in an arc across the top. Kadin squinted to make out the scratched-off calligraphy. *M-A-G-I... Magic Shoppe!*

Her breath caught, and she peered into the dusty window, looking for any sign of life in the building. She thought she saw a hint of light from the back, and this was enough for her to reach for the door handle.

What are you doing? the part of her that didn't seem to control her body shouted. *You need to go* home. *And if magic* is *real, you can't mess with it. Dr. Combs said it was* dangerous. *And you're not a real detective. You need to find a husband, not a murderer.*

But her internal protestations did no good. She wanted—no, more like *needed*—to go inside. To find out what she could about what had killed Queen Callista. Or what so fascinated Duke Baurus. Or... She wasn't sure she even had a real reason. She just knew if she walked away without at least trying to get more information, she would regret it.

The rusty hinges squeaked as she pulled open the door. She stepped over the threshold and coughed as thick air filled her lungs. The floorboards creaked as she inched forward, closer to the ancient wooden bookcases laden with musty tomes and odd-looking antiques. Kadin ran her fingers along the cracked spines of the leather-bound volumes, trying to sound out the foreign titles in the dim moonlight shining in through the grubby windows. Some of the words she recognized as Minskorian, Ruathalese, or Astrevian, but others bore strange pictographs she had never seen before.

On the other side of the room stood what had once been the shop's main counter, if the ancient pewter cash register atop it was any indication. Something crusty had formed on the glass of the case in front, but she could still see tarnished necklaces, cufflinks, and snuff boxes laid atop faded beige velvet. She wondered if the objects possessed magic or if they were gimmicks to con those rich enough to pay more for an item that *might* have magic. Judging from the state of the shop, neither method had prompted much in the way of sales.

"Kadin Stone."

Kadin jumped as a baritone voice spoke her name. She spun around and beheld a tall, thin man with grey-streaked red hair a few shades darker than hers stepping out of the shadows. The lines around his eyes and mouth placed him at about the age her parents would have been, had they not died more than fifteen years ago. He peered at her from over his wire-framed reading glasses with an expression she couldn't quite place—a combination of satisfaction, resignation, and perhaps fear.

How did he know my name? Her mind spiraled, combining this man's recognition with the feeling of need—or *destiny*—she had felt when she opened the door to the shop. Somehow the thought made her insides quiver, as if her whole life was about to change, and the feeling terrified her.

She shook herself back to reality. *It's some kind of parlor trick they play on customers. Trying to make buyers think the store is magic.*

The man stepped closer, and the sole light in the room flickered, creating a pattern of shadows across his face. "My name is Daimon Gates. How may I help you, Miss Stone?"

Kadin swallowed, her mouth dry. "I-I wanted to know about magic."

He stared at her until she turned her eyes from him to focus on a dusty phonograph in the corner. "So ask a mage," he said.

Her gaze wandered across several jars on a shallow, backless set of shelves that looked as though they belonged in a mad scientist's lab at the cinema. "I don't know any mages. As I understand it, there aren't any in Valeriel anymore." She glanced back at him.

His face didn't flicker, as if his deep-set brown eyes and slightly too-large nose were made of rock.

She took a deep breath. *In and out. You have every right to be here.* "Look, if you can't help me, that's fine. If you could point me to someone who can help, that would be even better."

He looked her up and down, but not in the appreciative way men often did. He seemed to be evaluating her worth. "You don't seem to be lying." His body deflated in visible relief. "Maybe they aren't back."

"Pardon me?"

He straightened. "Nothing. Why are you here?"

Kadin felt a wave of irritation rise in her, and she decided to go with it. Anger seemed safer than her fear, which made her feel as if the floor was about to drop out from under her at any moment. "I work for Valeriel

Investigations, and we are investigating a homicide that may have involved magic. I thought maybe someone here might know more than me about it. Which would be anything at all."

He barked out a laugh. "You're a detective? Investigating magic?"

"Well, a detective's aide, actually..."

"Then you have no doubt heard the cautionary tale of Dexter Corkscrew." His tone was caustic. "And in case you haven't, I'll sum up the moral. Detectives should stick to shootings, stranglings, and stabbings and leave magic alone. The Society does not react well to outside interference."

The acid in his tone seemed to combine with that in her stomach, and they roiled together into a hard ball. "Right. I mean, I understand. But someone murdered the queen, and I don't think the Imperials are going to let that go."

Gates's mouth dropped open, and Kadin realized what he had said. "Wait, the Society of Mages *did* do something to Dexter Corkscrew?" she asked at the same time that *he* asked, "You think someone murdered the *queen* with magic?"

She realized she had given him confidential information about the case. *But it doesn't matter. No one but me—and maybe Dr. Combs—thinks magic was involved. And no one would believe me as a source anyway.*

He must have mistaken her silence for determination because he sighed. "You'd better come with me. This is going to take a while."

I should go. I need to get home before Octavira gets upset, and I shouldn't go anywhere with a man I don't know in a place as creepy as this.

Almost without her approval, Kadin's feet led her after Gates past the row of bookcases that looked as though they had not been touched, much less dusted, in at least ten years. Gates stopped in front of a door at the back of the store and glanced around, though what he thought might lurk in the shadows, Kadin didn't know. He pulled out an old-fashioned iron key and used it to open the door.

Gates had cleaned the room on the other side in the past year, possibly even in the past week. *Or I suppose someone else could have done it. But somehow I don't think he lets many other people into this room.* She stopped that train of thought in its tracks and examined the room around her.

Bookcases full of leather-bound tomes in a variety of languages lined one wall, and glass display cases filled with common-place items sat along the other three. *Like the room outside.*

She would have known when he closed the door, even if she hadn't heard it. She felt as though some outside force had choked her, even though she could still feel herself breathing.

She put a hand on her chest, to ensure herself that her lungs still worked. "What is this place?"

Gates studied each of the glass cases in turn. "This is the largest collection of magical items in Valeriel. Possibly the whole world." He sat down in one of the red leather chairs in the center of the room and motioned that Kadin should sit opposite him.

Kadin sank into the chair, gaping at the items around her. *These things are magic? Then what's outside?*

Gates ran his finger along the metal beads on the arm of his chair. "I have spent the last twenty-seven years acquiring magic objects and storing them here. This room itself is one of the first magical artifacts I came to own, one of the few that can be used by a non-mage. The room guards itself against intruders unless you have the proper key, and when the door is closed, it blocks all magical access to the outside. That is probably why you find it so discomfiting."

Her head shot up. "I'm not a mage. Why would I feel magic?"

"No, you aren't a mage." He pursed his lips and looked as though he wanted to say something, then shook his head. "Nonetheless, everyone has at least a small connection to one of the three powers, and this room blocks that. I found it unsettling at first, though now I find it rather soothing."

Kadin couldn't imagine finding the shut-off feeling anything other than stifling. "What about the items outside? Are they part of your magical collection as well? Because this one doesn't appear all that big, for the 'largest collection in the world'."

"Ah, well, looks can be deceiving." Gates reached over and poured himself a glass of water from the pitcher sitting on the end table. "There are not many magical items in the world. Most magic comes from the mage himself, and he rarely wants to put it into an object that anyone could use. Mages usually only imbue items when they plan to give up their power and want to save a bit for an emergency. Magicking something is chancy, however, because anyone can use that magic later. Accessing the power usually involves a ritual specified at the time of the object's creation, known only to the creator. But sometimes word gets out, or someone performs the necessary sequence of events accidentally. The results can be... unpredictable."

Kadin gave the display cases another wary glance. The items looked so... sedate. But she supposed they were encased behind glass in a secret vault for a reason.

Gates took a sip of water. "As for the items outside, they are non-magical antiques or replicas of the things in this room. I sell them to people with no abilities who want to say they have a magical item or some such. The objects with actual power are not for sale."

Kadin shifted in her chair. She didn't approve of conning people into purchasing fake magical items, but if actual magic devices were dangerous, perhaps dishonesty was the wisest course of action. “The Society of Mages doesn’t mind that you keep the items here? Don’t they want them for themselves?”

“Well, for most of the time that I’ve collected, the Society has been absent from Valeriel.” He cocked his head to the side, then shrugged. “But I think most of them are grateful for the service I provide. After all, even to another mage, in some cases especially to another mage, these items are quite dangerous. A watch imbued by a red mage is, quite literally, a ticking bomb, set to go off when touched by another mage. There are a few pieces a mage might be desirous of possessing. The thimble in the second case there, for example, can enhance a mage’s power. The Society may resent me holding on to such an artifact, but they would be unlikely to try to enter this room to retrieve it.”

Kadin nodded. She wouldn’t rush to re-enter this room once she departed, and she wasn’t a mage. “You said you knew about Dexter Corkscrew. Did the Society actually take away his sanity because he was uncovering their secrets?”

Gates swirled his glass in a circle and stared at the ripples that formed in the water. “I don’t know. He may have been delusional from the start. There is certainly no proof that he wasn’t. However, I can tell you that if he had been of sound mind and sought to sully the reputation of the Society, they would have had no moral qualms about silencing him for their own protection.”

He knows more than he’s saying. “So people do die by magic.”

Gates set his glass down on the end table with a clink. “Mages each have one of three different powers. Red magic destroys, blue magic stops, and green magic grows. Each potential mage is born with a tendency toward a particular power, which gives off an aura other mages can see. The limit of each one’s power is dependent on the imagination of the caster. For example, if a blue mage wished to kill someone, he could stop that person's heart. A red mage could burn a hole through a person's aorta, and a green mage could cause a massive tumor to grow in the victim's chest cavity."

Interesting, but that doesn't answer my question. "So if someone appeared to have been suffocated but with no apparent mark or poison, the mage could have done something to the person's lungs that wouldn't be discernible from the outside."

"Yes, the same principles would apply to asphyxiation."

Kadin's breath came faster. This could be the break Combs was looking for. "But if you were to look at her windpipe, there would be evidence that it had been blocked by something?"

Gates considered her for a long moment, as if trying to decide how much to tell her. "In the case of a green or red mage, I would imagine so. A green mage would have to grow something to block the passage, or else swell the trachea until it closed off. A red mage would most likely burn a hole in the windpipe or destroy the air sacs. A blue mage, however, could kill without a trace, since he would simply stop the lungs from functioning."

Probably not a green mage, then, Kadin thought. *Combs would have noticed a swollen windpipe or growth. But would he have noticed a hole in her windpipe? Or something that had destroyed her lungs?*

Gates took a deep breath. "Miss Stone, if you don't mind, I need to ask about this hypothetical 'she' to whom you keep referring. You implied earlier that you are investigating Queen Callista's death. Do you believe a mage killed her?"

Kadin met his gaze. "You think it's unlikely."

"I think it unlikely that anyone in the Society would be that brazen," he said. Kadin opened her mouth to ask another question, but Gates held up his hand. "Miss

Stone, you probably have dozens more questions about magic and the Society, but let me assure you that it is in your best interest, not to mention mine, if I don't give you any more information. Look elsewhere for your murderer if you can. If the Society of Mages as returned to Valeriel—and especially if they have been brash enough to allow one of their members to kill the queen—believe me when I say the consequences for everyone will be dire."

CHAPTER 12

HOW MUCH SHOULD *I* INCLUDE? Kadin stared at her typewriter. She had typed up her conversation with Olivan, whom she had to admit might not be the most reputable of sources, though he was at least as reliable as the average gossip columnist, but she couldn't decide what to do about her interview with Gates.

Leave it out. She gave the return level a resolute pull, and the carriage rattled back to its starting position. She twirled the piece of paper out of the machine and held up her handiwork for inspection. After a quick spell-check, she slid the paper into the manila folder with her other notes and dropped it into her desk drawer. *Not that anyone is going to see it.*

She opened the file on Lord Landis Imbolc that Olivan had lent her yesterday. She had skimmed through some of the articles the night before, but she wanted to get a better picture of his character. She spread out the pictures, grouping ones with similar themes—his family, his fashion, his politics, his rumored paramours. She worried at first about getting the glossy clips out of order, until she noticed that Olivan had numbered each in the corner with a black ballpoint pen.

That's Ollie all over. Organized to a fault and leaving nothing to chance.

Kadin tapped her pen on the desk. She had all the pieces laid out before her, but somehow they added up to... nothing. Olivan could make staid Octavira's toes curl with his sordid tales of the Imperials, and Lord Landis had all the usual stories: irresponsible spending, drunken cavorting, getting involved with inappropriate women—Queen Callista, for one. But such misbehavior only elicited mild frowns from the nobility. Somehow, though, Lord Landis's playboy ways seemed calculated, as if he wanted to appear rebellious, but not *too* rebellious.

I wonder if any of the Imperial reputations are real. Her eyes fell on a picture of Lord Landis and Duke Baurus. *What about the duke? He seems so straightforward, but maybe he's as calculated as the rest of them.* She picked up the image of the duke smiling so broadly it seemed to jump from the page. *All that emotion he showed me. Surely it can't be fake...* A shudder ran through her at the thought.

She shook her head and slapped the picture back down in Olivan's file. *That doesn't matter. I need to know about Lord Landis, and there's nothing* real *here. I need to talk to him. Or someone who knows him. His sister, perhaps.*

She had arranged the clippings in a pile in the proper order when Inspector Warring thundered into the office with such bluster that he sent the glossy pages flying everywhere. Kadin slid off her chair onto her knees and began to gather her papers.

"Fellows, I'm taking White off the queen's case for the next few hours." Warring's voice boomed through the office. "We've got more cases coming in than ever. Seems everyone wants to hire the king's detectives. Ordinarily I'd be grateful for the business, but we're stretched a little thin. This new case seems cut-and-dry—probably don't even need us, case seventh and all. What's the status on the queen?"

Kadin craned her neck to look into her boss's office.

Fellows cleared his throat. "We have a few promising leads, and we're wondering if perhaps the death wasn't a homicide after all—"

Kadin almost dropped the articles in her hand. *Not a murder? But... it has to be!*

Warring took a threatening step forward, and Fellows jerked backwards. "Save your excuses. Get me Baurus DeValeriel. Today, if possible. Yesterday, if not."

Warring brushed past Kadin, and she clutched her clippings to her so they didn't fly away again. *Great. Ollie's going to kill me for wrinkling them.*

Warring stuck his head back in the office and pointed at Kadin. "You. You're new?"

Kadin pushed herself to her feet, catching her heel on the leg of her chair and nearly falling flat on her face in the process. "Yes, sir. I'm Kadin St—"

"Go with White on this case. He may need an aide on this one." Then he was gone.

Wow, someone thinks I'm here to do work. She pushed down the burst of excitement in her chest as she grabbed her notebook and bag and started out the door. *Wait. You're going to see Dahran, remember? Your would-be future husband?* She took a minute to smooth her green skirt and to make sure the seams on her stockings were straight.

Kadin met Dahran outside the kitchen, and he gave her an appreciative smile. "Looking good, Miss Stone."

Kadin felt heat rush to her cheeks, and she hoped that the result was a charming blush and not a bright red face. Though she supposed she had no reason to be ashamed. She had chosen the scoop-necked dress because it flattered her, and she knew how well her shoes defined her calves. "Oh, you can call me Kadin."

"Don't mind if I do." Dahran held the lift door open for her, and Kadin scooted in.

"So, what's this case about?" she asked once the lift was on its way.

Dahran's almost-too-white teeth flashed in the dim light. "A woman was shot in her brother's nightclub. It sounds like a case seventh, though, so it shouldn't take too long."

"A case seventh?" Kadin thought back to her aide training, certain that they had covered the term. "Isn't that when the victim refuses an investigation?"

Dahran leaned against the lift wall. "When a family refuses an investigation, we don't have much to do. We'll be back before lunch, and it should be a quiet Friday afternoon. We can probably even leave early if we want."

Kadin tried to convince herself the dead feeling in her chest wasn't her heart sinking. "Don't you have a lot of work to do, finding Duke Baurus?"

"Oh, sure." The lift dinged, and Dahran held the door open for Kadin. "But he's a prominent figure. He'll have to come out of hiding eventually. Where can a duke go without someone recognizing him?"

I'm pretty sure he has the means to spend the rest of his life on a beach in Astrevia, or at least until they sign an extradition treaty. But he'll probably stay in town until Queen Callista's murder is solved. "Don't you have other leads to follow? Other suspects?"

Dahran laughed. "No, generally when your prime suspect disappears immediately after the murder, instead of appearing with assistance and a plausible alibi, we can assume he's guilty. Of course, even if he has an airtight alibi, he's probably still guilty. Complex investigations only happen in dime store novels."

Kadin felt that familiar pit re-form in her stomach. *I have to tell him what I know.* "Look, Dahran. I mean, Detective White..."

Before she could finish, Dexter Corkscrew stepped in front of her and blocked her path.

"I'm handling the forensics on the case at Pinky's." The small man gave Kadin the hairy eyeball. She wished she knew what about her upset him so much. His distrust of her seemed to pre-date her mention of the M-word.

Dahran snapped his fingers to get Corkscrew's attention. "Why are you coming? Where's Combs?"

Corkscrew hefted a black bag and ambled toward the door. "They don't let Jace handle case sevenths anymore." He looked over his shoulder, offering a genuine smile. "Don't worry. I've got this. I called us an autotaxi."

Kadin followed Corkscrew and Dahran out to the vehicle. Dahran claimed the front seat next to the driver, and Kadin crawled into the back next to Corkscrew. Judging by the cracked black leather seats and sickly sweet smell that permeated the cabin, Corkscrew had selected the worst autotaxi company in the city.

Last time I let the crazy man pick the vehicle, Kadin thought, but she instantly regretted it.

Corkscrew's tuneless humming blended with the droning of the engine as the autotaxi stopped and started its way through the busy Business District. After several blocks filled with men in tailored grey suits, the old brick and limestone buildings gave way to the more modern lines and colors of the Triangle. Kadin usually came to the avant-garde area of the city at night, as it held the best bars and night clubs, but even without the flickering neon signs, the white and pastel tiered buildings served as a contrast to the more traditional architecture of the rest of Valeriel City.

They passed a malt shop with an aqua and checkered pattern boasting 24-hour service and a brand new apartment building designed like a giant, round layer cake. Soon they came upon a garish pink nightclub with a neon green sign flashing "Pinky's!"

Corkscrew stopped singing. "We're here."

The autotaxi skidded to a halt, and the three detectives got out. As Dahran paid the driver, Kadin eyed the colored papers advertising last night's drink specials littering the sidewalk.

I guess no one got around to cleaning them up. Understandable, if there was a murder. She considered picking up a few of the fliers and throwing them in the trash, but when she poked at one of the sheets with her toe, the paper appeared stuck to the concrete with a substance she couldn't recognize. Her generosity didn't go that far.

Inside the club, the squeaks from Corkscrew's rubber soles twined with the clicks of Kadin's heels, and the harmony echoed across the cavernous space. A chalky scent filled Kadin's nose, and the bright spotlights that flooded the room made her squint, even as the solid black walls absorbed some of the glare. She barely recognized the place, so different did it look with no fashionable sideways men flirting, cavorting, and sipping pink cocktails with slices of grapefruit in them. A short, balding man with tears running down his red-streaked face and a taller companion with thick grey hair and a stocky build were the only people gracing the dance floor now.

Unless one counted the chubby dead brunette lying flat on her face at their feet.

Dahran molded his expression into that of a funeral director, sympathetic yet professional. "Hello, I'm Detective Dahran White, and this is my aide, Kadin Stone, and our forensic specialist, Dexter Corkscrew. We are very sorry for your loss and will do everything in our power to help you."

Oh, see, that's nice, thought Kadin as she pulled her notebook out of her bag. *I worried he'd be dismissive of the case, after what he said before.*

"Thank you." The man who had not been crying shook

Dahran's hand, while his other arm remained wrapped around his partner. "I'm Quind Hart, and this is Pinky Boxer. That's..." His voice broke as he nodded toward the dead woman. "That's Pinky's sister, Skella Best."

Dahran made a clucking sound with his tongue and scrawled a note on his pad. "Have you ever commissioned a murder investigation before?" Both men shook their heads. "Well, let me begin by explaining the process to you. I will ask you some questions, some of which may seem intrusive to you, and I will want to talk to any other witnesses. Meanwhile, Dr. Corkscrew will examine the body to try to determine the exact cause of death—"

"Ject shot to the head." The forensic examiner's voice held none of the sensitivity of Dahran's.

"—which he believes he has already determined, though he will do a few more analyses before making an absolute statement. He will also glean any other information that he can from the body itself. Once we have the forensic analysis, we will determine whether we have enough evidence for a trial or if we need to interview more people or further examine the premises." Dahran cleared his throat. "May I ask what kind of insurance you have?"

Pinky looked up, tears staining his puffy, red face. "We don't have insurance that covers her death." He let out another sob.

Quind patted his partner's shoulder. "Her husband Bryne Best has a policy that covers crimes committed against his family, but we don't think that he will want to pursue an investigation in this case." He looked as if he wanted to say something but thought better of it. "I called and informed him that you were coming over, so he should be by shortly, and you can discuss this with him."

Realization dawned on Kadin. *Case Seventh. They made it sound so harmless in class, but you should have known what it meant. You've heard Tobin rant about cases like this often enough. Husband kills the wife, then refuses an investigation. Happens all the time.* Kadin's breath came faster, her clinical acceptance faltering in the face of the blood caked on the back of Skella's head.

"In the event that Mr. Best declines an investigation, you, as an immediate family member, are authorized to commission one." Dahran handed Quind a card. "Please keep in mind that evidence that has not been verified by a certified investigation team is not admissible in Valeriel Courts. We have a variety of payment plans for those without insurance, though for a homicide we require a $5,000 deposit."

Tears began to stream from Pinky's eyes once again. "We never should have invested in that new club on the other side of the Triangle. We could afford the investigation if we..."

Quind glanced toward Skella's body. "We couldn't know this would happen."

"She was my sister! I should have paid more attention! I should have known..." Pinky looked up as the door to the club opened and a man in his mid-thirties sauntered in. "You!" Pinky's face contorted with rage, and he sprang toward the new arrival. "You killed my sister, you Deity-misbegotten son of a—" Quind grabbed Pinky's arms to restrain him.

Kadin inspected the newcomer. He was attractive enough, with dark hair and strong shoulders, but the coldness in his eyes lowered the temperature of the dance hall by a few degrees.

"My apologies for my brother-in-law." The newcomer stepped forward to shake Dahran's hand, and Kadin couldn't help but notice similarities in the studied neutrality of the men's expressions. "He is understandably distraught over the death of his sister. My name is Bryne Best, and as I'm sure these two gentlemen have informed you, I don't think that a full investigation is warranted in this case."

"Of course you don't!" Pinky lunged toward Bryne but couldn't break free of Quind's tight grip. "You did it! I know you did! She came here to hide from you! You've been beating her for years!"

"Hm. That would explain all these bruises." Everyone turned to look at Corkscrew, kneeling behind the body and holding up one of the victim's wrists. Kadin and, she suspected, everyone else expected Corkscrew to continue, but he let Skella's arm fall to the ground and returned to his examination without another word.

Pinky reached a hand out to Dahran. "Please, you have to help me."

The detective didn't flinch. "I'm sorry, Mr. Hart, Mr. Boxer, but in the absence of a deposit or insurance authorization, I am not authorized to conduct an investigation. You have my card, in case you change your mind at a later date, though I caution you to make your decision quickly, as evidence tends to degrade over time."

Kadin pretended she didn't see the slight curl to Dahran's lip as he turned away. *We should do something.* Someone *should do* something.

A hand slipped into Kadin's and give it a gentle pat. She started, then noticed Corkscrew had appeared by her side.

He had a faraway look in his eyes. "You'll get used to it." He blinked, and his eyes focused again. "Or maybe you won't. Not everyone does. They don't let Jace come when they expect a case seventh. He tends to yell." Corkscrew shrugged. "That's the only reason I'm on a case at all. He's better with people than me."

And that's saying something, Kadin thought, recollecting what she had seen of Combs's interactions with others.

Corkscrew ambled over to where Quind and Pinky were standing. He took the film out of his camera and handed it to them. "This has some pictures of the bruising. Sometimes you can get a few clicks in front of a jury before the defense declares the evidence inadmissible." He looked back over at the body and twisted his lips. "And CrimeSolve has a department that takes on charity cases. You probably won't qualify, but it wouldn't hurt to try." Corkscrew floated toward the door, leaving the couple to stare after him.

Kadin looked over to Dahran to see whether she should follow Corkscrew out the door, but the detective stood with his eyes closed and two fingers against his temple.

Kadin smiled to herself. *I guess Corkscrew's intercession wasn't his first. I wonder what Combs does that's so much worse.*

"Hey, Quind?" A man appeared in a doorway near the entrance. "There's someone on the phone for a Detective White. They want to know if he's still here."

Dahran raised his hand. "Yes, I'm here. Where can I take the call?"

After Dahran disappeared into the office, Kadin made an effort to smile at the people around her, but she soon realized that no pleasant expression would make the situation any less awkward. She murmured something polite and went to wait on the street with Corkscrew.

A few minutes later Dahran emerged from the club, his expression grim.

Kadin hurried over to him. "What's wrong? Who was on the phone?"

"Fellows." He clenched and unclenched his jaw. "They found the queen's guard."

"Corporal Strand?" Kadin kept pace with Dahran as he strode over to the autotaxi. "He was missing?"

Dahran gave his head a short shake. "No, her original guard. The one Strand replaced. They finally found him. He's dead."

CHAPTER 13

SECOND TIME TO THE PALACE *this week.* The red and orange leaves crunched under Kadin's feet, filling the air with their crisp scent, as a guard led Dahran and her through the thick woods on the back of the estate. They had dropped Corkscrew off back at the office, since, as the forensic examiner himself said, he wasn't fit for Imperial company. *Trinithy will freak.*

They crested a tree-lined hill and found Fellows, Combs, Inspector Warring, Captain Carver, and half a dozen uniformed guards standing around Kadin's second dead body of the day. The depressed area next to him remained clear of leaves, and as she got closer, Kadin realized the hole had served as the dead man's stereotypical shallow grave.

"...same thing that killed the queen, as far as I can tell," Combs was saying as the she and Dahran approached. "Of course, since I have no idea what killed the queen, I don't have much to go on."

Bile rose in Kadin's throat as a sickly sweet smell overwhelmed her senses. She stared down at the purpling corpse and realized that, unlike the two fresh bodies she had seen this week, this one had started to rot.

"Curses!" Warring glared at Fellows. "You said this

morning that the evidence indicated the guards may have overreacted when we assumed homicide. Does this look like natural causes to you?"

Fellows sniffed and scratched his nose. "I said that I thought we might have made an error suspecting foul play, given the absence of any evidence of injury or poison. Obviously I had not ruled out murder."

"Hello, everyone." Dahran flashed his handsome smile at the team. To defuse the situation, Kadin reminded herself, not to show off his unnecessarily white teeth. "Fill me in on what I've missed?"

Warring's lip curled, revealing a definitely-not-white bicuspid. "White. It's about time you got here. These two guards were out on some training mission in the forest." He thrust his arm at two of the uniformed men, who stood apart from the rest.

"We weren't supposed to go in so deep." The guard fidgeted with the hat in his hands. "But we got a bit lost. We were figuring out how to get back when Saunter here tripped over this weird mound. It looked as if someone had made a great big dirt pile, but no one's supposed to come back here. We thought we should investigate, so Saunter waited here, while I went back to find some help."

Saunter nodded. "A bunch more guards came back with shovels and dug up poor Tailor there."

"Carver called us. We rushed over. Combs examined him." Warring glared at Combs. "He thinks that whatever killed the guard is the same thing that killed the queen. Fellows was explaining to us how that means the queen was not murdered."

Harsh, but... Kadin had to wonder if Warring wasn't right to be annoyed. Since the interview with Lady Beatrin, she hadn't seen much dedication to the case from anyone but Combs.

"Maybe they were both killed by some new disease strain." Saunter took a step forward. "I mean, they were always together, it makes sense that they both would have gotten it."

As one, the entire party swiveled their heads and gaped at him. Fellows spoke first. "You think he died of a disease and then buried himself in the middle of the forest?"

Saunter's face flushed. "Well, maybe the queen did it after he died so no one would find out about the disease. Or maybe a *third* person with the disease hid the body—"

Warring whipped a hand up to stop the babble. "Combs, when was this man killed, and how long ago was he buried?"

"Well, I can't say for certain." Combs frowned at the body. "I would say, given the weather and apparent rate of decay, sometime on Sunday or early on Monday. Though it could have been later, because of the cold. I would feel confident timing his death before the queen's."

Fellows lifted his bowler, rubbed his brow, then dropped the hat back on his head. "He showed up for work Sunday but not Monday, so we can assume he was killed sometime between the shifts." Fellows made a note. "White, when we're done here, talk to some of the other guards in his barracks, maybe palace staff who would have seen him when he went off duty. See if you can narrow down when he disappeared."

Kadin watched as Fellows harassed Combs to get more information. *If the guard—Tailor—disappeared on Sunday night, it couldn't have been Duke Baurus who killed him. The king, his sister, the servants—they all think he killed her in a rage. But he didn't become angry with her until Monday. Though I suppose Tailor could have died Monday afternoon...*

"Kadin."

Kadin broke out of her reverie and remembered to put on a smile for Dahran. "Yes?"

Dahran grinned at her in return. "I've got to run to do some interviews now. Are we still on for tomorrow morning?"

If I can get Octavira to lend me her yellow dress. "Absolutely! I'm looking forward to it!" *Okay, so that was laying it on a bit thick.* She tried not to feel as though she *should* be looking forward to it.

"Great! See you then." With a little wave, Dahran turned and followed Fellows and some guards out of the forest.

Kadin, not wanting to be left behind again, clutched her coat around herself and started forward, but a voice stopped her.

"You're dating Dahran White? That was fast." She turned to see Combs looking at her as if she smelled worse than the body did.

Kadin stood up straighter and tried not to feel as though Combs had a point. "Yes. What of it?" *As if he has any right to judge anyone else's romantic partners.*

"Nothing." He snorted and returned his attention to the body. "Your decision."

Kadin turned on her heel and struggled to remain upright when the stiletto dug into the dirt. Which made it all the more embarrassing when she decided to turn back around. "Hey, Dr. Combs, wait!"

He arched his eyebrows at her.

Kadin eyed the two men left to stand guard over Combs as he handled the body. She moved closer to the doctor and lowered her voice. "You can take this body to the lab, right? So you can do the tests that you didn't get to do on the queen's, since they probably had the same cause of death?"

"Yes, the other guards went to call the transport vehicle." Combs squinted at her. "Though I'm not at all sure that the causes of death are the same, and this body isn't in the most pristine condition."

"Right." Kadin took a deep breath. "I was looking into the possibility of magic as a murder weapon—"

"You were doing what?" Combs raised his voice enough

that one of the guards took a step forward, but Combs waved the guard back. "I told you to drop that!"

Is he surprised at the direction of my work, or that I did work at all? "No, you told me you would not consider it as a cause of death and you did not think further investigation in the area to be wise. And I was going to drop it. But I found myself near a magic shop in Smoke Row, and I thought I might as well make a couple of inquiries. Anyway, I think there might be a way for you to test for magic."

"You couldn't test for magic, even if it did exist." He lowered his voice even further on the M-word.

"No, but you can test for some of the marks it leaves." She explained briefly about the three kinds of magic. "If the killer is a blue mage, we're out of luck, but a green or red mage would have to leave some trace on the lungs or windpipe that would account for the changes."

Combs blinked. "Miss Stone, do you have any idea how ridiculous this sounds? Magic comes in colors? I think somebody's having one over on you."

Kadin shifted her weight from one foot to the other. "Gates seemed to know what he was talking about. Could you at least look? What do you have to lose?"

"What do I have to lose?" He looked as though he wanted to reach out and shake her. "Our lives, if the Society of Mages exists. And our careers if it doesn't. Oh, but then I forgot, you don't care about your career, do you?"

I'm getting tired of everyone assuming that because I want to get married, I don't *want to do my job.* "Maybe not, but as long as I'm here, I'm going to solve the cases I'm assigned to, even if that means going down an atypical alley."

"I'm not saying that you're right, because that would be lunacy, but what if you are?" Combs ran his fingers through his hair. "You're saying that the person who did this can strangle someone from across the room, and clearly they had no compunction about murdering the *queen.* You wouldn't even be a bump in the road for someone like that. You're better off making the java and staying out of it."

Kadin looked at the ground. "Maybe you're right." *Maybe I am a useless girl, no matter what Tobin thinks. But someone killed Tailor, and that same person probably killed the queen, and whoever that is doesn't deserve to be walking around free just because he has a power that nobody understands.*

Some of what she was thinking must have shown on her face, because Combs's expression softened. "I do understand. But, the consequences here aren't making the company look bad or taking a few dollars away from the investors' bottom line. If the Society is real, and you go against one of their own, you could be risking your life."

I don't want to take on the entire Society! Just the one man who committed the crime! But maybe Combs was right and those things were one and the same. Maybe no good could come of finding a magical killer, even if he had killed one of the most prominent members of Valeriel society. *Maybe it's a good thing no one listens to me.*

But somehow Combs's threat didn't scare her as much as the idea that Callista's killer might get away with murder.

CHAPTER 14

I LOOK LIKE A BUMBLEBEE. KADIN watched her reflection cringe. She had convinced Octavira to lend the dress, on the condition that Kadin baby-sit for the next three weekends, but Kadin wondered whether she wouldn't have been better off confessing she didn't have a favorite racer. Such an admission couldn't do her would-be relationship more harm than three unavailable Saturdays.

She ran her fingers over the black-and-yellow-striped skirt and hoped the polka-dotted bust and halter neck didn't show too much cleavage. The getup wouldn't have flattered someone with dainty shoulders and a thin frame, and on Kadin it looked ridiculous. *What even possessed Octavira to buy it?*

She took a deep breath. *It's the only yellow dress I have. I'll wear it this one time, then switch my allegiance to whoever wins this drag.* She glanced at the clock. *Okay, I should have enough time to get the mud off my shoes before Dahran arrives.*

She rummaged through her bureau drawer, searching for shoe polish, and barely noticed the ringer chiming until Octavira called up the stairs.

"Kadin! Call for you!"

Kadin grabbed her shoes and hurried down the stairs, her stockinged feet sliding against the wood floors.

Octavira put her hands on her hips as Kadin passed. "Don't be long. I'm expecting a call."

Kadin dashed into the kitchen and picked up the headset from where Octavira had left it next to the phone. "Hello?"

"K, it's me." Olivan's voice was mixed with static.

Kadin wound the phone cord around her finger. "Hi, Ollie. It's not a great time. I have a date in—" she looked at the clock above the sink. "—fifteen minutes, and I still need to clean up my shoes."

"Clean up your shoes?" Kadin could picture Olivan's raised eyebrows. "Never mind, I don't want to know."

"Is this about Landis Imbolc's file? I can get that back to you on Monday." She had read through all the articles again the night before. All sources indicated Lord Landis had ended his affair with the queen approximately a year ago, and the most recent pieces claimed he had left town the day after her murder. He had taken a firm place at the top of her suspect list.

"What? No." Olivan let out a breath. "There's a party tonight at Slides that you can't miss."

Kadin stretched the phone cord across the kitchen and dropped her shoes in the sink. "Isn't it kind of last minute?"

"It's an emergency party," Olivan said. "Pinky Boxer's sister got killed yesterday—"

"Oh, yeah, I was there." She switched the ringer receiver to the other ear and turned on the faucet.

"You were *there*?" Olivan screeched. "Okay, I definitely have to rethink this working in homicide thing. This week alone you got to meet Pinky Boxer and the king."

Kadin couldn't tell which one impressed him more. "If you don't know Pinky, why are you planning his party?"

Olivan made a clucking sound with his tongue. "Planning parties is what I do. Everyone who's anyone in the sideways community knows that."

She grabbed a dish towel and ran it under the water, then squeezed out the excess. "But if that's the case, why don't you know Pinky Boxer? Wouldn't that be necessary networking?"

"Kadin, just because—"

"Does any of this have a point? Because I have a date in eleven minutes, and my shoes are still covered in mud." She used the cloth to knock the larger chunks of dirt off the soles.

"Yes." Kadin could almost see Olivan running a hand down his face to center his mind. "We need to raise money for Skella Best's investigation, so we're having a benefit tonight at Slides. If you value our friendship, you will be there at 8:00 pm. If that is insufficient incentive, the Dawban Steel Band is playing."

Dawban Steel was one of the up-and-coming performers in the city. "How'd you get them on such short notice?" She wrapped the towel around one of the stilettos and twisted it to rub off the mud.

"Kadin. Must you doubt my skills?"

Kadin swiped along the insole of the pump and waited.

Olivan sighed. "All right, the drummer knew the dead girl, and the band happened to be free. So will you come?"

"Wouldn't miss it." A loud rapping sounded from the living room. "Curses! I have to go. Dahran's here."

"Okay, bye."

Kadin hung up the ringer. She made a quick pass at the left shoe with the cloth, then grabbed both pumps and scrambled into the living room, where Octavira sat on the couch flipping through a catalog. "Tell him I'll be down in a minute! Sorry about the sink! I'll clean it up later!"

"What about my sink?" Octavira called, but Kadin was up the stairs, by mercy of her firm grip on the railing. She looked back and forth between the shoe polish and her closet. Should she take the time to polish the shoes or wear the ones with smaller heels?

Muffled voices came from downstairs. *I* cannot *leave Octavira alone with him. She's better at spoiling my matrimonial prospects than I am.*

Kadin slid on her inch-high pumps and grabbed her black coat out of the closet, hoping it stayed cold enough that she could leave it on through the drag. She took a few deep breaths so she wouldn't look frantic when she met Dahran and kept her movements sedate as she descended the staircase.

As soon as she saw him, Kadin gave Dahran a bright smile and tried not to think how out of place his red and black leather drag clothes looked next to the worn pink and blue quilt on the sofa in her sister-in-law's homey living room.

"Oh, you support the Red Phoenix, I see," she said, naming the DeValeriel family-owned racer whose colors he wore. After she had finished looking through the Landis Imbolc file, she had taken time to read the glossy Olivan had given her.

Dahran's gaze roamed up and down her figure, taking in the yellow and black fabric sticking out from under her coat. "And I see you're in full support of the Yellow Comet?"

"I figured I'd keep my support in the investigations business, since CrimeSolve sponsors him, after all." Kadin gave what she hoped was a flirtatious smile. "But you're welcome to try to change my mind." *Though I'm not sure DeValeriel red would look any better with my hair than CrimeSolve yellow does with my complexion.*

"Shall we?" Dahran extended a hand to indicate that Kadin should lead the way out, so she started forward, trying not to think about what he must be thinking of her backside. Full skirts were not a flattering look for her. Yet another reason not to borrow Octavira's clothes.

"Don't stay out too late," Octavira said as Kadin stepped out the door. Dahran paused for a moment at the door, presumably to say farewell to Octavira, but Kadin didn't turn back. She was too distracted by what was in front of her.

She hastened over to the shiny evergreen autocar idling by the curb. “This is one of the new Model Q’s! It’s the first autocar in this color.” She spun around to face Dahran as he came down the front porch stairs. “Is it yours?”

Dahran smiled and made a noise that sounded like “Mmm.” He reached past her and opened the car door to let her in.

Kadin’s shoulders slumped as she slid into the passenger-side seat. *That means it’s not his, but he wants me to think it is.*

Oh, no. You are not going down that path, another part of her thought. *This is what Trinithy warned you about. You always find something wrong with the guys you’re seeing. It’s* good *that he wants to impress you.*

Kadin forced herself to give Dahran a smile as he lowered himself into the driver’s seat. “Well, it’s amazing.”

“Not nearly as impressive as some of the vehicles we’re going to see today.” Dahran put the autocar into gear and pulled away from the curb. “The Amber Hawk is racing for only the second time with these new tires made out of a new, more elastic rubber...”

Dahran seemed content to talk about racing news as they drove. Kadin did her best to seem interested and make noises of approval at appropriate intervals. Meanwhile, she used his monologue to test herself on what she remembered about the drag participants. Flotilla Bank sponsored the Amber Hawk. The Fan family owned the Purple Jackrabbit, and the Orioles backed the Blue Tornado.

When they pulled up to the drag course and Dahran stopped the car, Kadin stepped out onto the large-stoned gravel that made up the parking lot and took a moment to be grateful for the small heels. The stilettos would have gotten caught in the crags. She pulled her coat tighter around herself and tried not to shudder as the cold wind wafted gasoline odor in her direction.

Dahran had come around the side of the car. He gave her a small frown, and she worried he noticed she had shrunk three inches since the day before. But when he glanced from her feet to the car, she realized that he had wanted to open the door for her.

Amateur mistake. Trinithy would be so ashamed.

They joined the horde of people pushing their way into the arena. Based on the predominant jacket color, the Red Phoenix had the biggest following, but sparks of blue, green, and amber dotted the crowd as well. Kadin even caught a few people who had dyed their hair to match the Comet's. Blaring trumpets and roaring engines filled the air, so, even though she watched him out of the corner of her eye, she almost missed Dahran speaking to her.

She cupped a hand over her ear. "I'm sorry. What did you say?"

"Can I buy you a drink?" Dahran pointed at the refreshment stand as they passed.

"Oh, sure." Kadin brightened the smile she had glued to her face. "Don't want to have to get up during the drag and miss the exciting bits!"

They joined what appeared to be the end of the queue, though Kadin didn't think they were in a line so much as an amorphous mass of people demanding beverages.

Kadin cleared her throat. "So, how goes the search for Duke Baurus?" *Deity save me, you did* not *ask about work.*

Dahran didn't seem to mind. "We've got some promising leads."

Kadin had to fight her eyebrows flying up. This was news to her. "Oh, did you talk to King Ralvin or Lady Beatrin again, then?" She wanted to clap a hand over her mouth. *Now you're questioning his methods? Very attractive, K.*

"Not exactly." Dahran's voice held the same displeasure

she had heard on so many dates before. Why, oh why, couldn't she keep her mouth shut?

Should I apologize or drop it? She tried to think what Trinithy would do, but, of course, Trinithy would never question her date's competence in the first place.

Dahran pushed forward the last few inches to the front of the crowd and snapped his fingers to catch the barmaid's attention.

"I'll have a brew, whatever's the darkest you have on tap." Dahran glanced back at Kadin.

She stepped forward. "A diet fizzy, please?"

The barmaid nodded, and a few minutes later she passed them paper cups filled with cold beverages.

The condensation on the side of the beverage slid down Kadin's fingers. She hadn't considered having to hold a cup full of ice in the nippy weather.

I'll drink it fast. She took a sip but nearly spit it out when the first carbonated drops exploded on her tongue.

Her expression must have given her away, because Dahran narrowed his eyes. "What's wrong?"

"Oh, it's not a big deal." She took another sip to show him, but her shudder gave her away. "It's not diet." *I can't* actually *feel the sugar coating on my teeth.*

Dahran's nostrils flared, and he grabbed the soda from her, sending little droplets of sticky brown liquid flying onto her coat. He whipped around to face the bar and slammed Kadin's fizzy on the counter so hard that soda and ice fell out in all directions.

"What is wrong with you?" Dahran shouted at the barmaid. "She specifically said 'diet'!"

The girl's eyes widened, and she reached out to take the drink. "I'm so sorry, sir. Let me get you another one."

Dahran's lip curled. "Deity, how stupid do you have to be to make a mistake like that?"

Kadin opened her mouth to tell him a different barmaid had poured their drinks, but something in the set of his jaw told Kadin she should keep silent. She offered the girl behind the counter an apologetic look, but the server didn't appear to be in a forgiving mood. When she passed him the new drink, he snatched it up and thrust it at Kadin.

"I hate it when they do that." Dahran gave a barking laugh. "If I were that poor at my job, there would be murderers walking around free."

It's just a drink. And didn't you let a murderer go free yesterday under the auspices of doing your job? But she clamped her mouth shut and nodded at him.

Dahran held onto the tickets, so Kadin wasn't sure which direction they needed to head to find their seats.

Not that I would know anyway. Someone jostled her and splashed still more fizzy onto her hand. *This place is a zoo!*

Dahran led them to a pair of seats inside the arena. Good seats, as far as Kadin could tell. They were five rows back and near the starting mark.

She lowered herself onto the orange plastic and took in all the sights of the track. The race didn't begin until 1:00 pm, and she had worried hours of waiting would bore her. But the pre-show seemed to be as much of a draw as the drag itself.

A band of at least a hundred members in bright white and gold uniforms and matching puffy hats marched across the field, changing their formation from a phoenix to a hawk to a comet—shapes to represent every racer. Strident trumpets burst out in time with rapping snare drums, while flutes whistled out a descant.

In front of the band, twenty young women in glittering costumes danced and did flips in time with the music. Kadin realized these must be the infamous drag girls she had heard so much about, whose job was to rev up the crowd's spirits, while wearing outfits the average Class D wouldn't be seen dead in. Each racer had his own team of girls, and judging by the blue and green sequins glinting off the current dancers' uniforms, they supported the Oriole-sponsored Blue Tornado.

Say something to Dahran, Kadin's inner Trinithy prompted her. *And* don't *mention work.* "So... do you have any family in the city?"

"Mm-hm." Dahran's gaze remained on the dancing girls, as they cartwheeled their way into their final pose. When the music stopped he turned to Kadin. "I'm sorry. What?"

"Oh, I was asking if you had any family in the city." Kadin could feel her cheeks getting red, and she hoped he assumed her blush was a response to the cold air.

"No, they all live in Oriole Territory." He flashed a grin. "Bet that's hard to imagine, me growing up in a mining town."

Kadin tried to imagine him in something other than the trench coat and fedora he'd worn to work all week—or, she supposed, the racing-fan garb—and came up blank. Somehow she couldn't picture him shoveling coal and smelting iron.

Before she could respond, his gaze snapped to the black-and-red-clad DeValeriel girls now making their way onto the field.

Kadin wrapped her arms around herself. *Maybe he doesn't want to talk. That's okay. We talked in the car on the way over, and there's plenty to see here.*

Kadin watched in fascination as more teams of girls performed intricate routines on the field. She didn't think that she could ever be that flexible, or keep such a big smile on her face for so long. But Dahran seemed impressed with their long legs and bouncing breasts, if the way he ogled them was any indication. Even so, Kadin couldn't help but get into the spirit of things. More than once she caught herself bopping her head to the music or humming along with songs she knew.

About half an hour before the race was scheduled to start, the girls vacated the fields, blowing kisses at their adoring fans, and a man in a brown tweed coat took their place.

"Greetings, everyone!" The announcer's voiced swooped between high and low tones. "Welcome to the Valeriel Drag."

The crowd cheered, and Kadin raised her voice with them. She glanced at Dahran, who clapped but didn't seem inclined to yell.

"Now, the moment you've all been waiting for." The announcer waved his arm as a drumroll sounded. "Your racers!"

The band sprang into action, and the audience jumped to its collective feet as eight men in brightly colored race suits ran onto the field. Kadin recognized the bright yellow hair on the one in the yellow and black costume, and some of the other faces looked a little familiar to her as well.

The drums beat a steady rhythm as the rest of the band quieted, and the announcer continued. "Hailing from the sandy shores of Barring, I give you the Grey Shark!"

The racer in the grey and white suit came forward to the front of the crowd waving a grey scarf. The spectators cheered again, and some of the fans wearing grey began to jump up and down. Kadin wanted to ask Dahran what was going on, but she would only prove she'd never been to the drag before.

The Grey Shark looked around the crowd, and after a moment pointed to a section of the audience. Kadin craned her neck to see, and as she watched, a young woman in a grey dress made her way to the front of the stands. The Grey Shark made a big show of bowing to her and giving her the scarf. The girl returned to her seat, a huge smile on her face, and the people next to her hugged her and hurrahed.

The announcer and four of the other racers repeated this ritual of choosing one girl in the crowd and giving her a scarf. *Must be some kind of chivalrous ceremony. Each knight grants a token to the lady he races for. It's kind of cute.*

As the Amber Hawk returned to his place in the line, after handing an orange scarf to a girl who was so pleased she was nearly in tears, the announcer stepped forward again. "No crime will go unpunished so long as he and CrimeSolve are on the case. I give you the Yellow Comet."

Dahran glanced at Kadin, and she remembered to applaud particularly loudly in support of her alleged favorite. The yellow-headed racer stepped to the front of the crowd waving a scarf the same shade as his hair. He pointed up in the crowd near Kadin. She turned to see who he was gesturing at, but when she felt a hand push her shoulder and a voice say, "Go on, honey," she realized that the Yellow Comet was pointing at her and the yellow skirt puffed up around her knees.

She tripped on her way down the stairs, and once again felt flames of embarrassment on her cheeks. But she couldn't help but laugh as the Yellow Comet made an elaborate show of kissing her hand as he handed her the scarf. She climbed back up to her seat with the cheers of the crowd to urge her on.

But as she slid back into her place, she couldn't escape Dahran's glare. "What was that all about?" he asked. "You're here with me."

The pleasure drained out of her. "I'm sorry! I didn't realize... I mean, he called me. Was I supposed to say no?"

Dahran clenched his jaw and looked away from her. Kadin thought about apologizing again and explaining that she was sure it didn't mean anything, but somehow she worried that might make things worse.

This is going to be a long race.

CHAPTER 15

KADIN STEPPED OFF THE AUTOBUS in the heart of the Triangle and hoped the night would go better than the afternoon had. Though she supposed her date with Dahran hadn't gone *too* badly, considering some of her past experiences. He hadn't spoken to her during the race, but once the Red Phoenix won the drag—beating out the Yellow Comet after the two had been neck and neck the entire last lap—Dahran had forgiven her. He had spent the ride home reliving the drag's most exciting moments, and Kadin had to admit she hadn't realized a drag could be so much fun.

All in all, though, she felt much more relaxed as she headed from the autobus stop to Slides. Not only had she gone home and replaced the yellow fright with her favorite black dress with silver edging along the surplice neckline, but she planned to spend the evening among sideways men, whom she didn't need to impress.

About a block from the club, Kadin ran into the end of the line of people waiting to get in. *Wow, Olivan sure put together a big event at the last minute.* As the queue crept toward the entrance, she could hear the steady pulse of rock music thumping through the walls. She smiled and tapped her foot to the beat. When the last Dawban Steel LP had been released six months ago, Kadin had almost worn it through before Octavira declared she couldn't listen to his gravelly voice another moment.

When she got to the door, she reminded herself the exorbitant cover price would help cover the cost of Skella Best's investigation, and wasn't the average attempt of a Triangle club to extort money from young sideways men who didn't have wives to support. She gave the bouncer a bright smile and ducked into the club.

Kadin could feel the drums pounding through her feet as she stepped inside the club, and the temperature was warm enough that Kadin decided to check her coat. Up on the stage, the lead singer, in all his black leather, rock-and-roll glory, swayed around his microphone. Throngs of people shoved by her in the packed club, and she couldn't make out any of the faces in the dim light. But remembering the purpose of this party made her imagine the space if it were as empty as Pinky's club had been the day before.

She focused back on the room when a blond woman in a pink dress and white heels careened toward her.

"Kadin!" Trinithy's arms wrapped around Kadin's neck. "I am so glad you're here!"

Drunk already, Trin? The blonde's affectionate exuberance was a dead giveaway to anyone who knew her.

Trinithy pulled back from the hug and linked her arm in Kadin's. "I've been waiting all day to hear how your date went."

The two girls approached a pair of men whom Kadin knew by sight as clubbing friends of Olivan's and Trinithy's, one bordering on freakishly tall with dark brown hair, the other slight and nervous with sneaky grey eyes.

Trinithy pushed Kadin in front of her. "You guys remember Kadin, right? She went to the drag with Dahran White today, possibly the most attractive single man who works at Valeriel Investigations."

The taller man—Kadin thought his name was Aran, but she always thought of him as Wannabe Ollie, since he could never quite pull off the quiff and mismatched colors the way her friend could—snickered. "Don't let Olivan hear you say that."

Trinithy laughed louder than was necessary. "Oh, you know what I mean. The best-looking rightways man." She snapped her attention back to Kadin. "So how did it go?"

I am so not in the mood for a lecture from drunk Trinithy. "Well, uh, it went all right, I guess."

Trinithy gave a sigh so large she almost fell over when her chest deflated. "Oh my Deity, Kadin. What went wrong this time? You didn't tell him his shoes were ugly, did you?"

The shifty man—Frit, Kadin thought—spit his drink back in his cup. "You told a date his shoes were ugly?"

I am never going to live that down. "Just once. And he *asked.* And they were bright orange, and he was wearing a blue suit. Those shoes were an abomination unto fashion."

Trinithy tried to roll her eyes, but in her inebriated state ended up rolling her whole head. "No one has as much trouble with men as you, Kadin. You are never going to get a husband at this rate. You have to make *some* effort."

The buzz of the crowd around her seemed to grow louder. "I guess the date could have gone worse. He just didn't seem to want to talk to me that much."

Wannabe Ollie shrugged. "Well, that's hardly surprising. So much going on at the drag."

"Right." *Should I tell them about the drink thing?* "Well, and there was a whole thing with the racers handing out these scarves..."

Three faces stared at her with matching expressions of horror.

Trinithy broke the silence first. "Kadin, please, please, please, do not tell me that you accepted a racing token while you were at the drag on a date with another man."

Kadin felt a bead of sweat form on her temple. "What

else was I supposed to do? He was pointing at me, and everybody was cheering."

Trinithy buried her face in the hand that wasn't holding a martini, and Aran and Frit burst out laughing. "You are hopeless!" Trinithy said. "Forget whether you like Dahran or not. You'll be lucky if he speaks to you at the office, much less asks you out on another date."

Kadin opened her mouth to ask what she had done that was so terrible, but before she could speak, a sandy, overly hair-sprayed head stuck itself into the conversation.

"Everyone's here? Everyone's having fun? It's a good party, right?" The ice clinked against the side of the glass in Olivan's trembling hand, and Kadin suspected he had been downing java all day in preparation for the event.

She gave him her best reassuring smile. "The party's great. The band is great." She glanced up at the stage and realized that the musicians had left their instruments on the stage while they took a break. "They were great. They will be great again."

Trinithy skipped past Kadin to grab Olivan in an awkward hug. "It's the best party ever! It's amazing!" On the last word, she threw her arms up in the air, sending Olivan's drink flying out of his hand and all over the front of Kadin's dress.

Kadin jumped back but was unable to prevent a scotch-scented wet spot from appearing over her stomach. "Trinithy! This is my favorite dress!"

Trinithy waved both her hands, and Kadin worried for a second the blonde might dump another drink on her. "Please. It's not the most embarrassing thing that happened to you today."

Olivan wiped Kadin's middle with a handkerchief. "Yeah, and it's alcohol, so it should dry fast. But maybe you'd better go to the ladies' room and try to clean that up."

Kadin navigated her way through the mob of laughing people who seemed content to dance to the generic audio blaring from the speakers while the band rested. She turned down the long, dark, empty hallway to the restroom and tried not to feel like the damsel in distress going off on her own in a horror cinema.

She used the paper towels in the ladies' room to dry off her dress as best she could, but judging by the odor, she wasn't the first person to have an alcohol-related accident that evening. She exited the lavatory hoping the scent of vomit had not stuck to her hair.

She started back down the hallway toward the party and didn't spare a glance toward the man leaning against the wall smoking until he called out to her. "Well, hello there, honey. And they told me only sides would be here tonight." He dropped his cigarette to the floor and put it out with the toe of his shoe.

Kadin planned to give him the humoring smile of a woman who doesn't talk to strange men in dark corridors until she noticed that the man was lead singer Dawban Steel himself. Up close, he appeared even more handsome than on his LP cover, with dark wavy hair, piercing blue eyes, and solid muscles under his leather jacket. She added a nervous giggle to her expression and made to move away from him even faster.

"Aw, don't be like that." He reached out and grabbed her elbow. She tried to tug it away, but he had a harder grip on it than she had expected. "I just want to have a little fun."

Oh, Deity. What was Trinithy telling me about Dawban Steel last week? Something about him and a girl... "Please." Kadin could hear the panic rise in her own voice as the pain shot up her arm from where he held it. "I want to go back to the party."

He pulled her closer and grabbed her other wrist with his free hand. "Come on. We can have our own party right here."

"No." Kadin tried to break away from him, but the

muscles she had admired held her in a firm grip. He thrust her against the wall. Her breath came faster as the length of his body pressed up against hers. She could feel the condensation in his gin-scented breath as he ran his lips down the side of her face.

I should fight. I know I should fight. Her breath came faster. The cool venom of terror ran through her nerves, paralyzing her. She needed all her energy to pull her cheek away. Again, his mouth found the corner of hers.

Her legs parted as his knee slithered between her thighs. Her skirt rode up. She crushed her body against the wall, as if enough pressure might make it disappear, allowing her to escape.

Deity save me.

"I believe the lady said, 'No'."

As the new voice spoke, Kadin felt the air in front of her face clear and the grip on her arms loosen. She turned her head to see a slight man with dark brown hair standing with his hand on Dawban's shoulder. The newcomer didn't look much like a savior, with his horn-rimmed glasses and an argyle sweater vest underneath his brown tweed coat. He was average-sized and didn't cut a particularly impressive figure, but he had to be strong to pull Dawban off her, and the Merchant's Guild ring on his finger hinted at the kind of money that one didn't want to offend.

Dawban sneered. "What's it to you?"

The man raised his eyebrow. Kadin felt sure she had seen him before, but she couldn't quite place where. "By all means, let's turn this into a physical altercation in the middle of a benefit. No one's going to accuse me of assaulting a woman. What about you?"

"Let's find out." Dawban's fist jutted out, clocking the other man on the side of the head.

Almost too fast for Kadin to follow, the man, whose horn-rimmed glasses had skittered across the floor, grabbed Dawban's arm and twisted it behind his back.

Dawban tried to wrench himself out of the grasp, but the other man's hold stayed firm.

The newcomer let out a heavy sigh. "Now are we done?"

From his doubled over position, Dawban spat on the ground, then nodded. The other man let him go.

Dawban sneered at Kadin. "You'll be hearing about this."

"I trust she won't." The man's gaze followed the musician as he stalked down the hallway. Kadin's savior retrieved his glasses from the floor and put them on. "Are you okay?"

Kadin didn't speak. With his glasses off, she had realized why the man looked familiar—she had seen him in a click in the main hall at the palace the other day. He was older now, but he had the same dark hair and thin-lipped frown.

The man blinked and took a step toward her. "*Are* you okay?"

Kadin realized what he must be thinking and shook her head. "No, I'm fine. It's not that."

He gave her a half smile, and if she had any doubts as to his identity, that expression blew them away. "Then what? Is there something wrong with my hair?"

"No." Kadin gulped. "You're King Ralvin."

The man froze, and his expression fell in slow motion from a smile into a look of dismay. Far too late to be effective, he let out a dismissive laugh. "No, I'm not. That's crazy."

Kadin crossed her arms. "That was convincing."

The king stepped forward and grabbed her arm in the place that was still smarting from Dawban's assault. He spoke in an urgent whisper. "How do you know that? You can't know that!"

Kadin's heart raced. *Oh my Deity. He* is *King Ralvin. And he's here because...*

Kadin's eyes must have widened a fair amount because something in her expression made the king look down at the hand that clutched her arm, and he seemed surprised to find it there. He let her go but kept the same savage intensity in his hushed voice. "You can't tell anybody. I'll do anything. Whatever it takes. What are you, some kind of journalist?"

"No, I'm—"

"Kadin?" This time the voice pulling her away from the man standing over her was one she recognized, though she wasn't sure she liked the trace of anger in it.

"I'm here, Ollie!" she said.

King Ralvin, his eyes begging her not to say anything, pulled away until his back lay against the opposite wall.

Olivan hurried forward when he saw who she was talking to. "Vinnie! How great to see you! So glad you could make it! Is everything all right?"

Does King Ralvin always look that pale without his makeup on, or is the lighting bad back here? Or is he that scared that I've found him out?

"Yes, everything's fine," the king said, a ghost of a smile gracing his lips. "It's just... I have to be going now. Great job putting this all together, Ollie."

Oh Deity. That's Ollie's flirtatious smile. Please tell me Ollie does not have a crush on King Ralvin, or whoever this alter ego is.

"Thanks so much!" Olivan kept the smile glued to his face until the king disappeared from view, then snapped around to face Kadin, a scowl marring his features. "What were you saying to Vinnie Royal?"

Kadin blanched. "Vinnie Royal? That's his name?" *Wow that's not a total give away or anything.*

"Yes, that's Vinnie Royal," Olivan hissed. "Member in good standing of the Merchant's Guild and one of the most prominent members of the sideways community. He's super rich, owns tons of shares in the *Valeriel Tribune* or something. *Please* don't tell me you harassed him the way you did Dawban Steel."

"I didn't—" Kadin's mouth dropped open. "Wait, Dawban Steel said I harassed him? Because I can assure you—"

Olivan clenched his fists. "Kadin, when I by some miracle manage to get a topname band to appear at one of my events at the last minute, the last thing I want to hear from the lead singer is that some red-haired sub-D is propositioning him in the hallway."

Kadin felt like a fish, opening and closing her blubbery jaw, but she couldn't seem to stop the motion. "Ollie, would I do that?"

"I wouldn't think so, but when I come to investigate, and I see you clearly upsetting another guest, I have to wonder what's gotten into your head." Olivan rubbed the bridge of his nose with his fingers. "Look, maybe you should go. I can salvage the rest of this night, and hopefully convince the Dawban Steel band to play at another sideways event sometime in the next ten years."

The pulse in Kadin's temple throbbed. She didn't know whether all the DeValeriels upended her temper or if one too many people had refused to listen to her that week, but she had never wanted to scream so much in her life.

Easy, her pragmatic mind soothed. *Acting out won't get you anywhere. Get out of here, and you and Ollie can talk about this like reasonable adults next week.*

She exhaled through her mouth. "You know what? You're right. Going home sounds like a great idea."

She stalked out of the hallway and back through the main room, where all the lights suddenly seemed too bright, and the opening chords as the Dawban Steel band retook the stage sounded twangy to Kadin's ear. *I'm burning that LP.*

She felt a shock of the cold breeze as she stepped out of the hot club into the night air, and the drops of sweat seemed to freeze where they trickled down her neck.

Curses! I forgot my coat. She spun back around to where she had exited, but the door had slammed shut, and the outside didn't have a handle. She considered getting in the queue to go back in, but the line stretched further down the street than it had when she arrived, and she doubted she could convince the bouncers to waive the cover fee. *I'll get it another time.*

As she headed for the autobus stop, a light blue droptop autocar slid up to the curb beside her and came to a halt.

She met the driver's eyes.

"Get in," said Ralvin DeValeriel.

CHAPTER 16

KADIN TOOK A HESITANT STEP toward the vehicle. *Should I go off alone with him?*

She considered the king's face, which looked more panicked than menacing. *Yes. I have to. I owe him an explanation. Besides, if he wants to have me killed, there's nothing I can do to stop him. He has more resources at his disposal than I can imagine.* She pulled open the passenger side door and slid into the autocar before she could change her mind.

Kadin had thought Dahran's autocar was nice, but it had nothing on the king's. She settled into a butter-soft brown leather seat as King Ralvin pushed the button that locked both doors at once. Clear jazz music pealed from the quality speakers.

Ralvin steered the car away from the curb in a smooth motion. "How did you know who I was?"

Kadin worried the wind might mess up her curls, but the autocar wasn't going that fast, and she didn't think anyone who mattered would see her anyway. "It can't be *that* difficult to figure out. There must be other people who know."

"No." The corners of his mouth turned down as he gave his head a curt shake. "No one else knows. This isn't some fly-by-night operation. I planned this identity for years before Vinnie Royal made any public appearances. I bought shares in the newspaper so that no old images of Ralvin DeValeriel would remain in the public eye. The plan was foolproof. So how did you find me?"

She wondered if he always clenched his teeth like that and thought that, if so, the royal doctor must have a full-time job dealing with the king's headaches. *But if I ran a kingdom and had a secret identity on the side, I'd be a little tense, too.* "Well, I knew that you were sideways because of your reaction when Dr. Combs came into the throne room."

Ralvin's brow furrowed as he steered his car into the left-hand lane, so she clarified.

"Jace Combs, the forensic expert? Requested to keep the queen's body? Blond hair? Blue eyes? Prettiest boy you've ever seen outside the cinema?"

His expression cleared in recognition. "Oh, yes." His lips curled up into a dreamy smile. "I remember him." He jerked his head toward her. "Wait. You were there?"

Kadin tried to stifle the irritation that was growing all too common this week. "Wow, you hear about how the Imperials don't even notice the little people."

Recognition dawned on his face. "Oh, right. You were the aide. K-something..." He scrunched up his mouth, trying to remember the name.

"Kadin Stone."

"And you noticed I was sideways." He cringed. "Was my reaction to the doctor that bad?"

Kadin smiled. *He's like Ollie.* "Oh, don't worry; the first time I met Dr. Combs, I nearly fell flat on my face. But none of the detectives noticed anything. About you, I mean."

Vinnie groaned. "I'm usually so good at not showing any expression when I'm being Ralvin. But, you know, it's not every day random gorgeous men walk into the throne room." His mouth formed a tiny "O." "Hey, do you think maybe he would...?"

Kadin sighed, her exhalation carrying all the tragedy of the situation. "Married."

"Really?" His head perked up, eager for more details.

"Yes, and to a total sub-D. You would not believe..." *Are you seriously sitting in a droptop autocar with King Ralvin talking about boys?* Kadin cleared her throat. "But that's not what you want to talk to me about. You want to know how I knew about your alter ego."

The king stopped to let a foursome of laughing club-goers cross the street. The two girls wore stylish dresses and their boyfriends' black leather jackets, while the men seemed impervious to the cold. "That was the top issue in my mind, yes."

The two couples stepped back onto the sidewalk outside Red Rock, one of the swankiest clubs in town. Kadin couldn't imagine ever feeling so carefree. "I saw a picture of you out of royal dress in the hallway of the palace the other day, and then I saw you here."

King Ralvin swore under his breath. "What picture?"

Kadin thought back to the image. "The one of you and Duke Baurus. You were teenagers, I think. But you still look like you."

The king set his mouth in a grim line as he stared at the road.

Kadin sank back in her seat. "Oh, come on. I cannot possibly be the only person to notice. It's obvious, once you have your glasses off."

King Ralvin kept his focus on the orange and white autocar in front of them. "Most people who have been in the palace hallway don't frequent side clubs."

"But people know who you are," Kadin said. "Ollie said Vinnie Royal is one of the most prominent members of sideways society!"

The king banged his hands on the steering wheel.

"And Ralvin DeValeriel is a statue!" He grabbed the wheel again, holding it tight enough that his knuckles turned white. "I didn't expect my disguise to work when I started the whole thing. I thought for sure I'd get caught, which would at least get it out that I was sideways. But it did work. I guess if you tell a big enough lie, it doesn't even occur to people that it's not true. No one even seemed to guess. Except for you."

"Wait. Callista had guards who followed her everywhere, so I imagine you do as well. How do you escape for hours at a time?"

He shifted the car into a higher gear as the traffic in front of them sped up. "I have a decoy. I pay his family a lot of money, and he's pretty much at my beck and call." Ralvin's lips quirked upward. "But don't worry. He doesn't make any political decisions."

Kadin rolled her eyes. King Ralvin didn't make any political decisions either. She looked out the window as they drove past the neon lights of a gentlemen's club. "Do you know where you're going?"

King Ralvin put on his left blinker. "I'm taking you to the Imperial Forest, where I plan to kill you and bury the body."

Kadin's heart stopped, and she whipped her head around to look at him.

He had a wicked smile on his face. "Kidding, of course."

Kadin let out the breath she had been holding.

He made the turn and then flicked his eyes to Kadin. "Seriously, though, you know my secret. What do you need to keep it?"

"What, do you think I'm going to blackmail you?" *Deity, I* could *blackmail him. I could get him to do anything I wanted. That never even occurred to me.*

His voice was flat. "Well, you did discover the biggest secret of one of the city's most powerful personages. That kind of information would be invaluable to a number of parties."

I wonder what it says about me that I didn't think of selling this to the papers. Am I a good person, or an idiot? "First of all, I did not intentionally uncover your secret. If I could figure it out, anyone could."

He snorted. "Unlikely. Few people are invited into the palace *and* hang out at parties hosted by Olivan King, Master of Ceremonies. Besides, I'm getting the impression that you are a... singular individual."

Duke Baurus said the same thing. But it's ridiculous. Most people in my life don't even trust me to work a java machine. "Fine. You want to know what my silence costs? The answers to any questions I have about your wife's murder."

King Ralvin raised his eyebrows. "So you *are* going to blackmail me."

Kadin crossed her arms. "Don't blame me. It was your idea."

The king stopped the autocar at a traffic light. "You know, when I hired Valeriel Investigations, I was told to expect an insufficient and cursory examination of the events surrounding my wife's murder. I'm starting to think I made an error."

Kadin tapped her finger on the armrest on the door of the autocar. "Why would you want to hire a company who wouldn't be able to solve the murder? Unless, of course, you expected to be a suspect."

The tires squealed as King Ralvin spun the autocar into the parking lot of a teal and white building with the word "Diner" sitting on the top in capital neon letters. "If you're going to question me about Callista's murder, I'm going to need a java."

A Dawban Steel song blared from the juke box as they stepped through the glass-faced door. Kadin had half a mind to turn around and walk out again, but she knew avoiding his voice wouldn't change the events of that night. Her heels squeaked on the black and white tiled floor as she and the king headed for a booth with red vinyl seats in the back corner. Not that they need have bothered. The java- and grease-scented restaurant was empty except for a teen girl with a high blond ponytail, poodle skirt, and bobby socks and her letter-jacketed boyfriend.

The king pulled a green menu from the holder at the side of the table and buried his face in it.

If he thinks that's going to stop my questions, he can forget it. "Why did you think you would be a suspect? The detectives thought you might have wanted revenge for Callista's promiscuity. I thought that was ridiculous, even if you hadn't been sideways. Everyone knew about her indiscretions. Even I knew, and I avoid those society glossies like the plague."

King Ralvin made a noise from behind the menu that resembled agreement enough that Kadin continued her train of thought. "I don't know if Fellows and the rest would have been so quick to dismiss you if they hadn't gotten so caught up in the Duke Baurus angle."

"Ah." The king put down the menu. "But they have dismissed me, so I can stop worrying about having another awkward conversation with the investigators."

Kadin fought the strange urge to stick her tongue out at him. "Which would be a lot less awkward if you were nice to them. But I suppose if you prefer avoidance to basic courtesy, you could call a case seventh. Though that would convict you in the court of public opinion."

"Not that the court of public opinion holds much weight when you take all efforts to have as little public persona as possible." King Ralvin folded the menu closed. "Would a reputation as a murderer hurt or help Ralvin's image, do you think?"

A waitress in a pink-and-white-checked dress with a matching hat and frilly white apron came over to the table and flipped her order pad to a clean sheet. "What can I get you?"

The king gave her a bright smile. "I'll have an order of pancakes and a cup of java, please."

The waitress jotted down his order and turned to Kadin.

"I'm good, thanks," she said.

King Ralvin tried to hand the waitress the menu, but she indicated he should return it to the holder by the window. He did so, then turned back to Kadin. "So what do you think? Should I take unofficial credit for offing my wife?"

Kadin put her elbows on the table and rested her head in her hands. "No. I want to know who really killed her." A thought struck her. "Unless it *was* you. Unless you killed her for a different reason. You didn't care about her sleeping around, but you might have cared about something else. She already knew you were sideways, I assume. What if she found out about Vinnie Royal as well and threatened to tell?"

King Ralvin snorted. "Callista? Find out about Vinnie? She would never have slummed it enough to hang out in his circles."

The words poured out of Kadin's mouth. "Or maybe you cared who she was sleeping with. You must have been under pressure in Imperial circles to produce an heir. The general populace would assume that any child she produced had at least a chance of being yours, and as long as the baby's father was your cousin, people would let it go. He would look enough like you, and Duke Baurus is almost royalty anyway. But she had ended things between the two of them, for real this time, and that could put a serious crimp in your lineage."

The king laughed, but he sounded nervous, as if he weren't quite sure how serious she was. "Callista ended things with Baurus all the time. He would rage and pout, and she would go off and sleep with some other people for a while, and then she'd take him back."

Kadin shook her head. "This time was different. You said Queen Callista seemed happy on the afternoon before she died. Duke Baurus thought she was in love with another man."

King Ralvin sat back in his seat, as if suddenly unconcerned about her accusations. "Callista? In love with someone? Please. The woman was biologically incapable of empathy. Where are you getting your information?"

Somehow the king's dismissal didn't rankle her the way everyone else's did, probably because he was questioning her evidence, rather than her competence. Kadin opened her mouth to tell him that she had met his cousin, but before she could, the waitress returned and set Ralvin's pancakes and java in front of him. The hilarity of the entire situation struck Kadin, and she giggled.

King Ralvin frowned at her. "What's so funny?"

Kadin gestured around her. "Everything. This entire situation. I cannot believe I am in a diner in the middle of the night talking to King Ralvin about a murder that no one wants me to solve."

The king glanced around the room to make sure no one was paying attention to them, but the teens at the counter were lost in their own conversation. "First off, I'm Vinnie, not Ralvin. Ralvin doesn't go out in public without wearing face paint, and often a stupid hat. And he definitely doesn't have pancakes with detective girls who suspect him of killing his wife. And what do you mean no one wants you to solve the murder?"

Kadin buried her face in her hands. "Well, you don't, for reasons I'm not entirely clear on, since whatever else you say, I don't think you killed Queen Callista, if only because you haven't killed me and hidden my body somewhere. The entire team thinks I'm useless because I'm a woman and because I mostly got the job in hopes it would help me meet a husband. And, well, maybe that's true, but that doesn't mean I can't do my job. And Dr. Combs seemed willing to talk to me about the case, but he thinks I should stay out of it because investigating magic is dangerous."

"Magic?" King Ralvin—or Vinnie— raised his eyebrows. "You think magic was involved in Callista's death?"

Kadin could tell from the look in his eyes that he knew what she knew, that Baurus DeValeriel wanted magic more than anything else in the world. "Well, maybe..."

Vinnie spread his hands out on the table and gave her a steady look. "Did you ever think that maybe everyone's better off if you never find out who killed Callista?"

Better if we never find out? But how can justice be a bad thing?

Her disbelief must have shown on her face, because Vinnie looked away from her and wrung his hands. "Look, I'm not saying that she deserved to die or that I wanted her to die or anything like that. But... Well, she was a horrible person, and maybe whoever killed her had a good reason for it. Or at least a comprehensible reason. And maybe the world is better off without that person being locked away for ridding the world of a selfish, spoiled, and useless woman." He looked back at Kadin. "I realize that this is hardly a noble motivation on my part, and you don't approve. But could you at least try to understand?"

No, I don't understand. If everyone took matters like this into their own hands, society would fall apart. She took a deep breath. *But that's not what he's saying.* "You think Duke Baurus killed Queen Callista."

Vinnie sighed. "I don't see who else could have. He was so angry that day, and I should have noticed his rage was worse than usual. But he gets angry all the time, and he always gets over it. I tried to reassure him that Callista would take him back, that she always took him back, but he seemed so convinced that this time was different. I didn't think he planned to *make* it different. I should have stopped him. I should have realized..." His face crumpled under the guilt. "He shouldn't have done it. Obviously. That's a huge understatement. But she used him so badly, again and again. How much was he expected to take? And Baurus, for all his flaws, is worth fifty Callistas."

Kadin stared at Vinnie until he met her eyes. "But what if Duke Baurus didn't kill Queen Callista?"

"Hasn't even occurred to me." Vinnie picked up his silverware and began to cut his pancakes. "The timing would be too coincidental. I mean, even Callista couldn't get two people mad enough to kill her in one day."

Kadin shook her head. "Maybe not, but the facts don't add up. Several witnesses, including yourself, attest the queen still being alive long after Duke Baurus left the palace, and even after Lady Beatrin claims that he left the Oriole estate, allegedly much calmer than when he arrived. I suppose it's possible he rethought everything and got angry again, but several witnesses saw him leave the palace earlier in the day, and none of them described his departure as 'quiet.' If he had been enraged, could he have snuck back in without anyone noticing?"

Vinnie looked unconvinced. "Baurus usually regrets things that he does and says when he's angry, but not always. Like at Beatrin's wedding, when he called Frasis an ignorant pig and punched him in front of everyone." The king smiled at the memory. "Well, Frasis rather deserved that. He said disparaging things about his new wife's honor quite loudly. But Baurus still won't apologize to Frasis—or even Beatrin, for making a scene at her wedding—and swears up and down that he would do it again. He may well have done something similar with Callista, decided that he wanted to kill her while he was angry and still thought it seemed like a good idea once he had calmed down."

"Putting aside the fact that there is a rather large

difference between punching someone for being a jerk and murdering someone, the perpetrator must have planned the murder before the queen even talked to Duke Baurus that day. The queen's guard was found buried in the woods, where he had probably been since the night before she died. Someone had gotten him out of the way so her protection would be inadequate, and it's unlikely to have been the duke."

"I admit that's odd." Vinnie lifted a fork of food to his mouth. "But, seriously, this was far from the first time that Callista had upset Baurus. I can't think of anyone whom she enraged anywhere near as much."

Kadin tried not to be distracted by the sweet-and-savory scent of pancakes. Maybe she should have ordered something. "But she had inspired strong feelings in someone. She ended her relationship with Duke Baurus because she claimed that someone who she truly loved had come back to her after a year away. She must have had a great impact on him indeed, if he would come back to her after all that time."

Vinnie swallowed, and his fork clinked as he set it against his plate. "Wait. You really think Callista left Baurus for someone specific, someone she loved? Who could that be?"

Who indeed. "I was rather hoping you could tell me. I have a list of people that she... spent time with... last fall, but there's no news coupling her name with any of them lately. I can't believe this renewed relationship isn't connected to her death in some way."

"Wait a minute here." Vinnie took a sip of his java. "Where are you getting your information? I lived with the woman, and I don't have any kind of comprehensive list of her relationships. And I certainly never heard or saw any evidence that she was particularly attached to any one of her 'suitors'."

Should I tell him? "The entire world could get a list of

her suitors from the society glossies. But I got them from an interested party—Duke Baurus."

Vinnie set his mug down with a clunk, and the hot liquid sloshed up almost to the rim. "You spoke to Baurus? You mean after the murder? Even I haven't seen Baurus since then."

"Well, I certainly didn't talk to him before the murder." She took a deep breath. *Okay, cards on the table.* "I ran into him at the palace when the investigation team was leaving the day after the queen died. He was in the queen's library, where he threw a book at my head. The next day he came by my house to apologize for attacking me and to let me ask him some questions. He told me that Queen Callista left him for another man, and I've been tracking down these alleged suspects ever since. The only one I still need to question is Lord Landis Imbolc, who is out of town indefinitely." She let out a breath, relieved to have finally told someone.

Vinnie snorted. "Callista was not having an affair with Landis Imbolc."

"Duke Baurus seemed pretty sure..."

"Oh, I bet he was." Vinnie smirked. "Baurus was adept at tracking down every activity of Callista's, but he can be surprisingly clueless about many things. Like the fact that Landis is sideways."

I read that whole thick file several times... "Are you sure? Because the glossies have never even implied any such thing."

"Well, it's not public knowledge." Vinnie ate a bite of pancake. "If Chaise knew his son was sideways and unlikely to produce heirs, it would break the poor duke's heart. Which would cause him to break rocks—or his son's face—with his bare fists or something. But if Baurus thought that something was going on between Landis and Callista, then something was going on. It just wasn't an affair."

"So what was it?"

He took another mouthful of food and chewed it. "I don't know. You'd have to talk to Landis, or maybe his sister Elyesse. She usually knows about his goings-on."

That's what I planned to do anyway. Well, if the detectives let me have plans. She took a moment to watch Vinnie eat before she voiced her next request. "I want to know where Duke Baurus is."

"You think I know?" Vinnie's voice was light, but he refused to meet her eyes. "I told you, I haven't seen him since the murder."

"Maybe not, but you can tell me where he is."

Vinnie watched the silver tines of his fork as he shifted pieces of pancake around on his plate.

Kadin sighed. "Look, I don't think that he killed anyone, but the detectives are focusing all their energy on trying to find him, and they won't consider another suspect until he's brought into custody. If I can convince him to turn himself in, we can clear his name and figure out who really killed her."

Vinnie ate several more bites of food, and Kadin wondered if he planned to ignore her until she changed the subject. "I don't know for sure," he said at last. "I honestly haven't seen him, and it's not as if we worked out a contingency plan in the event that one of us was ever on the run from the authorities. But he's probably at his house in the Merchant District."

"He has a house in the Merchant District? What, the estate in the Imperial District isn't enough?"

Vinnie took a sip of java. "Most of us do. It's a stupid trend that's been going on for years. Sort of a private way of sticking it to the Merchants—we can buy houses in their district, but they can't buy property in ours. It's all under aliases, but I think most of them know we do it. You can see that I find having a secret house and identity worthwhile, and I would imagine Baurus has reached the same conclusion."

Kadin pulled a napkin out of the holder and took a pen out of her purse. She slid both over to him. "Address, please."

Vinnie scrawled something on the napkin and pushed it back over to her. "The house is owned under the name Camus Wrench."

Kadin folded the napkin and put it in her bag. She tried not to feel bad as Vinnie hung his head. "It's for the best."

"I guess." Vinnie pushed his empty plate away from himself. "Now, unless you want me to sell out any more of my relatives tonight, come on. I'll give you a ride home."

Vinnie paid his bill, and he and Kadin strolled out to the autocar. As he opened the door, he met her eyes over the top of the vehicle. "You're not going to tell anyone who I am, are you?"

Kadin studied the unassuming man across from her. No one would ever guess he held the kingdom in his hands. "Your secret is safe with me. I promise."

Vinnie pulled out of the parking lot, and for most of the ride they were silent except for Kadin giving directions to her house.

When they were almost there, she thought of something. "Hey, Vinnie? Do you know what it means when the racers give you a scarf at the drag?"

"You mean the tokens at the beginning?" He adjusted the clutch as they went up a hill.

"Yeah, those."

Vinnie turned the autocar onto Kadin's street. "If he wins the drag, the girl with the token has to go to dinner with him."

Kadin groaned. "I think I may be worse at dating than anyone else in the city."

Vinnie pulled up to the curb in front of her house. "Try being a Merchant with a secret identity. I can never tell if guys like me or are only after my money. And they never understand why I can't go out when the Assembly's in session."

Kadin pulled open the door and stepped onto the sidewalk. "Thanks for the ride. And the information."

"Yeah." Vinnie shifted the autocar into reverse. "See you around."

When Kadin entered the kitchen, she found Octavira waiting for her.

Octavira peered out the window, watching the autocar pull away. "Was that another man driving you home?"

Now she thinks I'm promiscuous? Kadin took a glass out of the cabinet and got some water from the tap. "This one's sideways. His name's Vinnie Royal."

Octavira's eyes bugged. "Isn't he a Merchant?"

Kadin paused in lifting the glass to her mouth. "You know him?"

Octavira shrugged. "I've heard the name. What were you doing with him?"

"Oh, nothing." She took a sip of water. *The worst date ever, followed by the worst party ever. Oh, and meeting the king's alter ego. And it may not have been my strangest day this week.*

CHAPTER 17

KADIN KNOCKED ON THE STATELY off-white door of a brick house with a neat evergreen hedge. The Merchant District lacked the prestige of the Imperial District. The houses stood closer together and had small, well-maintained lawns instead of independent parks, but this part of town was still a step up from the rest of the city. The air smelled of crisp autumn leaves and mowed grass instead of gasoline and garbage, and the autocars purred down the street instead of clunking. Kadin could spend the rest of her life working as a detective and never earn enough for a down payment on such a residence.

After a moment Kadin heard hesitant steps on the other side of the door. A man with a wrinkled face and tufts of white hair over his ears opened the door and looked at her with wary eyes. "May I help you?"

Kadin cleared her throat. "I'm here to see Camus Wrench?" She couldn't quite keep her voice from going up at the end, turning it into a question.

"I'm sorry." The butler gave a small bow. "He is not in residence."

He's a good liar, but I don't buy it. "I'm sure you've been told to turn away anyone who comes to the door, but he needs to talk to me."

The butler did a good impression of a sturdy road block for such a frail-looking old man. “I am sure he does, and I shall be sure to tell my master that you came by when he returns.”

Kadin noticed he didn’t ask for her name. “I have it on good authority that Mr. Wrench—and I think we both know that’s not his real name—is here, and I’m going to have to insist upon seeing him.”

The butler turned up his nose at her tone. “I’m afraid I’m going to have to ask you to leave. Good day, madam.” He moved to close the door.

Kadin stuck her high-heeled foot in the door jamb. She couldn’t believe she had figured out where Duke Baurus was but wouldn’t be able to see him. “Please! You have to let me in!”

The butler sniffed. “Madam, if you do not remove your foot, I shall be forced to contact Mr. Wrench’s private security force.”

Kadin’s breath came faster. *Oh my Deity, what am I doing?* “And if you don’t let me—”

“In the name of all that is sacred, what is going on out here?” A tall form created a sinister shadow behind the butler, and Kadin realized the duke had come into the foyer.

She waved her hand to catch his attention, as if he hadn’t already noticed her. “Duke Baurus!”

A thunderous cloud descended on his face. He grabbed the door and whipped it open, as the old man faded into the background. “You! What are you doing here?” asked the duke.

You showed up at my house without warning. I thought I’d return the favor. “I needed to talk to you.” Kadin pulled her foot back and made an effort at composing herself. “You need to turn yourself in.”

Duke Baurus gave a barking laugh. “Why would I do that?”

Kadin glanced at the brick houses lining the street. A black autocar slowed as it passed, and Kadin could see the passenger's face pressed to the window. The man trimming the hedge that bordered the lot also seemed interested in the conversation. "Do you want to have this conversation in the middle of the Merchant District?"

The duke started and looked down at himself, as if remembering he was supposed to be in hiding. "Not really. You'd better come in."

He pulled the door open a bit more, and Kadin ducked in under his arm. She tried not to stare at the expensive paintings and the intricate stone flooring as he led her into a sitting room decorated in DeValeriel red and black, with some warm brown tones mixed in to soften the effect. Kadin wanted to lower herself into one of the plush red chairs, but she thought standing would make her argument stronger.

Duke Baurus glowered at her. "I didn't kill Callista! I told you that!"

Kadin met his glare and once again found that she couldn't bring herself to fear him. "I know, and I don't believe that you did. But the investigation team is under orders to bring you into custody as soon as possible."

He took a step closer, his hulking form trying to appear menacing, but the amusement in his hazel eyes belied the effect. "Then where are they? Why are you here on your own?"

"They don't know I'm here." She kept eye contact with him, communicating with her entire posture that he didn't intimidate her. "I thought I'd give you a chance to turn yourself in and save your dignity before I told them where you were."

His smirk nearly made Kadin growl in her throat. "That's cute, but I don't think so," he said.

"I'm trying to give you a chance!" Kadin closed her eyes and took a deep breath. "If you turn yourself in and tell everyone the story you told me, they'll have to recognize the flaws in their case."

He looked at her as if she had suggested he run down the street naked. "You're serious? You have got to be the stupidest..." His eyes lost their humor and flashed with anger. "Do you honestly think that the investigation system works that way? If they can get me into custody with sufficient evidence that I committed the murder, they aren't going to look for someone else! They want this case done and settled, and I'm a convenient scapegoat. How naïve are you?"

"I don't know. How naïve are you?" Kadin could hear the frustration in her tone. "Do you think you're helping your case by hiding out from everyone and refusing to come in for questioning?"

"How is getting myself locked up and interrogated by people who will do anything to get me to confess going to be any better?" He took another step forward.

This isn't going anywhere, which is fair. The investigation system hasn't seemed too interested in justice this week. He stood so close to her that she had to arch her neck to look at him. "Because as long as you're on the loose, they're going to spend all their energy looking for you. Do you want the trail to go even colder while they're chasing a dead end?"

Baurus crossed his arms. "And what if they don't decide to look for someone else? What if I end up convicted for murder?"

"You're going to tell me you don't have the means to bribe your way out of prison and run away to Astrevia?"

He didn't look convinced.

She let out a long breath. "Please, Your Grace, I need you to trust me."

He stood there for a long time studying her face, as if trying to determine whether or not he could, in fact, trust her. After a moment, he nodded. “Okay. I’ll do this your way.”

Kadin let out an audible sigh of relief. “You’ll turn yourself in first thing tomorrow?”

His mouth set in a grim line. “Unless I convince myself that it’s a bad idea before then.”

Deity save me from impulsive Imperials. “If you do that, I’ll be back at your door with some enforcers next time.”

He smirked. “Maybe I’ll skip town.”

She shook her head. “If you do that, you’ll never find out who killed Queen Callista. You’re better off listening to me.”

He reached out and put a hand on her arm, and she felt goose bumps form around the spot where his warmth pressed through. “I’m listening to you. I’ll be there.”

The next morning, Kadin had finished typing up her notes from the weekend when Inspector Warring stormed into the office. Since her papers stayed on the desk, she had to assume his mood was positively gleeful. Warring glanced at Fellows’s office and noticed that the detective had not arrived yet.

Warring pointed at Kadin. “You. Fellows’s aide.”

“Kadin Stone, sir.” She didn’t know why it bothered her that he seemed to think of her as more of an object than a person. At least he thought she was an object capable of performing basic job functions.

He waved a dismissive hand. “Fine, Stone, then. Get together the team’s notes on this DeValeriel case. I want to see what you’ve got.”

Well, at least I know where Dahran’s office is now. She got up and wandered down the hall.

She found her probably-never-would-be husband sitting at his desk. “Inspector Warring wants me to get everyone’s notes for the case.”

"Of course he does. It's Monday morning, and he wants a report of all the major cases first thing. Any good aide knows that." Dahran grinned at her to show he was kidding, though she suspected he wasn't.

"Okay." Kadin took a hesitant step into the room. "Well, can I have your notes so that I can give them to the Inspector?"

Dahran held up a thin folder with a cluster of rumpled papers in it. "Sure thing. I've had them ready for you since Friday."

I can't tell if he's mad at me or not. But I guess a better question is, do I care?

She gave him a smile as she reached out to take the folder, in case she did care. "Thanks."

As she headed back to Fellows's office, she narrowly avoided bumping into Combs.

"Oh, I'm sorry." She took a quick step back.

He grabbed her arm to steady her, pulling her toward him in the process. "Miss Stone. I was looking for you. I..." He broke off, studying her face, as if trying to decide whether he could trust her.

Kadin felt a strange tingle at being close enough to his handsome face to feel his breath whisper on her cheeks. She'd had so many men stand close to her this week. Dawban Steel, who she hoped never to see again. Duke Baurus, who she didn't know what to think about. And now Combs. Yet she'd managed to keep her distance from Dahran, whom she still planned to marry.

Combs lowered his voice to a whisper. "I ran those tests you were talking about, did the full autopsy I couldn't do on the queen's body. I found... I think you were right. The victim's throat wasn't damaged, but inside... His air sacs looked as though someone had burned them away."

Kadin gasped, all thoughts of handsome men gone from her head. "Then I was right. The murderer *did* use magic."

Combs looked up and down the hall, as if making sure

that no one was listening to them. "I have the report right here. In fact, I have two reports. One states exactly what I told you, and one says that I could find no cause of death. I'm trying to decide which one to give you. You're collecting notes for Warring today, yes?"

Kadin nodded and looked him straight in the eye. "We have to tell the truth. If the Society of Mages is killing people, we have to hold them accountable."

"You're right, of course. Though you'll forgive me if I hope we never find the killer, and this evidence never sees the light of day." He handed her the piece of paper and reached out as if he were going to touch her cheek, but then thought better of it. "Be careful, Miss Stone. I don't think this path leads anywhere good."

He's probably right, she thought as he walked away. But somehow she couldn't bring herself to be scared of the Society of Mages. They seemed too murky and nebulous. One murderer wielding magic seemed much more manageable.

Kadin returned to her office and flipped through the file that Dahran had given her. "Disaster" was the most positive word she could think of to describe it. The folder was full of smudged handwritten notes on various sizes of paper, and arrangement of the pages appeared haphazard at best.

Inspector Warring probably won't mind waiting an extra hour for legible notes. She sat down at her typewriter and organized Dahran's and Combs's reports into the case as she believed the detectives saw it, holes included. In addition to the speculations about magic, Combs's analysis indicated that Tailor had died sometime on Sunday night—long before Duke Baurus encountered Queen Callista.

Should I put my *notes in? Fellows wouldn't want me to, but Warring* did *say he wanted the findings of everyone on the team.* Feeling a rush of daring, Kadin pulled out her folder on the case and inserted the pages where she thought they best fit. She hoped Duke Baurus had turned himself in by the time Warring read the case file, or he would wonder how and where she had questioned the primary suspect.

Fellows came in as Kadin finished up. She went to get a steaming cup of java and delivered it to his door. "Do you have any notes for Inspector Warring?" she asked as she handed him the mug.

Fellows took the java but didn't look up at her. "I went over all of that with White on Friday."

Kadin nodded and headed to find Warring's office. She only wandered around for a few minutes before finding the right door, and she handed the case file to Warring's aide, who, judging by the quality of his suit, might have been better paid than Fellows.

She headed back to her office, wondering if she should try to make further progress on the case. The only lead she had left was Landis and Elyesse Imbolc, and she couldn't muster up the nerve to schedule an appointment with them on her own.

Midway through the morning, Fellows called Dahran into his office, and Kadin spent the next hour wondering how they planned to do any investigating if they spent the whole case sequestered in a windowless room.

Around the same time she was considering finding Olivan and Trinithy for lunch, Inspector Warring surged into the office and banged open Fellows's door. "How did you get him to do it?"

Kadin turned around in her chair in time to see Fellows frown. "How did I get who to do what?" he asked.

"How did you get Duke Baurus to turn himself in?" Warring shook his head and laughed. "I was beginning to think we'd need an international manhunt to find the guy, but a couple of hours ago he came into our offices himself. I'm surprised you haven't been up in my office claiming all the credit yet."

"Yes, well..." Fellows glanced at Dahran, but Kadin knew the junior detective wouldn't have any insight. "We know how to get things done."

Warring made a disbelieving noise. "I don't know about that. Have you seen this file?" He threw the folder in his hands onto Fellows's desk. "I have to give you credit for organizing your notes for once instead of handing me a collage of hand-written scribbles, but the case has holes all over the place. So stop congratulating yourselves and interview Landis Imbolc before I decide to interrogate you about why you pursued the DeValeriel angle so hard." Warring headed out of the room and yelled over his shoulder. "And tell Combs to get me a real cause of death. Magic, indeed!"

Fellows uttered a few flabbergasted monosyllables at Warring's retreating back. Dahran said, "Where did he...?" before dead silence filled the room. Kadin felt two pairs of eyes on her.

"Miss Stone?"

She pasted a bright smile on her face and turned to look at Fellows. "Yes, Detective?"

"Do you know why Duke Baurus turned himself in?"

Kadin's grin slipped a little. "Possibly because I told him that it was in his best interests to do so."

Dahran's mouth fell open, and she worried the little blood vessel at Fellows's temple might explode.

Eventually Dahran spoke. "But... But... how did you *find* him?"

Kadin's heart pounded, and she could feel her lungs quivering. "Oh, he owns a house in the Merchant District under a different name." She shrugged as it if were no big deal. "Once I found out about it, it seemed logical that he would be there."

Dahran shuffled through the file Warring had dropped. "He has a house in the Merchant District? But... I've been investigating him all week, and I haven't found anything of the kind. How did you learn that?"

"My source... prefers to remain anonymous."

"Anonymous?" Fellows's booming voice made Kadin wince. "You're an *aide*, Miss Stone. You don't get to have anonymous sources."

Would it be worse to tell them nothing or admit I talked to the king on my own? "I'll try to keep that in mind for the future, but I swore secrecy on this matter. Isn't the important thing that Duke Baurus is in custody?"

Fellows's cheeks puffed up, and his face reddened. "Miss Stone, I realize that you are new to this position." Fellows's tone indicated he was being patient with her, as one would be with a child who had done something to infuriate him. He planned to dismiss everything she said as irrelevant, but he still needed to put her in her place. "So I will explain the hierarchy to you. Every decision that is made while you are working on this case, who you question, when you question him, when you take a break to eat, and especially who you convince to turn himself in, is made by me. If you think that you by some miracle have an idea that I have not considered, you bring it to my attention, and I decide whether it has merit. Understood?"

"All right, Detective. It's just..." Kadin looked at the floor.

"It's just what, Miss Stone?"

She turned her head back up and looked him in the eye. "You wouldn't listen to me."

Fellows glowered. "And I suppose you can tell me why Inspector Warring doesn't think that Duke Baurus killed the queen." From his tone, Kadin couldn't tell whether the worse answer would be "No" or "Yes."

Kadin took a few steps forward, until she was almost in the room with the detectives. "Duke Baurus was our primary suspect because a number of witnesses had seen him angry with Queen Callista on the day of her death.

But the murderer killed the guard the night before, before Duke Baurus was angry. Any jury is going to demand his motive for killing the guard on Sunday night."

The detectives exchanged glances.

"She's right," Dahran said. "We should have thought of that."

Fellows leaned forward. "And I suppose, Miss Stone, that you know why Warring wants us to interrogate Landis Imbolc."

Kadin nodded. "Yes, sir. It's because—"

Fellows stopped her with a hand. "Save it, Miss Stone. White, take her over to the Imbolc estate and get some information from them." He grabbed the case file out of Dahran's hands. "It seems I need to familiarize myself with my own case."

CHAPTER 18

"IT'S PROBABLY BETTER THAT I ask the questions," Dahran said as he and Kadin strode past the lavender-draped bronze statues on the Imbolc estate. They had called ahead, and while Lord Landis was still out of town, Lady Elyesse had agreed to see them. "I'm the detective, after all."

"All right." Kadin balanced her high heels on the brick walkway that ran through the manicured lawn. "What are you planning on asking her? So that I can prepare to take notes."

Dahran came to a stop, apparently realizing he had no idea what this meeting was about. "Well, about her relationship with the queen and Duke Baurus." He resumed walking, having regained his confidence from what Kadin assumed was an endless well. "Did you have other questions?"

She hurried along after him, repeating Trinithy's advice about feeding men's egos in her mind. "I heard a rumor that Queen Callista was having an affair with Lord Landis Imbolc about a year ago. I wanted to ask him about that, but he's been out of town. I thought that maybe his sister might know something..." *Also, he's sideways, so he wasn't having an affair with the queen. And Lady Elyesse knows all the details of her brother's business. But I'm not sure I can repeat that, and you should be able to get the information I need without knowing.*

Dahran flashed her an arrogant grin. "Well, that should probably come up when I ask her about her relationship with the queen, but I'm glad to know beforehand."

Kadin resisted the urge to roll her eyes.

The bird-like woman who answered the door informed them that Lady Elyesse had asked that they be escorted to the library. The housekeeper led them down the third elaborate hallway Kadin had seen this week, this one decorated in Imbolc purple and bronze. *Fourth,* she supposed, *if I count Duke Baurus's house in the Merchant District.* The dark metal gave the corridor a masculine feel, but a feminine floral scent wafted through the air. Kadin suspected the suits of armor and mounted stags' heads were the influence of Duke Chaise Imbolc, while the accompanying vases of flowers and bowls of potpourri were his daughter, Lady Eylesse. Kadin wondered what role Lord Landis played in the trimming, or if he kept his tastes as secret as his sexual orientation.

The library was quite dark for a room where one was expected to read fine print, but a reading lamp shone above Lady Elyesse's shoulder. The young Imperial appeared at ease, though her soft brown hair and white dress seemed at odds with the mahogany poker table and studded leather chairs. Lady Eylesse's book of choice, a pristine paperback with a green and white cover, did not have the same erudite appearance as the many leather-bound tomes that lined the walls, but looked more as though it belonged in Queen Callista's library.

But what fit in least was the friendly smile that lit the lady's face, which lacked any trace of the arrogance Kadin had come to expect from Imperials.

"Thank you, Halla." Lady Elyesse nodded to the woman,

and then turned her beatific expression on Kadin and Dahran. "Please, have a seat."

Kadin stared at the book in Lady Elyesse's hands, certain she had seen it before, though she couldn't place where. *Diamonds in my Mind,* the title read, and that meant nothing to Kadin. She didn't frequent bookstores, and Octavira only approved of cookbooks, and the occasional biography of some Merchant's wife who had been instrumental in maintaining the status quo. Kadin looked down when she realized she was staring, but Lady Elyesse was focused on Dahran anyway.

The detective gave the noblewoman his handsome smile. "I'm Detective Dahran White, and this is my aide, Kadin Stone. Thank you so much for meeting with us."

"Oh, it's not a problem." Lady Elyesse leaned forward, her big blue eyes opened wide. "You wanted to ask me some things about Callista. It's so sad, what happened to her. She was such a vivacious person. We're all going to miss her so much. Please, ask me anything. I want to help in any way I can."

Lady Elyesse liked Callista, Kadin wrote with some surprise. Even Duke Baurus had not described her in so positive a manner, but no doubt the description said more about the woman in front of Kadin than it did about the queen.

Elyesse is such a sweetheart. One hates to disappoint her, Lady Beatrin had said.

She was talking about... a book? Kadin thought. *A book Queen Callista had and Lady Elyesse wanted.*

Dahran made a few marks on his notepad. "Lady Elyesse, could you please tell me about your brother's relationship with Queen Callista."

The lady bit her lip and glanced down at her hands. "I shouldn't... I mean, Landis told me in the strictest confidence... But I suppose this is for a murder investigation." She sighed. "I can count on you to be discreet, of course?"

Dahran gave a solemn nod.

"My brother Landis is sideways." Lady Elyesse almost whispered the word. "I know it's accepted these days among the common folk, but Imperials... Well, my father still expects Landis to produce an heir, and Landis wants my father to be proud of him."

His father is proud of a playboy? Kadin though absently, but her mind focused on Lady Elyesse's book, trying to place it.

The lady took a sip of the light brown beverage in front of her. From the scent, Kadin imagined it was herbal tea. "In order to hide the truth, Landis has a sort of... arrangement with some of the other Imperial women," Lady Elyesse said. "When he wants to spend time with a lover, he finds an Imperial woman who wants to have a secret affair of her own. They then use each other as alibis. If Landis's name was coupled with Callista's, it meant that she didn't want anyone to know who she was really seeing."

Someone unsuitable, even for an affair, Kadin thought.

Dahran opened his mouth, no doubt to ask some further question about Landis Imbolc's affairs.

Kadin spoke before he got the chance. "My lady, would you mind telling me about the book you're reading?"

Lady Elyesse's brow furrowed, and Dahran looked at Kadin as if she had asked the lady to stand on her head in front of the palace.

Kadin cleared her throat. "I realize that it might not seem important to the case..."

"No, that's all right. I mean, I don't see how it could be related to... what happened to Callista, but it is related to her, at least a little bit." Lady Elyesse considered for a moment. "Callista, Beatrin Oriole, and I are—were—in the habit of exchanging books, as we all read the same things, and there's no point in buying three copies. Beatrin and I always tried to lend to each other first, simply because Callista... liked to take her time with them."

Kadin suspected that a ruder person would have said that the queen borrowed them and then either forgot or didn't care that other people wanted them.

"Anyway, this book came out a few months ago, and I was in the middle of something else. I knew Callista was desperate to read it, so I told Beatrin to give it to her first." Lady Elyesse sighed. "I didn't want to bother Callista or Beatrin too much about it, but it had been a few months, and I wanted to read it, so I might have been a little bit hard on poor Beatrin. And after Callista... passed on... I decided to buy my own copy. I feel bad, now, over putting so much pressure on Callista. I wish the last time I had seen her that I had been nicer to her. I didn't need to bring up the stupid book." A tear fell down her face and she looked down, ashamed.

Queen Callista took a lover, one she had to hide from society, and she didn't hide any of her lovers from society. And that book...

"Lady Elyesse, is this the only book of Lady Beatrin's that you were waiting for Queen Callista to return?" Kadin could hear the quiver in her own voice.

"Yes." The noblewoman leaned back a bit, no doubt wondering why Kadin was focusing on books in the middle of a murder investigation. "As I said, Beatrin usually let me read her books before Callista, but in this one case... Miss Stone, are you all right?"

Kadin supposed her face was probably pale at that moment. "Yes." She gave what she hoped was a reassuring smile. "Lady Elyesse, may I use your ringer?"

The lady furrowed her brow but nodded. "Of course, if you need to. It's in the other room; I can show you."

As Kadin got up to follow the lady out, Dahran grabbed Kadin's arm with what she could only assume he did not realize was pain-inducing pressure. "What are you doing? I told you that I would do the talking, and you didn't even ask her any of the things we talked about."

Kadin tried unsuccessfully to pull her arm from his grip and nearly fell over in the process. "You can ask her more if you still want to, but I already got the information I came here for."

Dahran looked at her with a mixture of astonishment and scorn. "You came here to find out about the reading habits of Imperial women?"

He loosened his grip on her arm, and she was able to wrench it free.

"No," she said. "I came here to find out who killed the queen. And now I know."

CHAPTER 19

HALF AN HOUR LATER, KADIN and Dahran's autotaxi pulled up in front of the palace. She had called the guards, and the king must have given them her name because as soon as she asked, they readily agreed to gather King Ralvin, Captain Carver, and Herrick Strand to meet in the queen's chamber. Dahran had called the Fellows, since Kadin figured her boss was more likely to listen to his fellow detective than to her.

Kadin had to stifle a laugh when the guards seemed dubious about letting Dahran in until they heard her name. She told them to let the rest of the team in when they arrived, because she didn't want to think about how angry Fellows would be if the palace staff denied him entrance to his own murder investigation.

Fellows and Combs piled out of an autotaxi before Kadin and Dahran got to the door.

Fellows, a scowl on his face, hurried over to them. "What is all this about, White?"

"Ask her." Dahran pointed at Kadin, looking no more pleased than this superior. "She said she knew who killed the queen and hasn't told me a thing since."

"Miss Stone." Fellows turned his less-than-pleased expression in Kadin's direction. "Did we not have a discussion less than two hours ago regarding your role in this investigation? One that forbade exactly this sort of behavior?"

Kadin took a deep breath and tried to look contrite. "We did. However, given some new evidence that has come to light, I thought that you might appreciate the opportunity to re-question some members of the palace guard. As quickly as possible."

"What new evidence is this, White?" Fellows asked Dahran.

Dahran ran his fingers through his hair. "I told you. I have no idea. You told me to go with her to visit Lady Elyesse, so I did. Your aide and the lady had a discussion about the Imperial women's appalling tastes in paperbacks, and before I could ask any further questions, Miss Stone insisted that we come here. I'm sure Lady Elyesse thought we were quite wasting her time."

A strange expression came over Fellows's face as he puzzled through his fellow detective's words. He had been an investigator for a long time, and Kadin knew that something in him recognized that what Queen Callista read was in some way relevant, though he couldn't quite put his finger on it.

But that didn't make him any less impatient. "So we are here because...?"

He didn't address Kadin, but she answered, and this time, he listened. When she had finished, he opened the palace doors and strode down the hallway and up the plush-carpeted staircase toward the queen's bedroom without another word, leaving the rest of the team to scurry after him.

A few minutes later, everyone involved in the case had assembled in the queen's gold-and-white bedroom. Kadin hadn't thought the space could be more crowded than it had been the last time she'd been there, but apparently it could.

King Ralvin stood in the corner, garbed in full royal attire complete with robes, face paint, and shoes that, despite the lack of heels, may well have been less comfortable than Kadin's from the other day. She couldn't see a trace of "Vinnie Royal" in his visage, not even when he glanced at her. But she supposed he had become skilled at hiding.

Captain Carver, Corporal Strand, and a few other guards stood at attention in their puffy hats. The members of the investigation team did their best to look as if they knew why they had come to the palace, though Fellows was the only one who succeeded. Kadin assumed the posture of a diligent aide, several steps behind her boss, notepad at the ready.

Fellows cleared his throat. "I'm sure you are all wondering why I have assembled you here. I have a few more questions regarding the death of our beloved queen, and I shall try to make this as quick and painless as possible. Corporal Strand, I wonder whether you could again tell me why you happened to be acting as the queen's bodyguard that night."

Strand glanced at his captain, who nodded his approval. "Her night bodyguard had failed to report, and someone had to take over, so they sent me. I'm not sure why."

Fellows made a sharp mark on his notepad. "Nor am I, considering what a shoddy mess you made of the job. After all, as the queen's bodyguard, your primary duty is to stay by her side, and yet you abandoned her. Would you mind explaining your decision to disregard your superior's order?"

Fellows glanced at Kadin as he said those last words. *I sure hope he's looking at me in complicity as an investigator and not chastising me for my behavior this past week. After all, which one of us solved the murder?*

"I... I..." Strand looked from side to side, seeking help from his fellow palace guards.

Captain Carver looked to the impassive king, but when support didn't come, turned to Fellows. "Please, Detective, is this necessary? Corporal Strand has already answered this question for you, and for the palace guard, several times. While we are no happier than you about the situation, he has submitted to disciplinary action, and we are not in the habit of subjecting those who make errors of judgment, however severe, to extensive emotional barraging."

"I do apologize, Captain," Fellows said, though not a hint of regret laced his words. "I assure you, I would not assail the corporal's delicate sensibilities without a good reason. Clarifying the details of that night is crucial to my investigation. So, Corporal Strand, if you would humor me and explain one more time."

Strand closed his eyes and winced. "She wanted some book from downstairs in her library. She insisted that she needed to have it right away."

Fellows nodded, flipping back in his notebook as if to confirm this with some note he had taken before. "And what book was this?"

Strand's eyes widened. "I... I don't... So much happened since that..."

Fellows looked up from his notebook, a glint in his eyes. "Come now. This book was so important that you left the queen without any protection in the middle of the night. I realize recent events may have rendered it immaterial, but you must have had a name or a description in order to retrieve it."

Strand's breath began to come faster. "I don't... I mean, the book was important at the time, but... She said it was the only book unshelved in the library and that she needed to finish it that night because Lady Elyesse Imbolc wanted it, but I can't remember the exact title."

"Was it *Diamonds in My Mind*?" Dahran asked. Despite having heard Kadin's story downstairs, he seemed to only now be putting all the pieces together.

Strand gave the involuntary smile of someone who has been reminded of something on the tip of his tongue. "Yes, that's it!" Then his face fell. "It was a stupid novel. I should have insisted that I accompany her to retrieve it or that she summon another servant or that Lady Elyesse wait an extra day for it..." He dropped his head into his hands as he trailed off.

Fellows nodded and wrote this piece of information down in his notebook. "So, to confirm the events of that night as you portrayed them, Queen Callista asked for you to retrieve a book, *Diamonds in My Mind*, that she needed urgently. You went down to her library to fetch it, neither heard nor saw anything malevolent or unusual, and returned to the queen's room to find her dead. Is that correct?"

Strand nodded without raising his head. "Yes, that's exactly what happened."

Captain Carver frowned at Fellows. "Please, Detective, we have heard all of this before. I was under the impression that you wanted to gather some new information, but I must insist that you either broach a new subject or stop this interrogation."

"I quite agree, Captain, and, with your permission, I have only one further question to ask the corporal." He waited until Strand raised his head before asking the question that he knew would be paramount to the case: "Where is the book?"

Strand froze as everyone except for Fellows and Kadin involuntarily looked around the room, which, with the exception of the missing body, looked exactly the same as it had the night the queen had been murdered. Clothes and jewels were scattered everywhere, and a ball gown pooled next to the queen's bureau, but not a book was in sight. As the various members of the palace guard came to the realization that no book was in evidence, they all took a step away from Strand, who continued to stare at Fellows.

"Since you seem to be drawing a blank, allow me to answer the question for you. The book is where I saw it when I came to investigate a week ago: downstairs in the queen's library."

He *saw it?* Kadin thought. *More like* I *saw it—when Duke Baurus threw it at my head. But I guess it doesn't matter who takes credit for solving the case.*

"Would you care to revise your story, Corporal?" Fellows took a step forward and met the man's eyes. "Perhaps I can do it for you. Back when you worked in the palace, you fell in love with Queen Callista, and she returned your feelings. Then you were transferred out of the palace, at which time you ended your relationship. But things were not over between you, and a year after your transfer you decided to kill her bodyguard in order to be reunited with her. But clearly something went wrong between you. Maybe you were angry about her year of faithlessness, maybe you had a disagreement. Whatever happened, something made you decide to strangle her. To deflect blame from yourself, you made up a plausible story involving the queen's notorious insistence that things always be exactly as she wanted them, and you didn't have to pretend to be upset, since you did have an emotional attachment to her. Does any of this sound familiar, Corporal?"

Strand's blank expression curved into an amused smirk. "Not precisely, Detective."

Fellows raised an eyebrow. "Would you care to clarify the tale for me, then?"

Strand laughed aloud, and Kadin could not believe that this was the same man who had seemed so incompetent and distraught a few moments before. *But, then, there's no accounting for the emotions of a man who would kill the woman who loved him—especially when she was the queen.*

Strand leaned forward, as if to whisper to Fellows. "Sorry, but I think I'll keep the details of this tale to myself. And if you're wise, you'll let it stay that way."

Fellows chortled. "I'm afraid that's not possible. Corporal Herrick Strand, I am taking you into custody for the murder of Queen Callista DeValeriel."

Strand shook his head with an expression of mock regret. "I did warn you, Detective."

He gestured with his hand, and Kadin's world exploded into the worst pain she could remember experiencing. She felt as though someone had splashed acid onto her abdomen and the corrosive substance was slowly eating away at her skin. As she doubled over in pain, she pressed her hand to her gut. The touch increased her agony, and she realized her stomach was covered in burning sores. She couldn't muster the energy to look up, but based on the sounds she heard, she assumed that everyone else was suffering the same injury.

Magic. The queen was *killed by magic. Only Baurus DeValeriel didn't do it. Herrick Strand did.*

A part of her wanted to thing about everything she had heard about magic in the past week and consider the critical ramifications. A larger part wanted to pass out from the pain causing her knees to buckle. But the deepest part of her knew that while the team lay incapacitated, a murderer was escaping, and in order to catch him, she needed this pain to *stop.*

A rush of cold burst through her, coating her entire body in an icy chill. When it subsided, the burning sensation had subsided. She could still feel gashes across her abdomen, but her skin was no longer eroding away.

She grabbed Fellows's ject out of its holster and pointed it at Strand, who was strolling out the door, whistling a jaunty tune.

"Stop right there, Corporal Strand."

He stopped whistling and whirled around to face her. All amusement vanished from his face as he looked from her to her colleagues. "Who are you?"

"I am Kadin Stone." She raised the ject to aim at his head. "I am the woman who is taking you into custody for the murder of Queen Callista DeValeriel."

"Not tonight, Miss Stone." Strand waved his finger at her as though she were a naughty child. "But I'm sure I'll be seeing you around."

The ject heating up in her hand was the only indication that something was wrong, but she noticed the sensation in time to toss the weapon away from herself. The last thing she remembered was a piece of an exploding ject rushing to her head before she passed out.

CHAPTER 20

KADIN DIDN'T RECOGNIZE HER SURROUNDINGS at first. She lay on a white and gold canopied bed, which may well have had silk sheets. She looked to her right and saw Combs sitting there, fiddling with some gauze and medical tape.

"What happened?" She reached up to touch the throbbing spot on her forehead.

"Don't touch that." Combs grabbed her hand and pulled it back down to her side. "You've got quite the gash on your forehead. It's not that deep but it's bleeding quite a bit. If you're lucky, it won't scar." He put a piece of folded gauze on her head and began to attach it with the tape.

Just what I need. A scar on my face. "The last thing I remembered was..." The gun exploding. Strand escaping. Everyone on the floor in agony.

Kadin sat up straight. "Oh my Deity, is everyone all right? Did he kill anyone?"

Combs moved so that he could keep applying the tape. "Everyone's fine. I don't think Corporal Strand had any intention of killing us. He just wanted to escape. Though we're all going to have to keep an eye on the sores. They won't be pretty if they get infected."

Kadin slumped back on her elbows. "But he got away."

Combs smoothed the last piece of tape on her forehead and sat back. "Yes. But he had to reveal that he used magic, which I'm sure the Society of Mages did not intend. With any luck, we won't be hearing from them again for a while. We have time to prepare, though I'm not sure there will ever be anything we can do against them."

Kadin stared at a fold in the sheets. *I could do something. Back there, when we were all in danger, I made it stop. But what did I do? And how?*

Combs stood and put his supplies into a black bag. "Come on. The king has summoned one of his personal autocars for us to take back to the office."

"One of his autocars. Of course." As she followed Combs from the room, she wondered how many cars Vinnie Royal had.

Kadin remained silent on the ride back to the office.

I caught a murderer. Well, almost caught a murderer. I solved a crime at any rate. A major crime. I never thought I could do that. Wouldn't it be amazing if I could do that all the time?

Do what, Kadin Stone? A harsher voice came to the forefront of her mind. *Solve murders? Be a detective? There's never* been *a female detective in the whole history of Valeriel. You're lucky you get to be an aide, and you might not even be that after Fellows fires you for interfering in his case. And even if you get to stay, he's going to retire in a few years, and you'll have to hope someone else takes you on. Until that person retires, and someone else has to take you on, and the chances of that happening go down the older and less attractive you get. Meanwhile, you'll still be living in Tobin's house. You need to get married. You need to go crawling back to Dahran White and beg him to give you a second chance. There aren't any other options. Not for women. Not in Valeriel.*

But maybe... The first voice, the one she internally

chastised, didn't seem to want to let go. *Maybe, until then, I can solve murders.*

Kadin stepped out of the autocar determined to write up her account of events at the palace before finding Dahran to see if she could coax an invite to the next drag. She was so distracted, she didn't even notice the large shape rushing toward her until it had lifted her from the ground and spun her in the air.

"You saved me!" said the man holding her aloft.

After a moment she found herself in a stationary location about a foot off the ground, looking down into the grinning face of Duke Baurus DeValeriel.

"Your Grace..." Kadin tried to remain as dignified as she could in her current position, in spite of the duke's infectious smile.

He laughed. "Kadin Stone, you have saved me from a lifetime of undeserved incarceration. I give you official permission to drop all titles."

"Um... okay..."

"Baurus," he prodded.

She took a deep breath. "Baurus?"

"Yes, Kadin?"

"Would you mind putting me down?"

He laughed again and lowered her to the ground. "I do have one condition, though."

"And what might that be?" She couldn't imagine what else he might want from her.

"I want to know how you found me."

"Oh, that." Now it was her turn to giggle. "I asked your cousin."

Baurus's eyes widened, and his smile dimmed a bit. "Ralvin gave me up?"

Kadin looked down at her shoes. "Well, he may have been under the impression that I was in possession of a certain piece of information that he didn't want the general public to know. And he might also have thought that, if he didn't tell me where you were, I would reveal that information to some interested parties."

Baurus's mouth fell open for a full minute before he began to laugh. "You blackmailed Ralvin?"

It sounds so much worse when he puts it like that. "Well, not exactly. I mean, I never planned to... I didn't even think... I..." She sighed and dropped her hands to her sides. "Yes. Yes, I blackmailed King Ralvin." *Melting into the ground would be great around now.*

Baurus gave a great guffaw. "Bay!" Baurus called to someone behind her. "Kadin here blackmailed Ralvin into telling her where I was! Ralvin!"

Kadin spun around to see Lady Beatrin Oriole approaching them wearing a light green suit and expensive blue heels.

"Quite astounding." Lady Beatrin didn't spare Kadin a glance.

"Oh, don't be that way, Bay." Baurus's voice took on a wheedling tone. "I know you don't get to inherit all my property and such, but you have to be at least a little glad that I'm no longer suspected of murder."

Lady Beatrin didn't even blink. "Don't be ridiculous, Baurus. All the DeValeriel lands and titles are not worth the humiliation of having a murderer in the family. And speaking of family, word has reached Mother of this whole affair, and she is not amused."

Baurus deflated. "No, I imagine the Lady Augustille is quite put out that once again her son has failed to meet her exacting standards."

"Quite." Lady Beatrin shifted her purse from one hand to the other. "So if you are finished making a public spectacle of yourself, for the time being at least, I have an autocar waiting, and I would prefer to get out of here before the news clickers arrive."

"Your wish is my command." Baurus gave his sister a mock bow and then turned to Kadin. "I must depart.

Beatrin is right, as usual. I'm surprised the news clickers aren't here already. But I want to thank you from the bottom of my heart. I can't imagine what I would have done if you hadn't helped me."

As Baurus turned and walked away, Kadin glanced at his sister. Lady Beatrin looked Kadin in the eye and then turned her nose up in a pointed snub.

Kadin didn't know what the duchess's problem was, but since Kadin thought it unlikely she would have any dealings with the DeValeriel family in the near future, she decided to ignore it. She shook her head as she entered the building, grateful that as bad as her family could be, at least their problems weren't plastered all over the front of the *Tribune.*

Kadin entered the office building and rode the lift up to the fourth floor. As she stepped out of the elevator, she just avoided bumping into Dahran.

He held the lift door and looked her up and down. "Books, huh?"

Kadin gave a weak shrug. "I noticed it in the queen's library, is all." *And had it thrown at my head.*

"That's pretty good thinking." He gave her a condescending grin. "Hey, I don't have tickets for this Saturday's drag, but I do for the week after. Maybe you'd care to join me?"

Kadin hoped she looked excited, rather than flummoxed that he had forgiven her without any effort on her part. "That sounds great!"

"And maybe we can get dinner sometime, too. Need to keep you busy so you don't steal all those cases out from under us." He gave her a wink.

Kadin nodded. "Absolutely."

He's giving me another chance, she thought as the lift doors slid closed. *And that's a good thing... right?*

Fellows looked up when Kadin stepped into her office.

She took a deep breath, walked the last few steps into his office, and shut the door behind her.

I'm probably going to get fired, she thought. *But I can't be sorry I solved a murder.*

Fellows took off his bowler hat and set it on the desk next to him. "So, Miss Stone. It's been a bit of an interesting first week for you, wouldn't you agree?"

Kadin looked down at her hands. "Yes, sir."

"I asked you to do one thing, Miss Stone. You had exactly one job function."

"I did make the java, sir." *Well, most days. Actually, all days. Just because it was undrinkable the first day doesn't mean that I didn't do it.*

"You did," Fellows said. Kadin wanted to glance at his face to see if she could tell where this conversation was going, but she couldn't get up the nerve. "But you also took it upon yourself to investigate a high profile murder without any particular skill or authority. Can you offer any justification for that behavior?"

Kadin didn't know what to tell him. She didn't think he would believe that she had *tried* to stay out of the case.

She sighed. "You told me I could do whatever I wanted. I wanted to do my job."

Fellows took a deep breath. "Do you know why I only hire young women to be my aides, Miss Stone?"

"I'm sure I don't, Detective." *That's a lie.* Everyone knew why he hired young female aides, but Kadin didn't think it polite to say so.

Fellows stood up and came around the desk to stand in front of Kadin. "I've been here so long that I'm almost always put in a primary position on the major cases. I get a whole team of idiots reporting to me, and usually they don't have a brain between them. Oh, sure, they can handle a basic homicide with one obvious suspect, but give them any actual detecting to do and they stand around surprised that the universe expects them to do their jobs. I decided a long time ago that any employees under my control would stay out of my way."

Fellows put his finger under her chin and raised her head to look at him. "But you have demonstrated that there may be some people around here worth working with, people who can add more than what I can to an investigation. I never even thought to check the details of the guard's story."

"Oh, sir, I'm sure that's not true!" Kadin could feel herself flushing. "You're a brilliant detective. I've read about some of your past cases. You would have thought of the book eventually. Lady Elyesse happened to be reading it when I went to question her. I wasn't even planning to ask her about it."

"Stone, don't argue with me. I'm trying to give you a compliment. And I'm letting you keep your job." He gave a little snort. "I'm going to have an aide who *works*. This should be interesting." He walked back to his chair and sat down. "Now get out of here, Stone. These magic burns hurt like nothing else, and I've got the Deity's own mountain of paperwork to get through before I can go home tonight."

Kadin stepped out of his office, closing the door behind her. She closed her eyes and took a deep breath. When she opened them, she realized Olivan was sitting in her chair, and probably had been for most of the meeting.

Kadin groaned. "Ollie, I have had a worse day than you can possibly imagine. My head hurts, my stomach hurts, and I am absolutely exhausted. Could you please wait to yell at me until tomorrow? Or maybe next month, which is about when I think I will have recovered sufficiently to deal with anything emotionally straining?"

Olivan put his feet up on her desk. "I have decided to forgive you."

Kadin almost snapped that she hadn't done anything in the first place, but she bit back her words. "That's great to hear, Ollie, but I can't deal with this right now."

Olivan put his feet back on the floor and stood up. “Look, K, I really am sorry. I may have overreacted a bit the other night—”

A knock on the door interrupted him. The both turned to see Ralvin DeValeriel—*no, Vinnie Royal,* Kadin corrected herself—standing in the doorway.

“Hi, Vinnie.” Olivan’s face brightened into what Kadin recognized as the smile he got when he crushed on someone. “I thought we weren’t meeting for another hour.”

Oh, no, thought Kadin. *Please, please, please do not tell me that Ollie is dating Vinnie.*

“Oh, we aren’t.” Vinnie’s lips curved upward. “I came by to see Kadin and congratulate her on solving the murder of the century.”

Olivan raised his eyebrows. “News travels fast.”

“It does when you own shares in the newspaper.” *Or when you were there the entire time because the murder victim was your* wife. Kadin had done a little research on “Vinnie Royal” and had discovered that “shares” understated the matter. Vinnie Royal owned enough of the newspaper to control everything that went to print. She’d had to dig pretty hard to find the association, and she’d known about it beforehand.

“I’ve got a couple of things to finish up in my office.” Olivan gave Vinnie a dopey smile, but he turned to Kadin and hissed, “Be nice.” She was pretty sure Vinnie heard, but Olivan may have intended that.

As soon as she was sure Olivan was out of earshot, she turned and glared at Vinnie. “What in the name of the Deity are you doing? You’re dating Ollie?”

Vinnie shrugged. “He called me yesterday. He wanted to apologize personally for your behavior and assured me that you were usually quiet and self-effacing. I explained what had really happened with Dawban Steel, and he felt terrible. Then we started talking about some other things, and we kind of hit it off.”

Kadin looked at him with her mouth gaping open. "Is this some kind of joke? You can't date Ollie. He really likes you."

Vinnie stuck his hands in his pockets. "I like him too."

Kadin crossed her arms and lowered her voice, aware that Fellows could be listening from the next room. "And what's going to happen when he finds out there is no such person as Vinnie Royal? I have half a mind to tell him myself."

"Quiet and self-effacing, those were his exact words." Vinnie shook his head. "And you're not going to tell him."

"No." Kadin heard the resentful tone in her voice. "I promised I wouldn't, and I won't. And let me tell you, Fellows was not amused when I wouldn't tell him who told me where Baurus was."

"Well, I didn't come here to argue with you about Ollie. I came here to thank you for helping Baurus like you did. Everyone thought he was guilty, even me, but you managed to see past the obvious to the truth." He reached out his hand and put it on her arm. "If there's ever anything I can do for you, you only have to ask."

Kadin met his eyes. "You could end things with Olivan."

Vinnie looked stricken. "Do you really want me to do that?"

Part of her wanted to say yes, but Vinnie looked so upset at the prospect, and she knew from Olivan's expression that she wouldn't be able to talk him out of his new crush. Besides, they were both grown men who were capable of taking care of themselves.

"I guess not. But I do want you to remember that I can hurt you as badly as you can hurt him." She reached out and flicked a finger at his abdomen. As she expected, he cringed from the attack on his burns. "See you around, Vinnie." She smiled to herself as she strolled out, leaving him to stare open-mouthed behind her.

Jace Combs was in the lift when she stepped inside. "So how does it feel to solve your first case?" he asked.

Kadin laughed. "I'm fairly certain that all records will indicate that Caison Fellows was the lead detective."

"Oh, I'm sure they will."

They rode in silence for a moment until the elevator came to a stop, and Kadin started out into the lobby.

Combs nodded his head at her feet. "I see you're still wearing those shoes."

She looked down at her heels and then back at him. "Well, this is a different pair, but, yes, my heels are still high."

He reached out to stop the elevator door from closing and carrying him down to his lab. "You know, when we first met, I thought you were a silly girl, willing to destroy her feet to look pretty."

"Oh really?" Kadin tried to sound nonchalant, but his words stung.

"Yeah, but I changed my mind." He gave her half a smile. "Now I think you're the kind of girl who isn't going to be defeated by a pair of shoes."

Kadin considered his words as she watched the lift doors slide closed in front of his perfect features. She felt her own lips turn upward.

Maybe he was right.

ACKNOWLEDGEMENTS

So many people have helped on this book that I'm sure I am going to forget someone. So I apologize in advance and state that if I have talked to you since I started writing this in 2007, you have probably contributed in some way, and I thank you.

First, I thank my alpha readers, Kevin and Stephanie. They read the very roughest draft of Kadin Stone, which I can now say with some certainty was pretty terrible. And they still liked it enough to want me to develop it.

Next, all my beta and gamma readers, in no particular order: Mom/Ginny, Anne, Jason, Julie, Greg, Maddy, Ashley, Steve, and Mary. You have offered me constant support and advice, and this book would be far worse without your thoughts and contributions.

The team at Red Adept Publishing: In working on the Earthbound Angels series, you taught me so much about writing that has influenced these pages. And your feedback on *Catching a Man* was invaluable.

Streetlight Graphics: The cover and formatting are amazing. I could not ask for a better representation of a 1950s fantasy/mystery.

All my readers and reviewers: Thanks for your support as I branch out and "go indie." I hope this did not disappoint.